ADVISORY

This anthology is created for a mature audience and may contain
subject matter that some readers find unsettling.

For a complete list of Content Warnings, please see the last
page of the anthology.

PERSPECTIVES

Published by The NE1 World as a part of ASAP Comics UK
www.asapcomicsuk.com

Edited by Jessica E. Mondy
Cover Design by Kelsey L Connors

PERSPECTIVES

an anthology

FOREWORD

When I decided to launch The NE1 World with this anthology, it was already predetermined that ALL the proceeds would be going to charity and that it was for a cause that I hold close to my heart: dyspraxia. My son has dyspraxia, so I am more aware than most of the trials that someone who has the condition goes through on a daily basis. I reached out to the wonderful people at The Dyspraxia Foundation who do such incredible work to help people deal with the condition, and they are the charity that the proceeds will be donated to.

I was willing to do whatever I could to make this book a reality. What I needed was help. I needed good people. There are two things I've been sure of in recent times:

1. It's that good people exist, and they have helped make this book possible.
2. These creative people have shared something special—their stories—and I have the pleasure of introducing them to you.

Even before you flipped open the pages and started reading, you could see the work of a good person; the talented designer who gave her skill and time to create the beautiful cover that wraps this book like the perfect gift. She gave these things freely for charity. I want to thank her.

The editor who worked for hours with all sixteen writers to ensure that their stories were spellchecked, fact-checked, that things were grammatically correct, and for helping the writers make their stories the best that they could be. She communicated with them all in such a way that messages of respect and gratitude were sent from the writers. She did this all for charity. I want to thank her.

Every single writer that has been involved in this project has given you one of the greatest gifts possible—a part of their imagination. This is no small gift because they are giving to you a piece of themselves, a world that they brought to life. These worlds they share with you are much more valuable than people realise. Stories can empower you or bring you to your knees. They can make you laugh or cry. You could connect with a story in such a way that it may change your entire life. The world that was brought into being from one person's mind becomes part of yours. That's how powerful and precious their perspectives are, and they have given them without thought of material gain but selflessly for other people. I thank them from the bottom of my heart.

So the next time you're watching a film, reading a book or a comic, remember what was given to you. The next time that you think about your favourite character or superhero, remember they were a gift from inside the mind of another person.

Please join me in celebrating this book and those involved—enjoy every word, every story, every perspective.

P. A. Hayden
Owner and Founder of ASAP Comics UK

DEDICATIONS

All proceeds from this anthology
are donated to the Dyspraxia Foundation UK.

Mitch Larkins – For Laylee and Rowin.
Caleb L. Taylor – For Jeremy "Mandingo311." Rest easy, friend.
Martin Freznell – For Loot.
R. E. Misery - For that one friend who supported me.
Bracey – For my endlessly supportive wife.
Michael D. Nadeau – For my wife, Sheila… My everything.
L. A. Cunningham – For Brad and my parents, for the gift of time.
Frasier Armitage – For Lunarbelle and the boy.
Paul D. Nolan – For Marian. Thank you for your belief in me. RIP.
C. Vandyke – For my family and all the bad decisions we've made together.
D. W. Howard – For Connor, Caitlyn and Kiersten.
Tim Davis – For my family, who support me endlessly
Steve Sellers – For CC, who always inspires me.
Luis M. Cruz – For my mother, Jenny, and aunt, Wanda.
Micah Richards – For my kids.
Christian Prosperie – For those who have always supported me.

ASAP Comics UK would like to thank everyone
involved for helping to make this anthology happen.

TABLE OF CONTENTS

THE HUNTED
By Mitch Larkins

The girl darted through the underbrush, ignoring the limbs lashing at her face and exposed body. Night was falling, but she could still see as clear as day. The only thing blinding her was the sheer terror of the monster behind her. Cries of pain and roars of anger echoed through the forest, punctuated by the thundering boom of weapons. She wanted to stop, to turn back, to do something—anything—to help, but she was too small and too scared to do anything but run.

They had been out for a simple walk. That was all. A quick, evening stroll before nightfall. The girl had begged and pleaded to go out. She was even willing to go on her own. Her father had warned of the danger, of course. Of the dangers that stalked the woods. But the girl ignored him.

"I'm big enough!" she proclaimed. Her father had grumbled at that, firm his daughter would not be going anywhere today.

Her mother understood, though. Her mother always said her girl was wild, meant to be free to run through the grass, jump across the rocks, and swim in the creeks. To drown in the sounds and smells of the woods. Her father constantly had to hunt the girl down and drag her home when the hour grew late, when she had been too mesmerized by a trail of ants or the fluttering of birds. Her mother would come to her defence, as always, defusing her father's anger, while stroking the girl's soft, long, dark hair.

It was her mother who convinced her father that she would be going for a walk in the woods—and that their daughter would accompany her.

"My big, strong girl will protect me, won't you?" Mother said, with her warm, gentle smile. The girl had foolishly believed in her own strength, and that her mother told the truth. It never dawned on her that her mother would be the one protecting her. Her foolishness and bravado made her even more reckless. She ran off on her own, to find flowers for her dad. A handful of those golden solidagos would keep him from being too angry with them if they took too long. She had been the one to stray from their usual path. The safe route. It was all her fault they had been attacked. And now she was alone. Her mother lost to her.

The dark closed around her faster than she thought possible. If she didn't find where she needed to go soon, even with her great sight, she would be stumbling around like a pathetic fawn. Her lungs burned. Her heart pounded. She tried to make sense of her surroundings; everything looked the same in her panicked state. Had she been turned around?

"Girl!" a voice called out. "Come on out now! It's okay!"

The voice sounded gentle, but exhausted and hurt. She was almost curious and desperate enough to turn around and go to it, but shook her head against the notion. Had someone been there to help her mother during the attack? No. Although her memory was already blurring, she didn't think anyone else had shown up. Could it be a trap? It had to be. She had been told to run by her mother, to run home, and that's what she planned on doing, no matter who or what called out to her. She needed to be strong. Strong enough to get home.

She heard the crashing of clumsy running in the woods behind her, from the same direction as the voice. Heavy, fast footsteps ploughing through low-hanging branches. Heading towards her. Danger was coming at her and coming fast. With wide, panicked eyes, the girl searched around, picked a direction she thought would lead towards home, and leapt forward. It really didn't matter where she ran anyway, so long as she ran. Maybe she could get away from the predator closing in on her. It wasn't trying to hide its presence. It acted confident, as if it knew exactly where she was and where she was going.

The calls and shouts kept coming, the voice beckoning to her as the girl kept running. Whatever it was, it grew closer while she grew tired from her wild flight. Only after a momentary pause did she feel a stab of pain from her side. An ugly-looking gash caught her eye, with her precious life-blood pumping out of it. She must've been struck in the ambush. Or the initial battle before being knocked towards the forest. Tears welled up in the girl's large eyes. The wound ached. The pain was overtaking the adrenaline burning through her system, sapping what little strength she had left. Her muscles began to throb, forcing her to push off trees with both her arms and legs just to keep going. She refused to give up. She couldn't give up. She had to get home.

What began as a sprint slowed to a jog, then a breathless, staggering walk. Before long, the girl found herself collapsed on the ground. She panted and whimpered in pain and exhaustion; the tears were flowing freely now. With the back of one hand, the girl wiped her running nose before cleaning her eyes with her palms. She had to be strong. She had to continue.

The girl struggled to her feet, staggering another yard, then crashed back to the muddy ground. She was so tired, so weak. She had bragged to her father that she was strong. Her mother had nuzzled her and told her that she believed in her little girl's strength. Where was that strength now?

The crashing grew nearer. Had she gotten close to home at least? The girl looked around with tired eyes. Tall trees ended barely a hundred yards away. From there, an open, grassy field. The girl didn't know if she should laugh or cry even harder. She had almost made it. Lights twinkled across the field and smoke started climbing to the heavens. If she tried, the girl could probably catch a faint whiff of the hot-cooked meals being prepared.

"There you are," came an unfamiliar, deep, soothing voice. "Finally found you. We were worried about you."

The girl pulled herself up and lay against a tree. Her side hurt. Breathing hurt. *Everything* hurt. She blinked, trying to focus on who approached her. Was he here to save her?

"You gave a helluva chase." The man panted, his long weapon glinting in the evening light. "Like that other monster. It sure fought with the fury of hell." No, this one was not here to save her.

She tried to growl, to bare her tiny fangs, but it came out as a weak squeak.

"Was that your momma back there?" The man chuckled, leaning against a tree, catching his breath. "Well, you'll be with her soon. If you're done running from me."

The girl's ears flicked, catching the barely audible creak of tree limbs high above them. Despite her exhausted state, she found herself smiling.

"I—I wasn't r-running *from you,*" she said at last, looking up at the man defiantly.

"Oh!" The man reeled, taking a step back in surprise. He shook his head, regaining his wits and confidence before taking a step towards her. "Ohhh ho ho! It really *can* speak? You're gonna fetch us a nice pri—"

The man's eyes widened as some instinctual fear struck him. Some ancient, genetic memory from ancestors long dead told him he should not be standing there. Not standing over this tiny, humanoid creature. From behind him came a thunderous crash, shaking the ground, nearly toppling the man over. He staggered forward, barely regaining his footing. A heavy, vicious growl of absolute, unending rage rattled the man to his bones, sending a chill down his spine, and freezing his very soul. An invisible, palatable ocean of pure hatred engulfed the man, swallowing him up so completely, he felt he would drown in the open air. Every instinct told the man to run, just run, to keep running until he was two counties over and to keep running some more. The man pushed those fearful, screaming voices away. Not out of some bravado, but out of the sheer impossibility of this experience.

Spinning around, the hunter looked up to the shadow-hidden behemoth looming far over him. The beast was nearly as wide as the man was tall. The man's knees shook as strength and courage left him. The gun toppled to the ground with a clatter. All he could make out of the mass of fur and darkness were two pairs of very large, glowing, yellow eyes stacked on top of each other. The same four eyes the young female lying against the tree had. Except these were far larger, and burning in pure, indescribable fury. The man stood there as a black-furred arm the size of a tree trunk rose so high it blotted out the moon. Six thick, razor-sharp claws glinted in the light.

"I was running *to my daddy.*"

RITE OF DEVOURMENT
By Caleb L. Taylor

"Thanks for letting me and my brother stay here for the night," says a man whose dirty hair and clothes cling to him, hard travel apparent in his appearance. "I'm Cederic Warrick, and this—" he gestures to his companion, similarly stained in sweat, "this is my younger brother, Elias."

"I'm Osbert," a man with unruly dark-brown hair states. "You've not me to thank, but this man." He points to the giant black-haired man whose only warmth comes from lying near the fire, thought to be asleep. "He let me join him just a bit ago. He hasn't said much, I'm afraid."

The brothers kneel near the fire, timid initially, but they both try to get comfortable.

"Is he asleep?" Cederic asks.

"No, at least, not any longer." A raucous voice responds before Osbert has a chance to.

"Oh, well, I don't know if you heard me but—"

"I heard," he interrupts, his deep voice cutting through the night's ambience. "You and your brother are more than welcome to stay here." He clears his throat to remove its harshness. "As I told Osbert earlier, tell all who pass to come and get warm. And sleep as needed. I haven't much food, but take as needed there as well. I can hunt if need be."

"Oh, we won't eat much." Cedric gestures to his brother to take some food. "Most of our supplies were lost to the river. Fortunately, we managed to save some bread and meats, though we've just run out."

"As I said," their host maintained, while still lying on his back, "take as needed."

"We really do appreciate the generosity. We aren't far from home. If you, sire, are still here by dusk tomorrow, we can come back and reward you for these actions."

"No reward needed." He takes a moment to yawn, then raises himself to their level. Though only propped up with his arm, his head is high enough to look down on them. "And the name is Ailwin."

The men now have a better view of his clothing, tattered and undistinguishable. They are taken aback, for though his attire is not of the best form, his health contradicts and appears phenomenal. They all remain silent. Osbert stares into the fire while the other two, curiously yet aimlessly, cast their eyes around to the stars and woods, taking in their surroundings.

Ailwin busies himself by searching through a satchel as equally worn as his clothes, pulling out a wooden pipe. He fills the small, carved bowl with tobacco and uses a lit twig from the fire to light his pipe, all while humming to himself. He takes two puffs, then uses the opposite end of the twig to tamper the tobacco down. He leans back on his elbows and blows smoke into the night sky. He sings softly, "And oh, the young flower, she came and went..." None around the campfire dare make a sound, choosing instead to listen in silence.

"Have you ever heard stories of the Verren?" Ailwin asks, interrupting himself.

Cederic, Elias, and Osbert take a moment to think on the question.

"Aren't they..." Elias tries to answer. "Aren't they the ones who were supposed to have lived here before our time?"

"No," Cedric insists. "That can't be right."

"He is not too far from the truth," Ailwin responds. "You see, there's a time—known to us as the First Era— that we have little to no records of. The Second Era began when we 'woke up,' as some say, as this is when we have the most recordings. There are things of the First Era—loose scrolls, structures, and carved tablets—but nothing that gives a consistent understanding of that time."

His deep voice resonates well with the men, soothing them, lulling them into a state of full attention; listening to every word, fully enthralled, none make a noise.

"From what has been passed about, there was a time of peace until Gateways began to open across the land. These Gateways brought you to another world: Verra. But where our ancestors, the Ellri, hesitated to enter such things, the Verren from the other side did not." He shifted from his position, sitting up to move his feet flat on the ground and his forearms on each respective knee. "Now, there are several stories. I'm sure you've heard a few. Most deal with the eventual defeat of the Verren and their removal. I've got a story I'm sure few have heard close to." He stares into the fire, deep in thought.

"Do tell," Elias requests, eyes lit from excitement.

"Though it may be short, it does bring interest." Ailwin pauses briefly, an indecipherable look in his eye, before continuing. "During the time of the Gateways, these doors to another world plagued our land. Most able-bodied men were called to arms against the foreign beasts that emerged from them. In the midst of the Verren invasion, a boy, not even mature yet, was left as head of his house. He had a flock of sheep of which he was the shepherd. Throughout several weeks, his sheep dwindled in number. Started as a sheep a week, eventually a sheep every other day. He grew frustrated, left his mother to tend to his younger siblings, and sought out what took his sheep. He brought a club and nothing more. He heard a rumour of a cave that was said to house a Verren. Fearless and determined, he marched himself to the suspected home in a nearby mountain."

Ailwin stops to dig through his satchel, grabs a leather flask, and takes a drink. He then offers it to the others. The group accepts the flask and takes turns drinking. Ailwin stretches, then continues the story.

"He knew the cave. He played in it frequently as a child. So when he approached the mouth, he noticed the evidence of something living inside. He told himself that it was probably a fox or wolf; trying to convince himself he could handle what lay within. Those notions were lost as he approached and saw large footprints unfamiliar to him, two sets of completely different prints to be precise. He kept his courage and advanced."

Elias, his imagination enticed by each word, holds the flask in his hands tight to his chest, perhaps wishing to imbue some of the courage as spoken about in the tale. Enthralled beyond his normal capacity—seeing the story painted before him—he stares, entranced.

"As he entered, he remembered why he no longer played in the cave. 'Unsafe,' his mother warned; he would be 'foolish to return.' The loose rocks could easily slip and block any escape, if they didn't kill him in the process. There was already a cave-in once before, years back. His father cleared it out to mine the remainder. But at this point, the resources had been depleted months ago, and the cave abandoned ever since. He continued forward, as the loss of sheep was greatly affecting his family. He needed to solve this before his younger siblings starved. He kept that in mind as he pushed forward. The cave was dry and progressively became cluttered with various skeletons. He knew he was tracking the right wrongdoers. With his club ready, he walked onward. The scent of death was strong and repulsive, but he faltered not."

Ailwin stops to take a few long drags on his pipe. Elias realises he has been holding his breath and lets out a long sigh. Cederic and Osbert, while having retained a more stoic nature and composure, both readjust their positions on the ground.

"Now this is where numerous accounts separate: regularly I'd say he had a lamp or a torch, but as the story goes," he gives Elias a quick wink, "some say he was mystical, and his hand brought light to the cave. But it doesn't matter how the cave was lit, it only matters what came next. He crept his way through the death-riddled depths and entered a small chamber where he discovered the two Verren. Asleep, they lay still, but intimidating nonetheless."

"Wait." Cederic stops him. Cederic looks around the camp, gauging everyone else's expressions to see how they viewed the story so far. "Mystical? I can't get past that." He squints as he delves into thought. "His hand lit up?" He inspects his hands.

"I've heard of people who had powers," Elias states. "There's rumours of several people now that do magical things."

"I've heard stories too," added Osbert, subtly staring at his own hands as he flexes them then releases, letting out a faint sigh of disappointment after several attempts.

"Well, from my understanding, someone of maturity acquires full use of their magical abilities. He was nearing maturity, but not yet there, and as such had only gained the ability to bring forth minor energy to his hand. If the stories are to be believed, our ancestors had the most amazing gifts. But, for his lack of magical growth, he had the club." Ailwin takes a long, slow draw on his pipe before breathing out a thick cloud to combine with the smoke of the dwindling campfire between them. "May I continue then?" he asks as he cleans and sets his pipe down.

"Yes, please," Elias urges.

"The beasts slept, breathing heavily, and still most terrifying. As the prints had shown earlier, the beasts were noticeably different from each other. One was a dark brown reptile-shaped man, tail and all. The other's face didn't have as much of a snout as the other, but had long ears, four arms, and hooved feet. The boy was ready to end their reign of terror. He raised the club above his head and swiftly brought it down on the larger Verren—the snouted one. It hurt the beast, oh yes, and it yelped in pain. Unfortunately, that was not enough to kill it. Before the boy could strike again, the snouted one attacked him. With a quick stroke to the chest, the boy was hurdled across the cave. The long-eared one woke instantly from the yelp, and as the boy landed, it pounced, grabbed him, and threw him back across the cave."

Ailwin hears a gasp from the group and looks up to see Cederic elbow Elias in the side. Ailwin continues.

"The boy had lost his club. He lay on the floor, mangled. Between the hit from the snouted one that opened his gut, along with the colliding and sliding on the floor, he was not faring well. The beasts kept against the opposite wall of the cave, watching the boy. A voice echoed through the tunnel, asking if anyone was in the cave and needed help. The beasts looked towards the exit of the small chamber. The boy lay on the floor, bleeding out, when he noticed the beasts heading for the exit. He heard the voice once again, and his thoughts flooded with fear for what he may have done. Fear of what the beasts would do. He was worried about the man calling out, the boy's own family... He felt a warmth inside him, much like how he felt when he brought energy to his hand, though this feeling was far more significant. He did the only thing he could think to do; he brought his hand up and unleashed a stream of energy at the chamber's exit. And like that, the tunnel was blocked. The shift caused small openings in the roof of the chamber, allowing the moonlight to enter, but the openings were too small for anything to escape through."

Ailwin rubs his eyes. He is visibly tired, as is everyone else.

Everyone except Elias. "Is there more? Did he get out?" he asks.

"Even if there is more, we need to sleep. There's still a bit of travelling we need to do tomorrow." Cederic interjects before Ailwin can answer.

Everyone agrees, though Elias's agreement is reluctant. So much so that in the middle of the night, while everyone is asleep, he sneaks his way over to Ailwin and wakes him.

"I can't sleep. I must know what happens," begs Elias.

"Well, so, let's see." Ailwin takes a moment to adjust and recall where he left off. "So, the tunnel collapsed... He is trapped with the beasts. It wasn't long before the beasts realised that the boy was their only food source. And considering the unknown length of stay, they couldn't devour him entirely."

"So, they kept him alive?" asks Elias as he lowers himself to sit down.

"That's right. They found a way to keep him alive, so they could stay alive as well. From my understanding, they discovered that their blood not only sustained him, but healed him and suppressed his magical ability. As it goes, they ate parts of him, drank his blood for thirst—only eating minor parts mind you, limbs and such—and then they fed him and healed him. Their blood would grow his missing pieces back. If they ate his left foot? The blood regrew it."

"How—For how long?" Elias asks, disgusted yet curious.

"Years. Many, many years."

"What happened? Did he survive? Did he get out?"

"Oh, well, of course."

"How?"

"One night, after years of their eating arrangement, he woke in awful pain. He tossed and turned, rolling around in agony. He was in the worst pain he ever felt before; years of their torture did not equal what he now experienced. This continued for hours, and the beasts grew tired of his yelling. The snouted one grabbed him and threw him against the wall. The yelling stopped. His pain slowly dissipated and he was left with a feeling unlike any he had had before—power. A powerful surge of clarity and energy surpassing all else. He didn't know what happened, but he felt unlimited, strong, and...unstoppable."

Through the darkness, excitement gleams in Ailwin's eyes. The smouldering fire isn't the source, nor is it anything Elias could name—be it emotion or enjoyment, a satisfaction of what was to come, or the understanding of what occurred. Elias can't help but feel a similar excitement brew within him.

"The beasts watched him rise from the ground, healing the broken arm and leg quicker than he had ever before. The air thickened, weighing on the two who watched his return. A momentous resurrection that brought forth an imminent dread to the beasts, having sensed the change in him. Deeming him a threat, they attacked. With ease, he fought them off. Each swing of his fist decimated their flesh, breaking bones and unleashing their blood. Mid-scuffle, he threw the snouted one through the cracked roof and out of the cave. The long-eared one quickly left the cave through the new exit, saving its life. He went into that cave a courageous boy and left as something more than a man, altered into a being that could be seen as near-Verren. He left that cave with the sole intent to hunt those beasts down."

Silence hangs thick as Ailwin's words settle among them.

"He—He became one of them?" Elias asks in hushed tones.

"Well, not exactly," Ailwin replies, scratching his chin. "He inherited their extraordinary strength, as well as the regenerative properties allowed him from their blood. It became inherent in him, granting him an unnaturally long life beyond just the healing of wounds. But he retained all of his human looks, altering only upon his situation; hunger, anger, just something which draws passion." Ailwin stretched before folding both hands behind his head. "Yes, parts of him were still undeniably human, while parts of him, well, weren't."

"Wow," Elias whispers in awe.

Ailwin smirks, feeling rather pleased with the reaction of his audience. "Do you want to hear one more thing? One more fascinating fact before you fall back asleep?"

"Yes," the wide-eyed Elias emphatically whispers, a grin erupting onto his face.

Ailwin chuckles before rolling to his side, aligning himself with Elias's eyes. "Some scrolls from the First Era tell of people who created a process—a rite of sorts—the very process which accidentally occurred in the cave."

"What does that mean?" He can't quite understand, though he tries.

"If it weren't for their search for power, there is a good chance that he and those monsters would still be in that cave, feasting off each other for centuries." Ailwin squints. "The magic of those power-hungry people imbued that act, allowing his transformation."

After a few moments of intense introspection, Elias stands to leave, but he remains in place. The whirring of insects and animals becomes prominent as Elias silently stares at the ground. Ailwin closes his eyes then turns his head out towards the tree line behind him. "You've best get to asking the question that's idled you, else neither of us will get any sleep."

"Did..." Elias begins sheepishly. "Did they succeed?"

"The power-thirsty people? I've heard they were able to transform at least one." Ailwin opens his eyes, peeking over to give the young man a sly expression. "Apparently, that one was capable of performing the rite far quicker and simpler on his own." Sensing Elias had a million questions about to burst through, Ailwin held up his hand preventing a single word from forming. "That, my friend, is a story for another time. Now," he gestures to the empty bedding, "I've kept us awake long enough. Long trip, not much night left."

Elias's face saddens from disappointment, but he nods slowly and goes to lie down. As he strolls away, Ailwin hears him mumble to himself, "Can you imagine... I'd make a whole army, to help teach those monsters a lesson."

Ailwin suppresses a laugh as he rolls over and makes himself comfortable before closing his eyes, now radiant from inspiration and reddened by exhaustion. He waits until he can hear the resting rhythm of Elias before whispering to himself, "Surely I don't need that many." His jaw begins to descend, his lips separate, the moonlight glistening on his teeth as they elongate into sharp points, doubling his smile. "No, just a few."

ANUNA'S CHOICE
By Martin Freznell

"Now, when you dust the bookshelves, do not go into Master Gelsin's study. He specifically told me to make sure you understand," Mrs Mooney said in a commanding, flat voice.

Anuna was young, but she knew exactly what kind of person Mrs Mooney was: a small mind, tightly wound up in rules, regulations, and the petty power it lent her. It was far beneath her to tell a lowly witch like Anuna what her tasks were, but Mrs Mooney insisted on it. She enjoyed it. She uttered each command with a mixture of contempt and lack of interest; as if to say she was well aware Anuna would disappoint even at these menial tasks.

"Yes, Mrs Mooney," Anuna droned. She had a hard time focusing on the old crone. So, this was where she'd spend the next few weeks, in the library, among her best friends: books. All those wonderful tomes full of stories, magic, and wonder.

"Are you listening, girl?" Mrs Mooney snapped.

Anuna caught herself daydreaming, and struggled to remember what Mrs Mooney had just said. "Don't go into Master Gelsin's study," Anuna replied.

"Doesn't matter," she huffed. "I have the only key."

Old hag, as if that mattered! Anuna was at the start of her witching ways, but already she had no doubt she could take the feeble woman in a duel. Not that she needed to. She didn't need the key to open an old lock like that one. She could pick it with the simplest conjuration. Useless, wretched cow! However, she had to suffer the likes of her if she ever wanted to learn, and Anuna wanted nothing more.

Now, Gelsin, he was another story. He was a true mage, a real warlock. He'd shown her such wonders already and in such a short time. How much more had he to show her?

His sharp features, dark hair, and blazing eyes made him a veritable dreamboat. All the girls giggled and swooned at him. Anuna was no exception. But it wasn't his good looks that drew her in. It was his fierce command of magic. Master Gelsin suffered no fools, but to the select few—who possessed what he called "the gift"—his attention was undivided and his demands unwavering. Harsh, yes, but at his side she had learned so much. He'd look at her, and she'd tremble all over.

"Come along now, girl," Mrs Mooney said.

"Yes, Mrs Mooney."

She found herself desperate to impress him. Anuna wanted to be at his side; to learn, to grow, to become a commanding force just like him, an equal he could lean on. She looked back at the study as she followed the old whining woman towards the next task that awaited her.

* * *

Anuna practised the hand motions once more.

"Thi harr k'rill d'jaahr."

Nothing happened. She made the motions again, her face scrunched up, going over the whole process in her head. She did not understand what she was doing wrong or what she was missing. Perhaps the book on her lap was not the treasure she had hoped it would be. She read the passage on transmutation again.

Candles made of pig fat? Check. The symbol of constraint painted on the floor? Check. The air incensed with expensive smoke? Check. What was she missing? Perhaps the pig fat wasn't pure enough. There were bound to be chunks of flesh in there. Anuna shuddered. Making those candles hadn't proven exactly pleasant.

She picked up the doll she had put in the middle of her spellwork. Perhaps it's too complex, she thought. After all, the doll was comprised of several different materials. Maybe that's what was dispelling her efforts?

No. No, she knew, somehow, that wasn't it either. What could it be? Anuna flicked through the tome on her lap, looking for anything to help. After a few fruitless moments, she closed the book and hit her head a few times with the sturdy, ancient thing. She studied the golden letters on the leather-bound cover, tracing them with her fingers. All magic was essentially either kinetic manipulation (easy) or transmutation (turns out—really, really hard). Transmutation was also, strictly speaking, totally forbidden.

Anuna sighed and said to no one in particular, "What am I doing?"

This was crazy. She was being crazy. Insane, even. If she were to get caught, she'd be finished. Her life as a witch would come to an abrupt end. Meddling in the forbidden arts was akin to treason of the highest order. She'd be stripped of all rank and privilege. She'd be cast out of society altogether. What meaning could life possibly have without magic?

Anuna shuddered. There was just no way she could survive outside of the Circle, now that she knew about magic, about the real world. She looked at the old doll, Melanie, in her hands. The paint in its eyes had worn thin. She remembered a time when that doll was all she had; when that stupid doll was her only friend. Yet the magic of childhood had faded and now it was just a piece of plastic, an unwilling participant in her experiments. She hesitated before putting the doll back in the middle of the intricate symbol on the floor.

"Right, Melanie. I'm counting on you, old dear."

If she could change the doll's plastic into something else entirely, all of the risk would have proven worth it. After all,

Anuna reasoned, none of it made much sense: what was so devastating about transmutation anyway? It wasn't like—

"Ah, Miss Tatter, I knew I'd find you here." A deep, sonorous voice sounded into the attic.

Anuna's heart stopped. She'd made sure. All the students had left for the feast of Kanucha, as had all the teachers. There was only old Gammer fast asleep in his office. She'd made sure!

"Master Gelsin," she stammered, clambering upright and trying to deface the magical symbols beneath her, rubbing at it with her foot to no avail. She gave poor old Melanie a kick, sending the doll flying into the corner of the attic, as she hid the book behind her back, hoping beyond all hope that he somehow wouldn't notice. "What a pleasant surprise," she continued. "How can I help you this fine night, Master?"

Master Gelsin sucked in his lower lip, a smile poorly hidden on his beautiful face. He strode towards her, titillating her with his presence. He was, by far, her favourite teacher—no, person—on the whole planet. He was brilliant, gorgeous, and powerful. He made Anuna's teen-heart throb with torturous delights each time she heard him speak or caught a glimpse of his fine-ass physique, usually hidden beneath a dark, worn-down cloak.

Master Gelsin took off his hat, a dirty, leathery thing. He took his time, taking in the scene, as he walked slowly in her direction. His face betrayed no emotion, the smile on his face having waned. He stopped right in front of Anuna. His dark eyes staring down at her. Has he ever stood this close before? She would be excited if she weren't so utterly terrified. He reached behind Anuna and took the tome from her hands, thoughtlessly dropping his hat as he did. It slid down slowly, as if made of smoke.

"Not celebrating with your fellow students, Miss Tatter?" Master Gelsin asked.

"Actually, I was just about to join—"

Anuna was cut off from finishing her desperate lie, as Master Gelsin flicked his hand absentmindedly behind him, and the door of the attic slammed shut. She wasn't going to get out of this, was she?

"My, my, my. Cathar Bale's Guide to Ollimancy for Experienced Users, Miss Tatter?" He sounded amused, pronouncing 'experienced' with what Anuna understood as contempt.

"Master, I can explain!"

"The smell of pig fat, some inane symbols on the floor and," he sniffed the air, "a small fortune in bilzuac seeds and webtistle? My, my, Miss Tatter. My, my, indeed." He lowered his face and looked her straight in the eyes. "You wouldn't be attempting to conjure up the basics of illegal magics, now would you?"

"I— I—" she stammered, desperately trying to come up with an excuse so fantabulous she would somehow convince the most brilliant mind she had ever known that she was not, in fact, doing exactly that. "I was testing a theory?"

"A theory you say?" he said as he brought the tome to his face and sniffed at the pages, visibly delighted by the scent of the old leather-bound book.

"A wonderful read, isn't it, Miss Tatter? I suppose I didn't hide it well enough. In a way, this is all my fault, really. But you were saying something about a theory?"

"Well, yes, sir," she scratched her arm vigorously, fighting back the tears she felt welling up. Her stomach was a nauseating knot, her skin an itching nightmare.

"I'm listening. Do speak up, child," he said. He walked towards a dark corner in the attic and sat down in a dirty, dusty beach chair. He let himself down ungracefully and the old chair groaned as it blew out a cloud of dust. As he sighed contently, the dust that had billowed up dissipated in the gloomy light.

She hesitated for a moment. But just a moment. She knew if she waited too long she would falter, the tears would win, and she would have to face the music without ever being able to defend her actions. So she dared. She pushed on and began telling her master her true thoughts.

"We're taught that all magic is divided in two—kinetic and transmutative—and that the latter is too dangerous to meddle with. It's something I never understood. Surely, of the two, kinetic is the more volatile, the more destructive. After all, with kinetic magic we manipulate energy in all its forms. We conjure a gust of wind, for instance. A bit more complexity and we have ourselves a fireball, et cetera." She swallowed hard, catching herself in her explanation. She was good at explaining things. She was used to doing it all the time, actually, but she wasn't talking to an audience of gullible friends and students this time. She looked anxiously to where Master Gelsin was seated.

"Hmmm, yes?" he went. If anything, he sounded like he was urging her on, as if she was stumbling her way through an exam, and he was waiting for her to find the answer. His foot tapped once or twice.

Anuna continued, "Transmutation, on the other hand, is the art of changing the properties of objects or elements and so forth; meaning, we could, once mastered, change an object or substance into another substance. Perhaps without limit! Perhaps, indeed, we could change any object into anything else." Listening to herself, Anuna once again had to fight back tears. She had gotten too excited. She sounded woefully naïve and silly, hearing her own words spoken to the dimly-lit figure in the corner. She wished he would forgive her.

"Well, that is, hypothetically…" She trailed off into silence, looking at her shoes. In the corner of her eye she saw the discarded doll's legs shimmer, still very much made of plastic: not only was she caught, but she'd failed, utterly. Now she would probably never amount to anything. Ever. If this were an exam, she just flunked. The silence hung thicker than dust.

An idea struck her. Perhaps he could be persuaded if there was some truth to her ideas? She gritted her teeth. If she was going down, at the very least, she would give it her all.

"But two things occurred to me," she started speaking quickly, hoping not to lose her nerve. "Firstly, as stated previously, although the possibilities are certainly daunting, most of the practices we would categorise as transmutation are rather tame in comparison to any of the kinetic disciplines, say, the ability to manipulate fire itself or thaumaturgy. Animancy can make objects move! A subform of that, and you can literally resurrect the dead: a necromancer can field armies of corpses! Most of the disciplines and abilities we'd unlock via mastery of transmutation would be subtle, tiny even—"

"And your second objection?"

"Sorry?"

Master Gelsin's face became more pronounced in the gloom as he folded his hands on top of the tome on his lap. "You said two things occurred to you. What is the second?"

Anuna sucked in some air, gathering the courage to speak. "That there is only one discipline. That all magic is, in actuality, kinetic. All that is—all matter—is made up of energy. Meaning, the art of manipulating energy would encompass the ability to change matter at its, um, essential level?"

She grew silent. She had done the unthinkable. And now she realised, after listening to herself speak what she had never dared before, she had no real excuse. She knew that all too well. Just as she understood the punishment that would follow. She would lose everything.

"A curious book, this, don't you think?" Master Gelsin said. "Ollimancy, the art of manipulating matter through application of an excess in structure and, indeed, force. A useless discipline in all regards but one: as the so-called entry-level discipline in transmutation, it ends up in the hands of many—if not all—aspiring sorcerers and casters of magic with any real talent. But it never succeeds. And the futility of the endeavour dissuades all but the most astute.

The remarkable brilliance of this book is how it manages to evade any subject of import. Yes, the old master Bale certainly knew what he was doing when writing this hefty tome—filled with complicated matters of little consequence while at the same time deftly avoiding all that does matter."

He stood up from his seat and swiped the debris off his cloak, filling the dark room with dust and the smell of old, forgotten things. He approached Anuna and stood tall in front of the girl.

"In a perfect world, you would be correct, miss. I'll certainly give you that. In a perfect world this ponderous testament to inefficiency would indeed be part of the curriculum taught here at the academy." Anuna's chest rose. Perhaps there was hope for her yet? "But you're, unfortunately, quite wrong. On all accounts." She deflated once again at her impending doom.

He sat down next to her on the dusty floor, folding his legs as he did. He gestured for her to sit as well, which a confused and frightened Anuna did.

"There's truth to what you say," Master Gelsin began. "Indeed, ollimancy is a prime example of your theory. I can't deny it. You need a firm grasp of kinetic disciplines to even begin to come to grips with the basics of ollimancy. Doesn't add up, does it? Why would the very foundation of transmutation be so interwoven with a completely separate discipline? Your reasoning is not without merit, though, unfortunately, you came to the wrong conclusion. As I'm sure the author of this book intended."

He lovingly stroked the spine of the book.

Anuna blinked. Did she hear him correctly? She looked at the dusty old thing on Master Gelsin's lap. The book deceived deliberately?

"Obfuscation? But why? Why lie about..." she asked. The beginning of a thought was forming in the back of her mind, but she was far too rattled to think clearly. What was all this?

"It's a clever lie intended to trap young witches, such as yourself, or any other mage on a quest for more power. The laws that govern us are ancient, girl, and the reasons are as ancient and ponderous as this very tome. There is terrible power hidden behind these lies, Anuna. Absolutely terrible. That is why it is forbidden."

Anuna. He called her by her first name.

"Is that why you intended for me to find this book? To trap me?" she asked, no longer fighting back tears. She faced banishment from the academy at the very least. He was not at fault: she had broken these ancient laws and she would pay for them. But it was he who had led her to her demise, of that she was now certain.

She continued. "It's true isn't it? You did intend me to find it? Study it?"

He nodded.

"Why?!"

She had always looked up to him. She had worked so hard. Harder than anyone she knew and yet he punished her?

"Because you are my favourite student. Because you are brilliant."

She looked at him, dumbfounded. She could not believe for a second that he would manipulate her for some outrageous reason, something awful and puny and human. But if not one of those reasons, why trick her at all?

"Your first observation is wrong because you have not fully understood what you could accomplish with a grasp on both disciplines. But it matters not. It is your second observation that is fundamentally wrong. As I said earlier, in a perfect world you would be correct and all would indeed be kinetic in nature. You're not wrong that ollimancy is, in part, a kinetic discipline. But only in part. In that regard, ollimancy is just like its parent discipline, in that regard."

"Transmutation is kinetic? So I was right?"

"Kinetic, in part," he said, waiting for her to figure it out.

And she did. "Transmutation isn't its own division of magic at all. There's another discipline!"

He laughed, pleased with himself and his favourite pupil. "Exactly! I knew you could figure it out."

She was at a loss, but at least he was not angry with her, that much was obvious. He had intended for her to find the book and study it, yes, but not to entrap her.

"What discipline?"

The master gestured with his right hand for her to keep silent. He motioned with his left to the doll in the corner and it slid over, as if by an invisible wire. Another few motions, and without much effort at all, Melanie was walking upright, as if by its own will. Astonishing, Anuna thought. He didn't even have to speak any incantation out loud, so advanced was his skill.

"You mentioned another elaborate lie that has been taught, with as much effort as possible, to you and countless other academics and students of the arcane. What I reveal to you now is indeed quite perilous. Take this example I've just demonstrated. I've made your doll move. Easy. Parlour tricks."

Melanie marched up and down, like a little soldier. It saluted its owner, Anuna, who smiled nervously.

"As you yourself said, it's only a small step further to manipulate a corpse in the same way. You could master it in a month or two, I'm sure, if you were so inclined."

Master Gelsin looked his frightened pupil in the eyes. She saw a cruelty there she'd never noticed before; an iron resolve, at least as old as he was.

He made some complex motions with his hand and blew out a green mist, which covered the doll. He whispered words she'd never heard before and she saw the doll fall over. The old plastic melted as the paint peeled off and the plastic hair shrivelled, leaving a disgusting grey slop in its stead.

"Necromancy is not the art of manipulating corpses, as you put it. You were led to believe it is nothing but an elaborate form of animancy, the art of making objects move to the cadence of your will. Admirable, and certainly powerful, but surely quite dirty and unhygienic?"

He never took his eyes off her as he resumed his bizarre incantation. The goop on the floor, all that remained of her childhood companion, started to ooze and then pulsate.

Anuna held her breath in terror.

"True necromancy—the second discipline you seek—is the art of life and death."

A few green bursts of sheer power arced from his hands into the pulsating mess and, as it did, the doll raised its tiny arms. Tiny hands formed and fingers spread wide as the little body solidified into a living, breathing miniature horror. Melanie sat up and opened its eyes.

"They would have you live your life as another impotent, obedient cog in the machine. By the time you're thirty, all the spark has gone out. All that's left is the routine that will be your undoing."

Anuna choked up. She understood. The art of life was not forbidden, but rather it was hidden. Such incredible efforts, upheld throughout all that time. For it to stand apart from the lore of energy had so many implications, each possibility that opened up to her more fantastic. Essentially, energy was not all. There was something else, ingrained into the fabric of existence. Something that binds all that is together into a cohesive whole. Life. Death. It wasn't just the locomotion of parts as she had always assumed.

So many decades of lies. No, millennia? The powers contained within the lore would have to be truly awesome, terrifying, terrible. It had to be hidden. It had to. From all but the few. She looked at the terrible creation that sat between them. Part of Anuna missed the doll, now that it was gone. The disgusting creature filled her with nausea and Anuna realised one more thing: it was wrong. True necromancy, or whatever it was called, was at its core a vile art, withering and warping. The pitiful doll tried to stand up, a look of confusion and wonder on its grotesquely human features. But now, Anuna knew she had to make a choice.

Anuna bowed. "Please, Master, teach me everything."

UNORTHODOX METHODS TO SUCCESSFULLL COW AN APOTHECARY

By R. E. Misery

One way or another, Svar was going to make sure Yaniv moved out.

Mornings in Ashewood were always beautiful. Illuminating the town with an ethereal shimmer, the sun-streaked hues of rose and lavender across the azure of the waking sky, while a crisp breeze rolled in from River Yan down south. But the beautiful dawn had lost its allure these past few months. Skulker was ruining the ambience every morning by loitering in the shadows like a demon in the night.

Behind the double-storied brick shop at the crack of dawn, with his old key already thrust into the iron lock, Svar sensed Skulker approaching him before he even heard the older man's shambling footsteps.

"How much?" Skulker asked. His voice was hoarse from abuse. Too much Dragonsbane being washed down with cheap ale. The herbal drug and alcohol were deadly when mixed, could eat through soaked iron ingots at the turn of the sun. It was no surprise that the man was falling apart from the inside out.

Slowly, with his heart thundering in his chest, Svar pulled his key out from the still-locked door. Turning around, he forced a pleasant smile onto his face. Svar was nothing more than a simple florist who didn't want any trouble.

Skulker was only half his size, shambles of an old skeletal man with rotten teeth and hollow sunken eyes. He was wearing the same tattered outfit he had been wearing when he had first appeared over a month ago, the fabric falling apart at the seams just like his body.

"Sir, I've told you that I don't sell Dragonsbane. You need to go see Borea in the Temple of Life. She's a healer. She can help you," Svar said simply. He had already reported Skulker, as well as the others, to the town Watch. But if the afflicted refused help, there was not much the guards could do to get rid of them. They hadn't hurt anyone, had only lingered to the point of being an annoyance. There was no proof that the man was getting Dragonsbane from the shop on the main floor, either. The Watch had investigated, and now they didn't want to hear about it again, turning a blind eye.

Svar needed Yaniv to set up shop elsewhere. He'd been plotting ideas all week on how to convince the man to move to no avail. There had to be something Svar could do to peacefully drive the other man out.

Nodding, Skulker mumbled under his breath before turning away, clicking his teeth together as he hobbled back to the alley to loiter. Svar breathed out a heavy sigh, his hands trembling. It seemed there wouldn't be a problem today. At least for now. He reached to his chest automatically, fingers clasping around the circular charm hanging from his neck. It was packed full of chamomile and gentle herbs, but had only eased his anxieties for the first few weeks after he had bought it. Now it didn't seem to quell his racing heart at all.

Unlocking the back entrance, Svar quickly slipped inside, locking the door behind him.

The shop was a three-level building. The hallway from the back connected into the store on the main floor, as well as the tattoo parlour downstairs, and Svar's flower shop upstairs. A few months ago, Yaniv Vulbretch moved into the space on the main floor, turning it into an apothecary.

He appeared to be some kind of Warlock. Unsavoury customers like Skulker had begun to loiter out front of the shop shortly after Yaniv's arrival, looking for Dragonsbane.

Taking the old rickety stairs two at a time, Svar quickly locked himself into his shop before tending to his plants. His little plant shop had been thriving until Yaniv moved in. Gifted with a Seer's Insight, Svar could tell just by looking at a living thing exactly what nutrition it required, so he could care for any plant that came through his door.

"Who wants some water?" Svar cooed as he sauntered around his shop. In his hands was a clay jug full of local well water that he had personally treated himself. His plants deserved the best, after all. They soothed his nerves.

When he finished tidying his storefront, he quickly disappeared into the back, unlocking the storage room. Inside, Svar locked that door behind him too. Several little clay pots sat in a neat row on a table, just beneath the wide window that only got direct sunlight during the peak of the afternoon. Six baby Howlers were just beginning to sprout from the damp soil, no more than pinky-length sprouts. They would get him into a lot of trouble if he was caught with them, but at this age, they were still quiet and discrete. His buyer would take them right before they bloomed when there was no fear of them dying. They were sensitive plants after all. Exotic. With drooping grey and black petals akin to a wolf's snout, the plants characteristically vibrated in maturity, emitting a soft moan like a low howl. Svar hadn't asked what the plants were for. He didn't want to know. They were poisonous if consumed by men, but they were also used for suppressing Lycanthropy.

Satisfied with the state of his baby plants, Svar locked them back up before unlocking his shop doors, including the door to the beautiful balcony outside. In better seasons, when Dragonsbane addicts weren't trying to eat the herbs and petals he put out, the whole wooden balcony would be full of flora and blooming flowers instead of being left empty.

At noon, the door to Svar's shop opened, the bells chiming softly above. Svar glanced up from the table he was sitting at in the middle of the shop, plucking dead foliage from a sad plant. Both his smile and his fingers froze. This person wasn't a customer.

"Ram?" Svar asked, his grin still wide and friendly despite the man who was aggressively walking straight up to him. The owner of the tattoo parlour downstairs always made Svar nervous, and ever since Yaniv had moved in, Ram had been making more and more frequent visits. His forearms and neck were covered in thick, striped tattoos. Elegant lines slid up his neck, over his jaw up to his cheekbones, making him look like a Demon of Old. Svar always wondered if they were prison bands, but he was too afraid to ask. They were too nice, too neat and clean compared to the usual branding methods, but in Ram's line of work, he could have easily gotten them fixed.

"Hey. Hope you're not busy." Ram wasn't as tall as Svar, but he was more built and his fiery red hair was intimidating all on its own.

Svar easily smiled. He had seen enough of Ram lately that he wasn't as nervous as usual. "Nope. What's up?"

"I came up here because of Yaniv. Again. I kind of want to suck the life out of him," Ram said. He shoved his hands into the pockets of his black attire.

"Oh?" Svar asked, his thoughts automatically wandering to the Alchemist downstairs. He'd been cornered and verbally threatened twice already, but he still didn't know how to drive the man out.

Ram huffed an annoyed sound, red eyes narrowing on Svar. "I think we should finally team up and convince him to leave. He's a lop and bad for business. That man's tongue is as sharp as they come."

"I noticed," Svar said. "He's cornered me a few times to complain about the flowers. Says their fragrances are meddling with his wares and contaminating their properties."

"Oh? Someone from the Watch came by last night asking about the suspicious lurkers outside," Ram said. "I don't want the Watch coming around here. I have enough problems."

"Agreed," Svar said. Svar knew what he had in his storage room—plants that could both kill a man or help a cursed man—so he could only wonder what Ram was selling on the side. Maybe one day Svar would find out.

"So, are you a Mage? There's no way you're non-magical, not with white hair like that," Ram abruptly asked, the personal question catching Svar by surprise.

"Isn't it rude to ask that before telling me if you're a Mage?" Svar asked.

"If we were on a date, then yes," Ram said smoothly. "But this is more like an interview. I'll be hiring you as an accomplice, so I need to know. But now that you mention it, I would ask you out to dinner if the situation was different."

"Oh?" Svar laughed. "Are you shamelessly flirting with me?"

"Yeah," Ram said. "And?"

Svar stuttered, feeling his face heat up. "And—nothing. But you first. Are you a Mage?"

Ram chuckled. "I'm not a Mage, but I have a Seer's Insight. I'm skilled with curses. I can curse people and objects. I can seal trinkets and release seals and make complicated conditions. But curses are illegal over here and I'm trying to keep my neck above water, you understand? There's no business in it."

"Oh. We're the same then," Svar said. "I also have a Seer's Insight. I can see the needs of all living things just by looking at them. I usually just look at my plants, though. Plants are really simple and easy to care for. They lack complicated emotions and the ability to hold grudges."

"Cute," Ram said with a wink. "But we're not very useful against Yaniv. I know for a fact that he's selling Dragonsbane to non-magical people. I've already talked to him about it, but he's not very nice. So, I was thinking maybe you can try and talk to him? If I run into him, we'll just fight."

Svar swallowed thickly. He didn't like confrontation. "Yeah, I can go talk to him."

"Good," Ram said. "And while you're at it, figure out if he's a Mage or down on our level."

"Sure thing," Svar said.

But when Ram left with a short wave and a cheeky grin, sauntering out of Svar's shop back to the lair from which he had come, Svar's heart was pounding hard in his chest. Reaching for the little circular charm hanging from his neck, Svar couldn't tell if he was nervous about facing Yaniv or disappointing Ram.

At noon, Dmitri Earlon, a little Earth Mage with big brown eyes and wild brown hair, came in for his shift. Svar had been mentoring him, teaching him the ways of the plants and the dirt until Dmitri found himself a real Mage to take him under his wing. The second Dmitri entered the shop, Svar shoved a broom into the surprised teen's hands before disappearing into the back hallway that connected the shops. If Svar was going to confront Yaniv, he needed to do it right now.

With a tiny succulent in his hands, Svar nervously entered the apothecary.

"Hello." A very tall man with long blond hair greeted him from one of his shelves. He was displaying ominous charms and wards, little glass animals full of herbs and spices hanging from twine necklaces dyed a variety of colours. Svar felt overwhelmed just standing in the shop, could feel the energies from the charms mixing into one giant maelstrom of anxiety.

"Hi, Yaniv," Svar said. He shakily approached Yaniv's counter, setting the little succulent securely down. "I thought I'd bring you this little guy as a gift, but really, I wanted to ask about the non-magical people lurking outside."

"Ignore them," Yaniv said simply as he spun around. His voice had been commanding enough to make Svar freeze. Gold irises fixed on Svar like wolves on a bunny in the woods, pinning him to the spot. When Yaniv moved, he was silent. Suddenly in Svar's space, only hands apart, Yaniv reached out, scooping up Svar's hands into his own and turning them palm up. Curiously, golden eyes glanced down over the lines in Svar's skin, thumbs smoothing over the muscles gently. From the skin contact, there was a transfer of energy. Yaniv read something from Svar, and Svar read that Yaniv took good care of himself. His body's nutritional levels were in proper order, perhaps even perfect. As usual, his information didn't benefit Svar in any single way. It was frustrating.

"You're nervous," Yaniv said, his voice purring so pleasantly that Svar suddenly shivered. Yaniv pulled away, the smile still on his face as he turned around and plucked a charm from his wares. He spun back around, looping the blue-dyed twine necklace around Svar's neck and tying it, the glittering glass owl settling heavily over Svar's quickening heart. Perhaps it was supposed to be grounding. Svar reached for it just as Yaniv tugged off the old charm, holding it up for inspection.

"This one is dead. There's jasmine and herbs in the talisman I just gave you to ease that anxiety of yours. It should last longer than this one did, but your anxiousness is too powerful," Yaniv said. But then he smiled gently and Svar forgot why he had been here in the first place, why he had been angry with this man.

"I hope we remain friendly in the future," Yaniv said. He leaned in close so he could lower his voice, his warm breath tingling against Svar's cheek. "I don't think you'd like to have a problem with me, hm?"

"Yeah. Sure." Svar stuttered, suddenly wanting to be anywhere else but here with Yaniv.

Fleeing the shop, Svar immediately went downstairs. His head was spinning, his hand still wrapped around the charm. Pushing through the parlour door, Svar almost ran into a dark-haired girl with a mop. If Svar remembered correctly, the teen was a Water Mage and Ram's apprentice, and Svar had seen her upstairs flirting with Dmitri. Her blue eyes flickered up to Svar quickly, before locking on the glass owl hanging from his neck. She was distracted for a breath before she apologized and scampered away.

"I've seen her in my shop," Svar said after the younger girl had run off. He approached Ram's counter quickly. "She flirts with my apprentice."

"Amaya?" Ram paused what he was doing to look up, scandalized. "Flirting? Really?"

"Yeah, that's what I said when I first caught Dmitri flirting back. He's so socially awkward but they chat so much that I had to kick her out one day," Svar said with a laugh.

"Cute," Ram said. He finished counting the coins before giving Svar his undivided attention. "So... Did you speak to Yaniv?"

"Yes. His voice sounds like a curse and rubs me six ways," Svar said.

Ram barked a laugh, his eyes glittering in amusement. "Did he agree to chase off his lurkers so they'll stop scaring off our customers?"

"No," Svar said. "But he has a Seer's Insight like mine. Like when I look at you, I can see that you need a snack to fix that low blood sugar but your hydration is great. He looked at me and saw a chemical imbalance impacting my mood and gave me this charm to fix it."

Just for emphasis, Svar lifted the charm, letting the heavy owl dangle from the twine.

"He gave you a gift? Maybe there's a nice guy underneath that lop brain of his after all," Ram said, but his eyes lingered on the owl. "So his power is just as useless as ours?"

"Our powers aren't useless. Stop that. They can be used to help people," Svar said.

"The keyword is can," Ram said. "Yaniv doesn't seem to be the helpful type, and I'm sure he's got a trick or two up his sleeves."

Svar smiled anxiously. "I don't think he's going to leave. We might just have to drop it."

"Or I could just stab him," Ram said offhandedly.

Svar gaped. He wasn't sure if Ram was jesting or not, his eyes sliding back to those banded tattoos in suspicion.

"I'm kidding," Ram said, his voice getting a little more defensive when Svar obviously didn't believe him. "I won't. I have an idea, but I promise I will harm no living beings in the process."

"You better not," Svar said. "And you better not involve me. I'm done with this."

"Don't worry about it. Thanks for trying anyway. I owe you one," Ram said with a wink.

"Okay. Well, I'm going to go now." Svar laughed as he spun on his heel.

Upstairs, Dmitri complained about the lack of customers. Svar only sighed as he checked over Dmitri's cleaning.

"Where'd you get that owl? It's really neat," Dmitri said curiously.

"Yaniv," Svar said. "I think it was a peace offering."

Dmitri laughed at that before tending to the plants.

Idly, Svar pulled on his neckline, his heart still beating too fast. It didn't calm for the rest of the afternoon.

* * *

The next morning was a disaster.

Svar arrived later than usual, feeling cloudier than the sky, just to be harassed by Skulker once again. With his heart already beating frantically in his chest, his breath short, he caught Ram standing at the back door of their store with a bristled tool raised. Ram's right arm was bleeding as he leisurely painted blood seals into the door with his left. The red markings disappeared with each stroke as he covered every inch of the door, the runes whispering with power that Svar could hear from where he stood.

"What are you doing?" Svar hissed. His head spun. He'd felt nauseated when he'd gotten up and it had gotten worse. "Are you cursing the door in broad daylight? That's illegal."

"And selling drugs out his back door isn't illegal?" Ram asked, pausing in his work for only a second to gesture at Skulker. "That guy has asked me every single day if I will sell him Dragonsbane cheaper than Yaniv. The problem isn't the drugs Svar, it's the principle."

"The principle? Are you jesting? Do you have something to hide?" Svar asked. His voice cracked awkwardly. He was too old to stress like this.

"Do you?" Ram shot back.

"If you both have something to hide, maybe you should be a little more cautious." Yaniv was suddenly right there, hands away from Svar. "I have nothing to hide. What are you doing to the door?"

Ram glanced over his shoulder with his brush poised over the door, a single drop of blood dripping from the bristles. Apparently, honesty was the best medicine. Svar wanted to step forward and just wrap his hands around Ram's tanned throat the second the man spoke.

"I'm cursing the door," Ram said. "I won't tell you what kind of curse though, because that would ruin the fun."

Svar's blood rushed to his head. What was this fool saying out loud? Turning away, Svar pressed a hand to his forehead, debating if he was better off just going back home. He didn't have the energy to deal with this. He had been feeling odd all night. Weighed down. Fluttering between calmness and distress.

"Svar, don't leave," Yaniv said. "What do you hope to achieve, Ram? To bully me out of here? You have no proof that I'm doing anything illegal, while I'm sure at least *you* are doing something you shouldn't be. Those marks on your face tell me you're nothing but trouble, and if the Watch comes down here, you're the first person they're going to investigate."

"I think these guys lollygagging are proof enough. They'll foolishly ask the Watch for Dragonsbane themselves and sell you out," Ram said simply, finishing up his curse. He pulled a clean cloth from his pocket after, slapping it down onto his arm.

"If I were to call the Watch and report you for cursing the building, do you think you can defend yourself with a dud human spewing nonsense in the alley?" Yaniv asked, head tilting.

"He's not a 'dud human,' that is a living person," Svar said. "You're feeding his addiction and helping him ruin his life."

"You can call the Watch if you want. I've been an upstanding citizen," Ram said heatedly. "If your little Watch friends can find my work, I'd be impressed enough to admit to doing it."

Yaniv huffed. "Instead of squabbling like a whelp, why don't the three of us make a deal?"

"Nope. No deals. I'm just a florist," Svar said. "I don't make deals and I remember not wanting to get involved. I want nothing to do with this."

"Svar, come here," Ram said. His voice was clipped, those blood-red eyes snapping over to Svar so fast that they pinned him in place. Svar placed a hand to his chest, the fluttering of his heart dangerous. He hadn't had this much anxiety in years.

"You're being bullied too, I see," Yaniv said. His golden eyes didn't leave Ram.

"I'm not bullying him," Ram snapped. "If anyone is being bullied, I will admit that it's you. You're the only person being bullied here because your drug addicts are warding off our paying customers and putting us all in danger. You don't think the Watch hasn't come skulking around since you arrived?"

Yaniv chuckled darkly. "And you think I care if the two of you work here or not? If the building was empty, I would have bought all of it."

"So you planned to drive the both of us out in the first place?" Ram asked.

"I don't want anything to do with this," Svar said. His chest hurt. "Nothing at all. Call the Watch if you want, but I'm going upstairs."

Svar fled. He shoved past Ram to get inside the building as fast as he could, quickly going upstairs. Unlocking his door to get into his shop, he pressed one hand to his forehead before leaning back against the door. No, no, no, he couldn't deal with this kind of stress. He'd been shaky and a little delirious since yesterday, and he wasn't sure who was causing more stress: Yaniv or Ram.

After half an hour of scurrying around, trying to keep busy and calm his nerves, trying not to think about the Howlers in his storage room, Ram came up to visit.

The second Ram stepped through the door, Svar whirled around and waved a finger at him, stopping the man in his tracks. Svar couldn't even explain why he was upset. He just was. "Nope. I don't want to see you here. You're going to get both of us in trouble!"

"I know you're mad——"

"Yeah, I'm mad. Is Yaniv calling the Watch?" Svar asked. His thoughts were on the Howlers and the fact that he could get heavily fined, if not jailed, just for growing them. He had six when he wasn't even supposed to have a single one. They weren't native to this side of the country and had been all but eradicated in the wild north a few decades ago after a couple of bad Alchemists had gone mad, using the flowers to try and murder the High King and royal families. Their use as a poison outweighed their benefit as a control for Lycanthropy, mostly because half the population didn't even believe Lycanthropy existed.

"I doubt he'll call the Watch. Don't worry about it." Ram shrugged. "I'll deal with them if they come, it's not a problem. I'm the best of the best when it comes to curses so they won't find my runes. But I came here to apologize for snapping at you and—are you feeling alright?"

"What?" Svar asked. He backed up violently when Ram stepped into his space. Ram reached out suddenly, plucking up the glass charm from over Svar's chest. Svar instantly grabbed for Ram's wrist to stop him but he faltered.

Ram let the little owl rest in his palm, admiring the glass for a second before he closed his fist, sliding the twine loop from around Svar's neck. Svar gasped, eyebrows creasing. Weight lifted from his chest like he had finally unburdened himself, his frantic heart still thrumming desperately but settling down for the first time in hours.

"It's not cursed, but it's packed full of negative energy. He knew what he was giving you," Ram said. His voice was low. Deadly. A line creased in his forehead until he turned around and stormed away with the charm still in his clenched fist.

"Where are you going? What are you going to do?" Svar called. He stumbled after Ram into the hallway, lingering in his doorway.

"You sure ask a lot of questions for a guy who was really mad at me only a few breaths ago," Ram said, pausing at the top of the stairs to turn Svar's way.

"I wholeheartedly blame the charm for my bad behaviour until now. I have been freed," Svar said with a chuckle. "Now what are you doing?"

Ram barked a laugh. "Well, first of all, if the Watch is swinging by, I'm going to make sure I have nothing incriminating in my shop. And by that, I mean I'm going to hide everything in plain sight."

"Oh, Gods, that's a great idea," Svar said. His Howlers were still sprouting. He could easily hide them in with the other baby plants around the shop. "I didn't even think—"

"Oh? So you *do* have something to hide? I knew you had at least one devious bone in your body." Ram flashed Svar a sultry smile. "Second of all, I have an idea. Go hide what you need to hide. I'll be upstairs in a few minutes to explain."

"Okay?" Svar asked. He quirked an eyebrow, watching Ram turn away and quickly descend the stairs.

Unlocking his storage room, Svar stepped inside. It would disrupt the plants for a few hours to be moved, but in the end, it was necessary. He didn't have to worry about customers coming in and accidentally buying the tiny plants because there were no customers these days.

Pulling out all of his baby Howlers, Svar did just as Ram was doing, hiding the little sprouts among the other baby plants in his shop. To someone who had no idea what they were looking at, the baby Howlers looked just like the baby peperomioides Svar had gotten off a travelling merchant a month back. They had only begun to sprout, so mixing six more little clay pots onto the shelf wasn't that suspicious. There were no labels on anything, so the Watch wouldn't even notice them. Hopefully. Unless they had a herbalist with them or a forager. That would be Svar's bad luck.

True to his word, Ram popped back into the shop a while later. "You good?"

"I have nothing to hide," Svar said with a wink. He was in his storage room, cleaning up spilt dirt and rearranging his supplies to make it look less conspicuous. He really was just paranoid, Svar supposed, but now that the charm was gone from around his neck, he had to admit he was feeling a little better. Freer.

"Here's the plan. You're not going to like it, but the situation has turned a little bit dramatic," Ram said. He offered Svar an appealing smile, but it did nothing to ease Svar's stress. From his pocket, Ram pulled out the glass owl, raising it in the air by the twine.

"You want me to put that back on?" Svar asked. "Why?"

"I added an ingredient to it," Ram said. He hesitated to continue, his eyes straying to the charm. "You're not going to feel very well, but its effects won't last. The story we're telling is that Yaniv gave you the necklace intending to poison you. If we can't bully him out, and the Watch won't do anything about the lurkers on the streets, then we'll have to accuse him of bodily harm."

"This is all very convoluted just to get a guy kicked out of our building," Svar said. He didn't reach for the charm, eyes on it warily.

"Would you rather me just stab him and hide his body in the woods?" Ram asked. "No? Then put it on. When's your apprentice in? Noon? You should be feeling sick in the next few hours, just make sure you mention it to your apprentice."

"Dmitri will be in at noon," Svar said. He carefully reached for the charm, his eyes flashing up to Ram warily. "Will it kill me?"

"No," Ram said. He sounded confident enough to ease Svar's stress. "You won't wear it for longer than a day, so you'll be alright. Just put it on and trust me. Also, that curse I put on the back door forces only Yaniv to tell the truth if he's inside the building. I got all the front doors too. So if the Watch questions Yaniv and he doesn't know to withhold his information—"

"—he'll tell them what he's been up to." Svar finished with a laugh. It was smart. He glanced down to the little charm sitting so innocently in his palm, running his thumb over the smooth glass. It was a beautiful pendant. Too bad it would only be wasted once this was all over. Who would keep such a thing? Svar didn't plan to.

Taking a deep breath, Svar looped the necklace back over his neck, letting the glass settle against his chest. He instantly felt heavier, his mood souring on his exhale. His headache from earlier was back in the next breath, his heart rate picking up once again. How had he not noticed this yesterday?

"You better come and rescue me," Svar said. He didn't like this one bit.

For the first time since Svar had met him, Ram was frowning. "I'll be here. Just go do your work as you usually would. You don't have to do anything besides tell the guards when they show up that Yaniv gave you the talisman and that you're feeling sick."

"Yes sir," Svar said, but his stomach was already rolling and he felt ill.

Ram nodded, arms still crossed, before leaving to tend to his shop. Svar took a deep breath of his own before he got ready for the day, unlocking his doors incredibly late and watering everyone as quick as he could.

The morning dragged on. It seemed as though the passage of time had suddenly slowed to a stop. By the time Dmitri came strolling in at noon, excitedly chatting about the garden he had just planted at home, Svar had already thrown up. Sitting at the table with plants all around him, Svar leaned with his head in his hands, his eyes closed.

"Svar? Are you alright?" Dmitri asked. He rushed over, placing a hand on Svar's shoulder.

Svar only moaned. He didn't even have to lie about his condition. "I'm not feeling too well."

"I can see that," Dmitri said. His tone wavered in concern. "What can I do? Do you need anything? Should I go get someone?"

"Mm," Svar murmured. "Not that Alchemist. I think he did something."

"Okay," Dmitri said. "I'll be right back!"

Svar only hummed again. He couldn't tell how long it had been, more than a few breaths at least. But suddenly Ram was right there, reaching an arm out to gently shake Svar's shoulder. Belatedly, Svar realised that Ram had asked him a question, his thoughts trudging through mud and suddenly not understanding the common language.

Lifting his head, Svar stared blearily, his eyes narrowed. "What?"

"I said that you're looking rougher than expected," Ram said. He frowned. Carefully, he brushed some of Svar's unruly hair out of his face, placing the back of his hand against Svar's warm, sweaty forehead. He gently lifted Svar's hand, placing two fingers over the pulse point in Svar's wrist.

Turning over his shoulder to the apprentices in the doorway, Ram frowned. "Can you guys go find a healer?"

"Yup!" Amaya and Dmitri said, their voices high and worried. And with that, the two of them were gone.

"You better make this worth it," Svar whispered without any bite. His head was spinning just as fast as his stomach. Ram's attention turned back to him and Svar instantly knew by the frown on Ram's face that he wasn't supposed to be this sick this fast.

"I'll take you for dinner and drinks. I'll promise you that, at least that. For your valiant efforts," Ram offered. He grinned wide, but the smile didn't reach his eyes. "Here, can you stand? Let's get you outside."

Svar groaned. He couldn't stand, could hardly lift his spinning head. Ram reached for the talisman around his neck, carefully pulling it off. The weight on Svar lifted, but it wasn't enough. Svar didn't feel like it would ever be enough. Ram placed the charm on the table, and in the next moment, Svar heard the door open again. Blearily, Svar tried to smile as a woman in white robes knelt beside him, her voice gentle and questioning. But his vision faded quickly. The last Svar saw was Ram's worried expression.

* * *

Ram's plan had deviated. Svar shouldn't have been so sick.

Lingering a few paces away by the counter to give Borea, the healer, some space, Ram wanted to pace. But he didn't want to make the two young Mages in the doorway any more nervous than they were, so he refrained from moving. He was suddenly doubting himself, wondering if his addition to the charm had been too much. Had he put in too much? Was it something else?

Shortly after Borea confirmed that Svar's condition wasn't natural, a guard from the Watch entered the shop. Ram crossed his arms as the guard approached him with an apprehensive look. Ram was used to it. People were quick to judge him everywhere he went. He didn't want the guard to be here anymore than Yaniv did downstairs, but Svar was half-conscious and Ram was worried he had gone too far this time.

"I'm Samson Walcher. What happened?" Walcher asked.

Ram glanced over to Svar who was unconscious on the table, snow-white hair spilling around his head like an angel's halo. Borea was inspecting the talisman that Ram had pulled off of him, her eyes critical as she poked around its contents.

"Dmitri came down to my shop, said Svar was sick," Ram said. "I think the charm he had on made him ill. The Alchemist gave it to him yesterday, Yaniv Vulbretch. He hasn't been very…friendly since he set up shop. Svar and I confronted him about selling Dragonsbane and he's been rude ever since."

"Dragonsbane? Are you the one making all the reports and complaints?" Walcher asked, his tone souring at the mention.

"No. Someone's been reporting him?" Ram asked. He hadn't realised Yaniv had already been reported.

"Yeah. We get complaints almost daily, but there's nothing we can do," Walcher said.

Nothing you can do, or nothing you *want* to do? Ram grimaced, eyes sliding back to Svar.

"Is Yaniv here?" Walcher asked.

"Yeah," Ram said. "Yaniv's downstairs. We had an altercation this morning about the doors. He accused me of stringing up curses all over the building. I think he took one look at me and judged me for my tattoos if I have to be honest. I'm on my best behaviour! You just ask your captain; he's had no trouble from me, but I've had nothing but trouble with Yaniv. And now Svar too. Who's next? Our apprentices?"

Beside Svar, Borea stood up with a neutral look.

"One of these flowers in here is poisonous. The talisman is full of herbs that promote sickness and negative energy when they're combined. Judging by the petal shape and the black markings on one of them, it's likely a Mauve Mountain Flower. They're extremely toxic and it looks like a second flower was crushed into a powder. He may be suffering from acute poisoning," Borea reported. She glanced over her shoulder, turning her big eyes on Walcher. "He'll recover on his own, but I have elixirs that can help. It's only been one sun rotation, but he's not handling the poison well."

"He got the talisman from the scary Alchemist!" Amaya said, piping up from the doorway. "Svar came by the tattoo parlour because the Alchemist spooked him yesterday!"

"He took a succulent to Yaniv as a peace offering," Dmitri said. "Svar's nervous about him so he was trying to make nice. I think Yaniv did something while he was down there. He was acting weird all afternoon yesterday."

Walcher nodded, listening. His eyes flashed over Ram before he sighed. "I'll go talk to the Alchemist downstairs, then. Let's get this finally dealt with."

Ram gave Svar one more look over before following after the guard. He stayed far enough away that he wouldn't be scolded for being too eager to see Yaniv confronted. Downstairs, Ram lingered in the doorway to the apothecary, leaning against the wall to watch the exchange. Yaniv didn't look too surprised to see Walcher approach him. Golden eyes slid Ram's way, a smirk spreading on his face before the Alchemist turned his attention back to Walcher.

"You're Yaniv Vulbretch?" Walcher asked.

"Yes," Yaniv said. His smile was friendly but too wide. Too amused. He thought he had the upper hand, didn't he?

"You know Svar upstairs in the flower shop? Did you give him a talisman yesterday?" Walcher asked, hands on his hips.

"I did," Yaniv said. "What is this about?"

"Did you give it to him with the intent to harm him?" Walcher asked.

"Yes," Yaniv said. His expression changed, puzzlement crossing his features at the admittance, eyes briefly flashing from Walcher to Ram in anger. "I mean—"

Ram smirked, wiping the expression off his face before he could be caught.

"There are some concerning accusations against you," Walcher said. "What do you know about Dragonsbane?"

Yaniv laughed, his eyes narrowing. "I know enough about Dragonsbane. Everyone and their dog knows about Dragonsbane. What are you accusing me of?"

"Is there any in this shop?" Walcher asked.

Yaniv laughed, but he refused to answer. He crossed his arms, gold eyes seeking out Ram. "It was him! You cursed this building against lies, didn't you, Ram? Sir, if you need to accuse anyone of misconduct, it will be him right over there. He's selling cursed objects out of his parlour downstairs and he cursed this building too."

Walcher sighed. "Yaniv, I'll need you to come with me. We're going down to the Watch-house, just for a conversation. And you there, Ram, come down with your apprentices for a witness statement. I'll also need to ask you a few questions as well. I'll be in touch with Borea, so don't worry about your friend. No one is being arrested right now. We're just discussing. There's been a lot of complaints about this building lately."

"Of course. Anything you need," Ram said, raising his hands in mock surrender.

Yaniv spat, glaring. He cooperated with the guard, however, leaving Ram feeling a little disappointed with the turn of events. He had been hoping for a dramatic reveal, but perhaps this was fine all on its own. Oh well.

Regardless, Yaniv was dealt with for the time being. Even if he didn't face jail time, he'd at least end up on a watch list for Dragonsbane. And with Svar threatened, all eyes would be on Yaniv. Ram waved coyly as Yaniv was led out of the building, before going back upstairs. He hadn't foreseen the plan backfiring like this. He just hoped that Svar was okay.

"Will he be alright?" Ram asked Borea, lingering behind her shoulder once again.

"He'll be fine. If you could help me get him down to the temple, that would be appreciated," Borea said.

"Consider it done," Ram said. He beckoned the apprentices over, and together they got Svar down to the Temple of Life.

* * *

When Svar woke up, he felt like he had been asleep for millennia. His body was so sore that he didn't even bother to sit up, let alone move. An ache buzzed down to his fingertips and when he concentrated, he could tell his body was in desperate need of everything. Simply lolling his head over to the side, Svar blinked blearily at Ram sitting in the chair beside him. He didn't know where he was, figured he was probably at the nearest temple judging by the stone walls. He was tucked into a little tiny room just big enough for him on the bed and Ram beside him, no other furnishings, the ceilings high and domed. The thin blanket covering him was white cotton, only used by the priests.

"How are you feeling?" Ram asked. He looked amused, which could be a good sign. He was leaning comfortably in his chair, no sense of urgency in his body language. That was good. Svar sighed. His immediate stress eased.

Svar laughed. "Like I had the Magika flu ten times over."

Ram chuckled. "Yeah, I'd bet. Did you know you're sensitive to charms and drain their powers faster than the average person?"

"No," Svar said. He laughed. "Just my luck, hey?"

"Right." Ram laughed. "Borea said you should rest for the next couple of days. Yaniv is down at the jailhouse right now and all the lurkers have been taken in by the temple. If you want, I can borrow your key and let your apprentice into your store, if you trust him enough to let him run the shop for you until you're feeling better."

"Wow," Svar said. "My hero."

"Well, I'm kind of the reason why you're half-dead right now. It would be rude of me not to offer you any kind of help after almost killing you," Ram said. Svar didn't know him very well, but Ram sounded guilty. It made Svar laugh, a deep chortle that left him clutching at his stomach in pain.

"Oh," Ram said. "I also got you a gift."

Svar raised an eyebrow just as Ram pulled a little talisman from his pocket. Grinning like an idiot, Ram held it up for Svar to see the little glass fox head hanging from the blue-dyed twine string.

"No," Svar said automatically. He laughed, raising a hand to point at the charm. "I've had enough of those things. I don't even want to look at it."

Ram rolled his eyes. "Relax. You're way too high-strung. I got this from a friend of mine. Trust me, he wouldn't lie about its contents. He knows better."

As if to prove himself, Ram reached over, letting the little glass charm rest on Svar's chest. Unlike the heaviness of the owl Yaniv had given him, the fox head was lighter than expected, pleasant, like a crisp breeze rolling in from River Yan. There was something else too, a rippling power coursing through the twine that suggested Ram had tampered with the charm himself. Perhaps for the better. Svar reached up, fingers closing around the talisman in acceptance. "Thanks."

"So. You. Me. Dinner and drinks," Ram said. "I think you kind of earned it at this point. I mean, I almost killed you and I don't know if I should be ashamed of myself for being an enabler or if I should be worried about how foolish you are for actually listening to me."

Svar laughed. "Doesn't matter if you're an enabler or I'm just foolish. I could use a drink now and after all of this, you owe me one. So I'll accept."

"Good, it's decided. I should head back and let you rest. I'm kind of not supposed to be here," Ram said. He stood up, still grinning.

"Wait," Svar said urgently. "My plants. Tell Dmitri he can't sell any of the sprouting peperomioides."

"I'll tell him," Ram said. "Why?"

Svar smirked. "Maybe one day I'll tell you."

Ram fixed Svar with a suspicious look. "You better."

Ram left, leaving Svar to stare at the little fox head in wonder. It was a thoughtful gift and Svar appreciated it. But days later, when Yaniv slunk back into his apothecary, free as a bird and only fined for the minuscule stash of Dragonsbane they had found, Svar realised that the talisman was more than just a thoughtful gift.

Yaniv took one look at Svar in the back hallway before glowering. He silently turned away without saying anything for once. Good. But from where Svar stood with one foot on the step, he saw the biological drop in Yaniv as the fox head sucked away his nutritional values. A cursed object. An energy thief. It looked like Ram hadn't been joking when he had said he was skilled with complex curses. It seemed like only Yaniv was affected, but only in close quarters. Smiling, Svar went back upstairs and greeted Dmitri, excited to be back to work.

* * *

Later that day, Ram took a second glance at a tiny succulent on his counter that certainly hadn't been there a few hours ago. He paused what he was doing, reaching out for the plant, gently touching one of the thick leaves. Svar must have snuck in while he was busy in the back. It was a welcomed surprise to his boring day.

"Cute," Ram said to himself before his finger touched the little pot, a thought suddenly occurring to him. He narrowed his eyes. He should've done this in the first place.

Upstairs, Ram leaned against the door to Svar's shop, baring a wide grin at the other man. Svar paused what he was doing, floundering for a second before offering Ram a bright grin.

"How many clay pots do you have in here?" Ram asked in place of a greeting.

"I don't know," Svar said, his head tilting to the side. "A few hundred? Why?"

Ram held up his bristled tool with a devious grin. "I apologize for dramatically trying to poison you last week. Instead, my next bad idea is that we're going to suck the life out of our unwanted neighbour on a grander scale until he leaves of his own accord. You see, I will admit that I cursed that little charm I gave you against Yaniv specifically. It's a ward to make Yaniv feel uncomfortable around you, slightly unnerved. But if your whole shop was full of cursed pots, he'd feel sick every time he came into this building. Drained and dismal because the plants would be sucking the nutrients out of him. I think it would be enough to drive him out for good. I'll even throw in a resist-disease ward for your plants to thank you for letting me tamper with the pots."

Svar fixed him with a look, lips parted, speechless again. It took him a breath to find his words but eventually he laughed. He looked bemused. "After your last plan, I want nothing to do with this. But you have until Dmitri gets here to do your sneaking around. I think I'll go outside for lunch today so I'm not an accomplice."

"I guess I'm officially firing you." Ram laughed. "You were a great employee. Foolishly dedicated to the cause."

"Thank you. You make a nice boss, but I prefer being my own boss," Svar said. "Goodbye, Ram. Make sure nothing in this store harms me after, okay?"

"Of course. Goodbye, Svar." Ram said with a wink.

Once Svar was outside, turning a blind eye, and Ram's bloody tool was writing its first seal, Ram hummed to himself in amusement. He would make sure it wouldn't kill anybody, would make sure that the runes were hidden should the Watch come by again. Yaniv and his bad attitude would leave. Ram would make sure of it.

"Goodbye, Yaniv."

THE FEEDLINGS
By Bracey

The man shadowed the woman at a conservative distance, slipping quietly through the night as he moved along the city streets. Practised at stealth, an avid hunter, he had grown up stalking prey with his father in Carolina forests. It was a long tradition passed down from fathers to sons. The same held true for his very first rifle, inherited by his father from his grandfather, and finally passed down to him when he was deemed worthy of the prize. He had earned it after having learned the proper respect and maturity needed for taking an animal's life.

These lessons had been useful—if not perverted—for war in a far-off desert as a marine, where he was taught how to hunt and kill men. There was no thrill in those hunts, no excitement, merely necessity and survival. Dangerous things had to be put down for the safety of all. The man understood this, even if he hadn't liked it, and so had fulfilled his duty to the best of his ability. Sniper training had made him coldly efficient and infinitely patient as he stalked the woman, studying his prey intently while remaining unknown and unobserved with practised invisibility.

The man could not help but appreciate the irony of what he was doing this night. He had spent so much of his life as a hunter of one kind or another. Even when finished with three tours in Afghanistan and Iraq, trading out carbine and kevlar for a badge and a sidearm, he was still hunting—still hunting predators, still hunting men. He missed the innocent days of claiming animals only for their meat. It was something that both he and the natural world understood. It was the way of life in the wilderness. One was either predator or prey. That was acceptable.

Hunting men was different. There was an inherent wrongness in it that went against the natural order of things. Terrorists and criminals, however, betrayed the human condition. They turned their backs on the tribalism of the herd, the social order that allowed man to dominate the world. Those he hunted had always offended him because of this. He did his duty to remove the dangerous element from his community, no matter how distasteful the act was. He hated being forced to think like his prey in order to track them down. It was an unclean way to hunt. Not like the simple interactions of the woodland beasts. But then there was the woman he was tracking now. She was so very different and yet...

The woman was small, a delicate thing of barely five feet in height. Her pale features, large luminous eyes, and dark hair gave her the appearance of a porcelain doll. She had an air of such fragility, such vulnerability, that even the man who stalked her was moved by a need to hold her, protect her somehow. It seemed a natural reaction given her sex...and her condition. The woman was gravid and swollen, burdened from within by the weight of pregnancy.

That was not his task though, not this time. He could feel the weight of the massive handgun beneath his left arm, concealed beneath his coat in its shoulder rig. The revolver was a Taurus Judge, a true hand cannon with its three-inch cylinders nesting .410 shotgun shells within. The shells were filled with a combination of buckshot and copper disks, designed to do the maximum lethal damage to a human target. The man wondered if it would be enough.

Remembering the bloody bodies strewn about with inhuman ferocity, the man flipped the emotional switch he'd learned to toggle on and off in the service of his country. There was no room within him for fear or uncertainty or pity. It was the only way to kill a human and not rot your soul. You had to divest yourself from empathy. It was going to be far harder with this one as he observed the familiar waddle of a woman bearing multiple children. Reaching her building, she mounted the stairs carefully, her centre of gravity distorted by her condition.

As she passed through the threshold, the man rushed ahead silently and caught the edge of the door an instant before it closed. He slipped into the dark foyer and listened to the awkward tread climbing the stairs above. Reaching into his jacket, his fingers closed around cold steel and pulled forth the oiled weight of the Judge. The gun in his hand was a deadly comfort as he made his way upward.

The man rounded the top of the third-floor landing and crept down the hallway. He already knew which apartment was hers; he had been there twice already. Once to ask questions, and once because of an uncontrollable compulsion to see the woman again. There was something about her that continued to draw him near, despite his suspicions. Reaching out to test her door, it pushed open with no effort. Unlocked—a bad sign. The man felt a thrill of fear slither up his spine. He took in a steadying breath and slipped inside.

"In here, Detective Waller," called an elfin voice. Shit. No point in subtlety anymore. Waller entered the living room, gun raised. He found the woman standing there, hands cradling her swollen belly, a gentle smile on her face.

"I see you figured out enough of my secret to suspect me."

"Yes, Amanda," Waller replied. "I know you're responsible for the so-called Abattoir Murders. I just don't understand how, especially for," he gestured vaguely at her abdomen with the barrel of his revolver, "someone in your condition."

"Oh that?" she continued with a smiling glance to her enormous belly. "You remember how I told you I was having triplets? Well, the pregnancy was killing me. My precious babies were going to die." Amanda's hands caressed the domed curve of her belly, the gesture protective, loving, expectant. Her eyes sought out Waller's. Something about them, so deep, he could feel himself falling away, some of his will drowning in them. She smiled and continued.

"When the doctors first told me that the babies and I had almost no chance for survival, I found myself crying on a park bench, hopeless and doomed. Suddenly, there *he* was, this handsome stranger, offering me a handkerchief for my tears. Some might call him a vampire. To me, he was a saviour. It felt like a dream. I told him everything. He took me in his arms and promised that everything would be ok. All I had to do was look into his eyes…and I did. Now my babies and I will live—live forever. My mysterious saviour has disappeared, but I'd still like my babies to have a daddy. You've proven yourself to be so strong, so resourceful. I know that you will be perfect!"

From beneath her maternity dress came a terrible wet sound. Something fell from below the hem but it did not hit the floor, instead its motion was arrested by some invisible force. The first was soon followed by two more identical creatures. Grey and bloody, the full-term fetuses quickly rose to hover about their mother in a grotesque orbit, floating like ghastly carnival balloons, their severed umbilical cords dragging slick across the floor. Dead black eyes, exactly like their mother's, peered soullessly into Waller's. He squeezed his fingers around the Judge, but his hands still shook in disbelief of the utter horror before him.

"Go give your daddy a kiss, my babies."

The undead things flew at him. He stared into mouths stretched agape by rings of lamprey-like teeth, the lips pulled back into a shape that would leave wounds on him that he had become all too familiar with at the morgue. Waller began firing and screaming, understanding he was already lost.

GRANDMOTHER'S DOOR
By Michael D. Nadeau

Darren stared at the house with a sense of dread. He always hated coming here when he was little; the damned place radiated a nameless fear that he could feel deep in his bones. It was an old house—Victorian if he had to guess—and whenever his parents dragged him here he'd have nightmares for days. He walked up the stone steps reluctantly, knowing that he had to do this. His grandmother, Illa, had left him the house when she passed away. His parents were livid. He, however, wasn't surprised at the choice. She often fought with his dad and always took Darren's side in any arguments. He would miss his grandmother, even though her house gave him gooseflesh just by walking into it.

Illa was a kindly woman, short and wrinkled with age. To him, she had always been old. Every time he would visit, she would give him sweets to get him to do small things for her. Odd things here and there; sweep the porch, clean her pantry. Always telling him to stay strong, whatever that meant. There were far too many rooms for one old lady to live in, but nothing in the house was off-limits, except one place: the door in her room. He was told repeatedly to never open it.

She didn't have to worry. He never liked roaming around the house to begin with. He had never tried to investigate, that nameless fear keeping him locked to the downstairs rooms. The one time he had tried to spend the night, he was crying within two hours of his parents driving away. They had to turn around and come get him, which upset his dad something fierce. His grandmother didn't mind though. "You'll get used to it in time," she used to say. That was over ten years ago and his knees still shook looking at the front door, still not acclimated to the feeling of dread.

"You going in or what?" a light female voice asked from behind him.

"Eve, you don't know what this house used to do to me," Darren said, a weak smile on his face. Eve was his longtime girlfriend, and today she was also his moral support. She had long black hair and emerald eyes that you could lose yourself in.

"It's just a house—creepy as hell—but only a house."

"Yeah, well…" was the only comeback he had. He shrugged and walked up to the door, turning the knob and opening it. The creak of the hinges seemed to echo throughout the empty home and go on forever, sending a shiver up his spine.

"Why didn't your dad come to empty the house?" Eve asked as she whisked right by him.

"Because he's still fuming that she left the house to me and not him. She didn't leave him anything when she died. It all went to me and my cousin Anna," Darren said, walking in tentatively. His skin started prickling the minute he was fully in the doorway. "I got the house, and she got the money, what little there was, at least."

"How old was your grandmother?"

"She was ninety-five," Darren said, running his finger along the bannister. It came away clean as could be… Odd for a house that had been sitting untouched for years. His grandmother used to hire a maid, but stopped about four years ago when money started getting tight. *So who has been cleaning*, he wondered as he walked into the living room.

Eve followed him, admiring the various pictures adorning the walls. They showed Illa in different stages of her life, from teenager to old woman, always smiling and enjoying herself. Darren noticed, for the first time, that every single picture was taken here at the house.

"Not a bad life. Was she in a nursing home when she died?" Eve asked, her curiosity brimming. She was always a talkative girl, and when she found something new, she couldn't help but ask a ton of questions.

"No. She died right here, in the house that she loved. My dad said that for the last six months she had a couple of nurses that stayed with her, but she never wanted to leave the house and be in a hospital." Darren opened the living room closet and saw that most of the stuff had been boxed already. He had heard that his grandmother had started packing her stuff, but didn't realise she had gotten so much done. Illa had always loved her knickknacks. Nearly every flat surface in the house was covered with them; on shelves, cabinets, tables, you name it. Ordered from all over the world. Without them, the house looked deserted.

"Hey, there's a note for you, Darren," Eve said, sitting down on the couch. She opened it before he could get there and read it aloud.

Dearest Ren,

I'm sorry you never did come around to liking the house, but it is my hope that now you will finally conquer your fear and settle in here. Your father never had the gift to appreciate this place, and quite frankly, I liked you better than him anyway.
I've boxed up all of my boring collectables. Keep them or not, it's up to you. The photos and albums are in my bedroom for you to go through if you want, as are my clothes in neatly packed boxes. Remember my one rule though: Do not open the door.
If you do plan on selling the house rather than live in it, I understand. However, I have one condition. You must call the number at the bottom and use that realtor. They know the house and will make sure it goes to someone that will take care of it. I hope you remember the good times with me.

Love, Your Grandmother Illa.

Darren shed a single tear in the quiet that followed, not knowing how to take most of that. He looked at his girlfriend and saw that she was trying not to laugh. "What?"

"Ren?"

Darren sighed and shook his head. "It was her nickname for me... I was ten for Chrissake."

"When was the last time you saw her?" Eve asked, leaning forward with interest.

"The last time I was here was when I was twelve years old. After that, my parents never made me go with them since I could look after myself. I heard my grandmother always asked after me though," Darren said as he sat down next to her, taking the letter gently. "She did come to my high school graduation, though she looked pretty sick that day. I remember because she said she had to get back to the house right away once the ceremony ended."

Eve punched him in the arm, a trick she always did to make him smile. "Hey, let's go see this door!" she said, jumping up and racing for the stairs.

A cold hand gripped Darren's spine, its fingers sliding down slowly. This was the feeling he always got in the house. "No!" he called after her as she took the stairs two at a time.

When Darren got to the room, Eve was moving a stack of boxes from in front of the closet door, stacking them on the bed. "Eve, I do not want to open that door," he said in his matter-of-fact voice. It was the voice he used when they argued and he had had enough.

She stopped and looked at him, confusion plain on her face. "It's just a door, Darren. Why don't you want to open it?"

Darren looked at the plain white door with its black iron knob and shook his head. "I know you don't understand, but I have always listened to her warnings. It feels wrong to ignore them now, you know?" he said, sitting on the bed and opening a box.

"Okay. Here, let's at least look at some pictures." Eve sat down next to him and pulled an album out. "This must be your father's baby book," she said, opening it and looking at the pictures under the cheap cellophane. "Oh, is this your grandfather?"

Darren looked and saw a photo of a young man holding a baby next to a stunning woman, her hair done up in the style of the thirties. These pictures were even older than the ones hanging on the walls downstairs and he wondered why those weren't packed up as well. "I think so…" he said, taking the album and looking harder.

"When did he die?"

"He died when my father was very young. I don't know how. I want to say it was right after they moved in. My grandmother had inherited this house from her parents." Darren gave her back the album and pulled out a stack of random pictures, sifting through them, his curiosity piqued now, despite the growing dread of being in this room. There were a lot of pictures of his grandmother right in front of this door. Weird to be sure, but then he found one with his father in it as well, looking like he was sleeping standing up. His father had to be in his late teens here, with his eyes closed and head back as Illa smiled at whoever was taking the picture; again in front of the door.

Daaarrreeeennnnnn

Darren turned around, hearing a faint whisper, the syllables dragging like some sort of snake-like creature trying to talk. He shivered, the tingle of fear creeping higher up his neck. "Eve, let's go downstairs with these," he said, his eyes fixed upon the door as if it were going to explode any minute. It seemed to *lurk* there, as if it was waiting for something…something from him.

"Fine by me," Eve said, grabbing a box and walking by him. "Besides, the beer I brought is down in the car. I'm gonna grab it and bring it in if we're going to be here for a bit," she said, walking down the stairs.

Darren watched her walk out of the bedroom and risked another look at the door. He would've called it a closet, except his grandmother never had. She always called it the 'door,' never anything else. He could *feel* it, even now, somehow pulling at his soul. When he was in the rest of the house it was just a cold tingle up his spine, but now that he was in this room, he could feel the dread and give it a source. That dread was a deep twist in his gut that could physically move him if he let it. He got up and hurried towards the hallway, almost feeling as if he was angering the door by leaving. He almost ran down the stairs once he was out of his grandmother's room.

Darren came down just in time to see Eve come in with the twelve-pack and a blanket. He smiled as she looked at him, his fears melting away in the love they shared. He had been seeing her for about three years now, and he was going to pop the question soon. He just had to figure out what to do with the house first. He had actually toyed with the idea of keeping it on the drive over, but the minute he saw it at the end of the long driveway, he knew it was going to haunt him again.

"You alright? You look like you need a good drink," Eve said, throwing the blanket in the living room.

"I'm fine, just staring at this beautiful girl I know."

Eve turned towards the window and peered outside. "Do I know her? That bitch better not take my man," she said kiddingly. "Okay, champ, I'm going to go chill some of these in the fridge. I assume the power is still on for a bit?"

"Yes, the bill is paid up for the next month. I have until then to decide what to do with the house," he said as she disappeared into the kitchen.

Darren went into the living room with the box of photos and sat down on the couch. He pulled out one after another, looking at the photos of his grandmother when she was his age. It seemed unreal that she was so beautiful. Then he found a stack of pictures from even further back, ones that showed his grandmother as a child. There were only a few of them, taken around the house. He found one of a woman he didn't recognise, holding a baby in front of the door. The picture said "Ellen and baby Illa," the date on the back faded with age. His grandmother was so little! He went to the living room closet to see if there were more pictures down here. As he walked in, the door slammed shut behind him. He tried the lock. It wouldn't open. *What?* He pounded on the inside of the closet and rammed it with his shoulder, but it wouldn't give. He felt that cold grip of fear again, shivering even though it was warm in the closet. *Oh no... Eve.*

* * *

"Hey babe, come check out this door with me," Darren's voice called from upstairs.

Sweet Jesus, Eve thought as she raced up the stairs for a second time. *Can he make up his mind?* "Hold on baby, wait for me!" she called out. Eve ran into the room and saw that the door was still blocked by two boxes, though they were moved a little bit.

"Babe, I'm stuck in here! Help me out!" Darren's voice called from the other side of the door.

Oh God, he must've squeezed in there and the boxes fell against the door, she thought, kicking them away and gripping the doorknob. *But why did he change his mind? He was so adamant about the door... Like it scared him.* The moment she touched the cold iron handle and turned it, she heard a loud splintering crash and then Darren called out from downstairs, stealing what breath she had in her chest.

"Eve, stay away from the door!"

Her heart stopped, along with time, as the door that was never supposed to be opened moved towards her, breaking the seal that had been in place. Just as she tried to slam the door closed again, black tentacles burst out from around the edges of the door and gripped her arms, burning her flesh on contact and dragging her slowly towards the black void staring at her from within. Eve fought and screamed with all her strength, digging her heels into the rug and leaning back. A tentacle wrapped around her mouth to silence her and another grabbed a leg, knocking her off balance. She tried to scream as she felt her skin melt under the tentacles' grip, blood dripping down her arms and towards the floor.

Eve heard a disembodied voice fill her mind. It called her name from the void as the entryway seemed to grow wider. She was fully wrapped in the tentacles' grasp now, with no purchase of freedom.

Eve struggled as she felt the acidic grip tighten, her bones cracking under the intense pressure. Her leg was the first to break, then both arms as she screamed away into the leathery skin covering her mouth. Eve's sanity flew out the window as the tentacles broke her other leg, then her back. Blood flowed freely from her wounds and floated into the void—not a drop touched the floor.

Huuunnnnggrrryyyyy, the voice said, as a slurping noise came from the void. Eve was all but gone.

Darren sprinted up the stairs after breaking out of the closet, terror driving him forward when Eve hadn't answered him.

"Babe?" he called out. He slowed to a walk when he reached the top of the stairs, dread permeating from the bedroom in waves now. He knew the door was open without needing to enter the bedroom. Reluctantly peering into his grandmother's room, Darren saw the door standing wide open, a swirling mass of tentacles writhing in the opening. There was a cold wind blowing out of it and his tears fell reflexively as he fought down the bile rising in his throat. He knew Eve was dead without having to see her body. Fear froze him in place as he stared at the horrific thing in the doorway, his eyes wide with fright.

Hooouuussse...yooouuurrssss...nnooowww, the voice from the void whispered.

"What—What are you?" Darren asked, a cold sweat now breaking out on his forehead. "And where is Eve?" He knew the answer, but he felt compelled to ask. Something in his mind said he needed to show this thing that he was strong. Words his grandmother always mentioned: stay strong.

"We are Amon," they said in Eve's voice, her disfigured body stepping out past the tentacle mass and into the room. She was ashen grey and her arms and legs were bent at odd angles, yet she stood solid and upright. "You own this house and now have to feed us. We require one soul per year and, in return, the ghosts of those we consume will keep up the house and we will grant you a very long life," they said through Eve as her body moved awkwardly towards him, like a puppet. "Beget an heir, one that will take over for you when you finally die, and then we continue."

"And if—If I say no?" Darren asked, a small bit of courage growing in his broken heart.

"Then we will take the rest of your family; one by one. They will feed us until one succumbs."

Darren thought of his mother and father. Of his cousin Anna with her three young children. He couldn't let this thing have any of them. He knew what he would have to do…in time. "Fine, but you stay in there until feeding day. I don't want you whispering, or anything else, to anyone in this house. Agreed?"

"That is acceptable. Goodbye Darren," Eve's body turned and walked back through the mass of writhing tentacles as they caressed her body. "Oh, and Darren," the creature that used to be Eve paused at the threshold, "if it helps, she found the ring in your coat last week. She would've said yes." And with that the door slammed shut, sealing the thing in for another year.

Once the shock wore off, Darren collapsed to the floor, sobbing in fear and torment. His life was all but over, having to kill someone every year to feed this…thing. And

Eve... He cried until sleep took him, fitful nightmares consuming his every moment. *She would've said yes.* Those last words would haunt him for the rest of his days.

* * *

Everett got out of his truck and looked at the charred remains of the house his son had lived in for two years. Darren had never married and had taken to staying in that damned house like some sort of recluse, just like that old bag. He hadn't seen his son since he had moved in; Darren always saying that he was too busy to have company. Now it was too late, and Everett's grief was etched across his tormented visage. Shaking his head, he moved through the rubble to see if anything was salvageable, sifting through the ruins of the burnt down house. There had to be something left of his son to remember him by.

The fire department said they tried everything, but something had burned so hot that nothing they did could extinguish it. Nothing was found as an accelerant, just the normal things found in a household, though Everett never remembered his mother keeping cleaning chemicals upstairs. Everett worked until midday and finally got to the centre of the ruined house. He moved a charred beam, seeing a piece of white underneath. With a heave, he cleared what seemed like a door. It was intact, with an iron knob, the hinges melted clean away. *That damned door,* he thought as he remembered his mother always warning him of this thing when he was growing up. He searched for another few minutes and found a small box with a ring in it and smiled. *Darren never got rid of it.*

He pocketed the box and walked back to his truck, his heart heavy. As he was driving away, something made him look back. He saw the white door stark against the charred beams surrounding it. He pulled over. *I need a new door for the basement.*

JUST A SECOND

By L. A. Cunningham

The red and white checked paper ripped away, revealing a pita full of spiced meats and pickled vegetables. The passenger door opened, and Nick looked over as Dean folded his too-tall body into the car.

"Well? What did you end up getting?"

Dean pulled a long package out of a plastic bag. "I got the donair, too."

"Nice choice, man. You won't regret it. They don't call Sam 'The Donair King' for nothing. I mean, the chicken shawarma is good and all, but nothing rivals his donair."

Dean tore the paper and took a bite. Nick waited for his reaction.

"Holy shit," Dean finally said after swallowing his bite.

"Right?" Nick turned his attention back to his own prize. He brought the pita up to his mouth and paused briefly to take in a long whiff of the spices and garlic. A rumble came from just above his belt, and he bit into the donair.

There was no room for conversation when eating Sam's, and the two men ignored each other accordingly. Nick let that sweet sauce linger on his tongue—savouring it—when Dean went and spoiled the moment by speaking.

"Did you hear that?"

Nick swallowed and held still, listening.

"What?"

"You don't hear that?" Dean furrowed his brow.

Nick looked out the front window. The 'open' sign on the little donair shop was turned off, but the glow from the awning and a single street light still lit the parking lot. Nick scanned the area, but theirs was the only car left. The front of the shop was empty, and there was no sign of movement. Sam must've gone into the back. It was just them.

"I don't know what you're talking about, man." Nick went to take another bite, but the pita never made it to his mouth.

He'd heard something.

He listened. There was definitely something there. Some kind of ticking. He looked over at Dean, and Dean nodded, acknowledging that they both heard it now.

Dean turned around, looking out the back window. "It's getting louder. Like it's moving…"

"And coming closer…" Nick felt on edge. The uneven ticking didn't belong in this setting. "It's hard to tell which direction it's coming from."

"Should we call it in?" Dean looked over.

"A mysterious ticking?" Nick chuckled through his words despite his unease. "I think we need a little more than that to—What?"

Dean wasn't looking at him anymore, but past him. His eyes had gone wide, and he was fumbling for his sidearm.

Nick turned, following Dean's gaze out the driver-side window. The donair fell from his hand. "Jesus Christ!"

* * *

Joseph leaned back and took off his glasses. He rubbed the bridge of his nose and reminded himself—for not the first time—that he needed to get a new pair that didn't pinch his nose so much. Above him, the little window had gone dark, and Joseph sighed at the night sky beyond. It was late. He supposed he should go home and leave the rest of the repair until tomorrow.

Reaching for a pen, he opened a notebook and jotted down some notes so he would know where to pick up in the morning. He set the book next to the watch and placed the pen carefully next to the book. Tools were scattered everywhere and he returned each of them, one by one, back to its rightful spot. A dozen brass metal gears lay spilt across the table, and he scooped them up, pouring them back into a drawer.

He stood back, looking for anything else to put away, but he'd spent months compulsively organizing and reorganizing his shop, and he was all out of excuses to stay there and keep tidying. He sighed again, reluctant to spend another night in his empty house. The clocks were better company than his own lonely thoughts. A dark brown coat was folded across the back of a nearby chair, and he shrugged it on, checking for his wallet and keys. He glanced at his cellphone before dropping it into the front pocket of his jeans and, with one final look back, he clicked off the lights and closed the door. The front of the store was dim, but the lights were still bright enough to glint off the rows and rows of watches in the display cases.

The walls were lined with numerous clocks of various shapes, sizes, and materials. People asked him how he didn't go crazy working in a store full of constant ticking all the time, but he found it soothing. There was something calming about the rhythmic ticking of a clock. Each one set perfectly, marking the passage of time, synched up with every other clock. Time connected people, whether they wanted to be connected or not. It made him feel less alone. Time is one of the few things you can't buy and never seem to have enough of... And can't get back.

His face fell at that thought, and he put a hand to his chest, feeling the familiar stab of grief. He frowned and visualized his own heart, imagining it hardening. He'd wasted too much of his time longing for the past. He was done. He needed to let go and move on.

He walked to the front of the store and paused by the security alarm to arm it. But his fingers stopped short of the buttons. He looked back into the dimly lit store.

Something was off. There was a ticking that wasn't matching the others. His eyes moved over the clocks on the wall, letting his eyes focus his ears.

He took a step back into the store and slowly made his way along one wall, trying to pinpoint the source of the ticking. The rhythm was unusual; it almost reminded him of a heartbeat. He shook off the thought while he ran a hand along one of the cases, feeling the dead eyes of the clockwork toys staring up at him. A couple of dozen metal animals silently begged him to wind them up and give them life, but he ignored their pleas. The out-of-sync ticking wasn't coming from the main part of the store. He wandered to the back room and pulled out his keys again. Turning the knob, he pushed open the door and flicked on the lights. Listening.

His feet carried him back to his work table, and he looked around. All of the clocks in the repair shop were usually broken, so there shouldn't be any ticking coming from inside. But there was.

Joseph followed the sound through the narrow rows of shelving, but it had grown faint. Finally, he found himself facing the back door into the alley and gave the deadbolt a turn.

Stepping out into the night, he looked up and down the alley. Dark, silhouetted garbage bins lined the backs of the nearby businesses, and a lone bike was chained to a gate, but there was no movement. And there was no ticking sound, either. Frowning and confused, Joseph retreated back into the building and locked the door behind him. He gave the room one final frown, went to the front, set the alarm, and left his store behind him.

The chilly air quickly found the bare skin on his neck. Joseph popped his collar and gave his zipper a final pull.

He looked left, then right, then watched as a solitary car drove by. The sight of red tail lights triggered memories he wanted to forget. He fiddled with his wedding ring while he stood there, not wanting to think about where its matching partner was. The car stopped at the next intersection, disappearing around the corner when the light turned green.

Joseph gave one last look at the store and started walking after the car. His mind wandered back to the watch he'd been working on, still trying to solve the problem that was no longer in front of him. There had never been a watch or a clock he hadn't been able to fix. His mind was built for solving problems with clockwork; even problems that weren't meant to be fixed with clockwork. He encouraged his thoughts to go back to his work for fear of where they might wander otherwise.

A ticking broke through his concentration, and he let his surroundings back into his focus. Jen's Convenience glowed at the end of the street, like a lighthouse breaking through his thick fog of thoughts. He had been so lost in his work, he'd barely paid attention to his walk home and was surprised he'd come so far already. But his surprise was quickly pushed aside by the continued ticking.

The street was mostly residential now, sprinkled with the odd store like Jen's. The ticking was the same irregular ticking he'd heard in the shop. He narrowed his eyes, peering into the night. Blue light flickered behind glass windows and porch lights sprinkled the street, but everything was still. He started to doubt whether the sound was even real. Maybe it was haunting him. There was no way that sound could still be real. Too much time had passed. He stuck a finger in his ear and wiggled it, hoping to clear the sound out of his head. But the heartbeat-like ticking remained.

He glanced ahead at Jen's Convenience and forced his legs forward. Before he knew it, he was running. Running from what, though? His past? His grief? His bad decisions?

The bell above the door jingled as he burst into Jen's. No one was at the till, but Jen's eldest son appeared from a hallway marked with an 'Employees Only' sign. Joseph straightened, hoping he appeared calm.

"Ah, Mr Collodi! How are you tonight?"

Joseph walked away from the door, but his eyes darted back to it before returning to Sonny.

"Fine, Sonny. How are you? How's Jen? Is she feeling any better?"

"Yes, Mr Collodi. She's just got a bit of a sore throat that won't let go, but she's already back yelling orders at us."

Sonny chucked, and Joseph forced a smile.

"Anything I can help you with tonight?" Sonny smiled and waited for an answer.

"Nope. Just going to grab a chocolate bar. Got to satisfy that sweet tooth."

"Yes, yes, of course." Sonny nodded as Joseph grabbed the nearest chocolate bar. Setting it on the counter for Sonny to ring it through, Joseph looked back to the door and the bell above, like he was expecting it to ring at any moment.

"Mr Collodi? Are you sure you're okay?"

Joseph looked back, forcing another smile. "Yes, I'm sure." He handed over the money and told Sonny to keep the change.

He paused before leaving, trying to see up and down the street through the glass panes, when he realised Sonny had said something. He turned back around.

"What?"

"I said have a wonderful night, Mr Collodi. It's nice to see you out and about again."

Joseph smiled awkwardly. "Yeah, uh, thanks. You have a good one too."

With that, he leaned into the door, causing the bell to ring overhead. He flinched but didn't look up as he stepped back outside. The cold air instantly found him again while he stood there listening. But it was just the normal sounds of his quiet neighbourhood.

Those normal sounds kept him company, but every nerve was on edge the rest of the way home until he was safe inside. He leaned against the nearest wall and rested his head against it, willing his heart to calm down. He took a deep breath and finally pulled himself away from the front entry. He threw the chocolate bar in the fridge, aware of how little appetite he had these days. Instead of eating, he filled the kettle with water and turned it on. A warm drink always seemed to soothe him.

He waited, staring at the countertops, mindlessly tracing the patterns in the granite, while willing his brain not to focus on anything in particular. He thought back to Sonny's last comment. Sonny was a good kid—always had been—but Joseph was tired of people's looks of pity and well-meaning comments. He resented them and their normal lives—and their happy families.

A thin whistle rang out, announcing it was time to fetch a cup and a teabag. As the whistle quieted, Joseph realised there was another familiar noise: a ticking. Almost like a heartbeat.

It was coming from the front of his house. Right outside.

Taking a step towards the noise, he whispered to himself, "It can't be..."

He started when a loud knocking came from the other side.

"Mr Collodi?"

Confused, Joseph strode forward and opened the door.

"Nick?" Then he noticed the small girl holding Nick's hand. She smiled at him, let go of Nick's hand, and rushed forward to hug Joseph's legs.

"Papa!" she said and pressed her cheek into him.

Joseph put a hesitant hand on her head, feeling the weight of the world fall back upon his shoulders, before looking back up at Nick.

"We found your, uh...your..." Joseph watched Nick struggle to find the right word. "Your... We found Penny. She was outside of Sam's. Scared the living daylights out of Dean and me. Especially Dean. Have you met Dean yet?" Nick ploughed on, not waiting for Joseph to answer, "He opted to stay in the car. I probably should've told him about Penny, especially with that new eye you added and all…"

Joseph glanced down again and watched as Penny brought her hand up to gingerly touch the eye Nick was talking about. Almost like she was self-conscious.

Nick carried on, "but I wasn't really expecting to have an encounter so soon. Not a lot of robots in our town, you know. I didn't think we'd see Penny out wandering this late. She get away from you?"

Joseph just nodded. The silence that hung in the air was filled with the irregular ticking sound. Nick seemed to be waiting for Joseph to say something else, but how could Joseph even begin to explain? So he said nothing.

"Well, have a good night, Joe. Just keep a watch out on that one, okay? We don't want your, uh, Penny, to get lost again."

Joseph's lips moved into something he hoped resembled a smile, and he thanked Nick before closing the door.

He stood there for a moment, watching as Penny crawled onto the sofa and found the remote to turn on the television. He walked over and sat beside her, but paid no attention to the show. Instead he sat there frowning, chewing the inside of his cheek, trying to solve a new problem. He'd driven her far enough out of town that her battery should've run out. Did someone wind her back up? Was it a compatibility issue between the AI and the clockwork? He'd always been unsure about pairing the two technologies. But he knew that the solution was likely the simplest one, as it usually was: Penny had figured out how to wind herself. And with that realization, the burden on his shoulders increased. He would have to do the very thing he'd wanted to avoid.

"Penny?"

She looked over at him.

"Yes, Papa?"

"Can we turn off the TV for a moment?" Joseph reached over and took the remote from her and clicked the power button.

He scooched closer to her, and she looked back at him questioningly with her one dark brown eye—an eye that looked so much like his daughter's. And from the other side—where the other eye should've been—a small clock face with delicate hands ticked in an irregular rhythm. Not too soon after he'd made Penny, he'd replaced her one eye with the clock face. On the outside, she was perfect; an exact replica. Too perfect. Because on the inside, she wasn't his daughter. She was a mistake made in desperation that he couldn't bring himself to undo. He didn't want to be alone.

As time went on, he'd needed that visual reminder that she wasn't real.

"Penny. You know I love you, right?"

"I love you too, Papa."

Hearing those words with that voice was a punch to the chest.

"Papa? Why did you leave me?" Her one eye showed her confusion and hurt, while her other eye marked their time together. The second hand of her eye matched the louder ticking that came from inside her.

Tears gathered along Joseph's lower eyelashes. "Can I check your motor, Penny?"

She nodded and obediently turned away from him. He brushed her hair off of her neck and unzipped the top of her dress, revealing a rectangular outline on her upper back. He opened the panel, and beneath lay an intricate system of gears and cogs and springs and metal ribbons. But in the very centre, nestled in the chest cavity, was a motor: her heart. Joseph delicately reached in, tinkered with a few parts, removed the motor, and relatched the panel.

"All done." The words came out in a strangled sob.

Penny turned and looked at him.

"I'm tired, Papa." Her smile was weary.

Joseph smiled back at her, and his tears overflowed. He pulled her into his arms and hugged her tight. "I know," he said into her hair. He kissed her head.

"Can you sing to me?"

He loosened his hold and looked down at her, the warm brown eye full of trust. He nodded and cradled her in his arms like he did when his daughter was younger. But when he opened his mouth, he couldn't find his voice. The tears flowed harder.

"What's...wrong?" she asked. Her words dragged out as her system slowed down.

He longed to say goodbye, but those weren't the words that came. "I'm sorry. I'm so, so sorry."

His gaze switched over to her clockwork eye. He could hear the ticking slowing and the gears coming to a rest now that there was no motor.

Joseph closed his eyes for a moment, and when he opened them again, the second hand had stopped.

HEAR NO EVIL
By Frasier Armitage

The photographs on the table screamed louder than any voice. Serena Wade flicked through page after page of camera shots, all of them riffing on the same tune. They showed a woman's body splayed at awkward angles, a pool of red soaking the carpet beneath the corpse. The recorder's whir percolated the sterile interrogation room, along with the stench of stale coffee and sweat. She twisted the file to the man opposite her, showing him the victim's remains for the last time.

"This is it. You won't get another shot at a deal," she said. "I know it was you. I know you were hired by someone to put a bullet in that girl. But if you give me the name of your employer, I'll make sure the prosecutor recommends a reduced sentence. You'll be looking at ten years instead of life."

Jason Green smoothed out his tie, straightened his cuffs, lifted his eyes from the photograph, and smiled. "What you have," he said, "is circumstantial, inspector. None of what you've shown me proves anything, except that you have a wild imagination and you'd make a terrifying photographer."

Serena slammed the file shut. "Look. It's your life. You can throw it away if you want. But that girl you butchered—she's going to get justice. You hear me?"

Green snarled through sinister lips. "Are you going to charge me with something? Or are we done here?"

She locked eyes with him, but he wasn't biting. Posturing wouldn't tease a mistake from him. No amount of red was going to prompt this bull to charge. A knock intervened, breaking her stare, and Julian poked his head around the door.

"Inspector, can I have a word?" Julian asked. It sounded more like an order than a question.

Serena rose from her seat and leaned forward. "Get comfy, Mr Green. I'll be back soon to take your confession." As she turned to leave, she snapped a surreptitious picture of him on her phone. His laughter followed her out of the room as the door clicked shut behind her.

"What is it, Julian?" she asked.

"Smith wants to see you. Now."

She grimaced and followed him across the precinct, past the myriad of desks where piles of paperwork hid coffee stains and discarded hope. Newspaper clippings lined the walls of the superintendent's office, alongside a host of certificates and framed medals emblazoned with the name "Ernest Smith." The Super slammed the receiver of his phone onto its base. He glowered at Serena with a look that could've cut diamonds.

"Inspector Wade, how many times have we been over this?" Smith said between gritted teeth.

"I felt it was worth bringing him in, sir." Serena stood statuesque, refusing to surrender to the shrivelling sensation in her stomach.

Smith rolled his eyes and rubbed his wrinkled forehead. "Do you know who that was on the phone? The head of the Crown Prosecution Service." Serena gulped. Whenever the head of anything got involved, it never ended well.

"Would you like to know why they were calling?" Smith asked, although Serena knew the question was pointless. What would he have done if she'd said no? "They were calling to complain about yet another one of your cases where there's zero paper trail on how you obtained the evidence."

"Sir, I can explain—" she started.

"Save it, Wade." He stopped her dead. "Every case of yours goes the same way. You bring in a suspect on sketchy grounds and waste our time getting nowhere in interrogation. Sure, after they've been released you usually find something solid on them. But you never explain *how* you got the evidence."

"Sir, I—"

"Blind luck, detective. Looks great on an arrest report. But how does a prosecutor explain it to a jury? There are protocols we need to follow, and you ignore them all!"

"I have good instincts," Serena said. "Is that why I'm here?"

Smith rested his knuckles on the desk, his chest deflating. "Listen, Wade. You're a great officer. I don't know how you get your arrests, and I don't want to know. But the jury does. The commissioner does. The Crown Prosecution Service does. You can't just pick up a suspect on a hunch. You know that."

"What about the tapes? The recordings?" she said. "I always come through."

Smith slammed his hands down on the desk and stood up so quickly papers flew to the floor. "You need a permit for recordings! You won't even let us see the machine you use to get these tapes in the first place." He sat back down and sighed. "It doesn't matter if you record your suspect confessing when you don't have prior authorization."

"So give me auth—"

"Two words, Wade: probable cause. Tell me, what do you have on this Jason Green guy to justify bringing him in today? Hmm?"

Serena held her hands tightly behind her back and stared intently at the wall behind the Super's head. "I just know," she said.

"You think any of that flies in court? These things have got to be by-the-book, or it's not admissible. Then the prosecutor needs to pull some kind of magic trick to convince a jury of guilt. Would you at least consider using equipment from the precinct to get these recordings? That way we could—"

"It wouldn't work, sir," Serena interrupted.

"It wouldn't? I mean, I—" Smith threw his hands up in the air before nailing Serena to the floor with another soul-crushing stare. "Look, Wade, I can't let you keep doing this. I want you to release this Jason Green guy you've got in custody. You understand? Or you might as well just hand in your badge."

Serena shrugged. "I get it, sir. Don't worry. I'll release him."

Smith raised an eyebrow. Silence settled between them, diffusing the lecture into an awkward rant. "It isn't like you not to fight me on this," he finally said.

Serena cocked her head and smiled. "Why should I, sir? I know how to take orders as well as break them. Besides, I've got everything I need from Green." She unconsciously placed a hand on her phone, secure in the pocket of her leather jacket.

"Alright, Wade. Dismissed." Smith rubbed a frown out of his forehead and got straight back on the blower to calm the nerves of the bigwigs he answered to. It wasn't unusual for the Super to dress her down, but not for the sake of procedure. He would have been the first to back her if she'd come to him with a hunch. But if the head of the CPS wanted good leads buried for the sake of paperwork, then she guessed Smith didn't have much of a choice.

Serena should've headed back to the interrogation room, but she marched to the stairwell and made for the exit.

Julian tracked her out of the precinct. "Psst. Wade." His whisper echoed down the stairwell.

Serena rolled her eyes and cemented a hand on her hip. "What is it, Julian?" She didn't have time to play fetch with the Super's lapdog.

"Aren't you going to release Mr Green?" Julian asked.

"Eventually."

Julian's eyes popped. "But, didn't you hear what he said? He ordered you—"

"There's nothing wrong with my hearing. I'll release Green. But he never specified when. I've got an errand to run first."

"But—"

"No buts, Julian. Or do you want Smith to find out you've been earwigging what goes on in his office?"

Julian's cheeks erupted in a beetroot blush, and he shrank back, leaving her alone. She rushed down the stairs, unchained her Ducati, and roared out of the precinct parking lot. She tore through the city, as if ripping a hole in it, while the engine's motor hummed between her thighs. Speed distracted her from Smith's tirade, from the fact she'd have to release that scumbag Jason Green. Letting him walk the streets meant he was getting one minute of freedom too many. And she was the cop giving it to him. Her sinews tensed, but the gush of wind whipping her hair and the grunt of the exhaust calmed her—kept her from doing something even more stupid than what she was about to do.

She skimmed the tarmac as she pulled onto her drive. Her phone buzzed, flashing Andrew's name in bright letters. Serena's nostrils flared. Her cheeks reddened at the thought of talking to him, but if she didn't get rid of him now, he'd just keep calling. Like any other pest, he needed dealing with.

She answered. "Not now, Andrew."

"Is everything alright, sweetie?" He sounded sicklier than a Belgian truffle.

"What do you think?" Serena yelled. "The bigwigs didn't have much of an issue with my methods until today. So be honest. It was you who made the call to your boss, wasn't it?"

Andrew paused. She knew he was smart enough not to try lying to her. "I just want you to be safe. I—"

"Save it," Serena said. "You prosecutors are all the same. You talk a good game, but that's all you are. Talk."

"Since when was it a crime to care about you?" he asked. "I don't want you chasing down blind leads that could be dangerous. Stabbing in the dark only ends one way. And I don't want to see you hurt."

Serena unlocked and slammed the front door behind her and stomped through the house. "Pack it in, Andrew. You made a jerk move. Trying to talk yourself out of it just makes it worse. This was a mistake. If you can't handle me chasing down leads, then we shouldn't see each other anymore."

"Serena, I—"

"No, Andrew. You blew it. You should've talked to me about this. But instead, you went over my head. The Super dressed me down for chasing my gut, all because you can't handle me doing my job."

"Don't do this, Serena. What we have, it's—"

"It's over. Just like this conversation. Don't call again."

She hit the red button on her phone and his name disappeared. Her fingers clenched the brittle edges of her handset and she closed her eyes, waiting for her breathing to steady and her chest to stop pounding. She exhaled, not wasting another drop of energy on that coward of a ex-boyfriend. After all, with Green's employer still out there, she'd need all the energy she could muster.

Serena opened up the photos on her phone to the last image she took. The pixels blurred as she zoomed in, but she could still make out Jason Green cackling in the interrogation room. She'd caught the side of his face. It should be enough.

Her leather jacket slipped from her shoulders as she opened the door to the darkroom. Its dim light bathed her in red. Inhaling that deep scarlet glow that permeated the air had always settled her, ever since she was a child and she'd stumbled into her mother's photographs developing on the line.

"You must be careful," her mother told her.

But Serena never listened. She blundered into every one of them, causing them to flurry as she ran. Her mother used to marvel at the way Serena stared at those old black and whites, tinted crimson by the cascading warmth of that faint, burning bulb.

"Why do you sit and stare at them for so long?" her mother used to ask her.

"Because," Serena would say, "they sound so pretty."

"They don't sound of anything." Her mother would laugh, but she couldn't hear them calling out. The voices. Her mother was too concerned about what the pictures looked like to notice them whispering through their 2-D faces.

Serena blinked away the memories, swept her hair into a ponytail, and loaded her phone into the specially designed cradle propped on her desk. Beside it, four trays of solution waited. She placed a piece of paper on the tray beneath the cradle and flicked a switch. After a few moments, she moved the paper into the first tray. Blotches formed, both on the paper and in Serena's mind. She recalled fragments of the first time she realised that the voices belonged to her alone.

Her mother stooped over the same desk Serena stood behind now. A photograph fell from its edge. Serena scooped up the photograph, but dropped it immediately and covered her ears. The voice was so loud that she screamed.

"What is it, honey?" her mother had said.

"That man. He's hurting her!"

"What man?" her mother asked. Serena pointed to the photograph. She couldn't take her eyes off it. Her mother shook her head. "That's just George. I snapped him mowing the lawn."

"No, Mummy. I can hear him. He's shouting at a lady. He's saying the most awful things."

"Saying what, dear?"

Serena glowered at the photograph. "You stupid cow, you think you can make a fool of me? You think I care how much you bleed? Take it. This is your fault. You forced me to do this. You—"

"Serena, stop it!" her mother chided her. "Where is this behaviour coming from?"

"He's saying them! Can't you hear the picture, Mummy?" Serena burst into tears and turned her eyes from the photo of the man waving back at her mum from his lawnmower. "I don't want to see. I don't want to hear it anymore." Her mother placed the photograph out of reach and cuddled Serena, her heartbeat taking the place of the screaming man.

Later that night, as sirens flashed through the curtains of their home, they watched George being taken by police. The body of his wife was rolled away under a white sheet.

"Why didn't the police stop him, Mummy?" she asked.

"The police didn't know," her mother answered.

"Could nobody hear him? Didn't anybody have a picture of him?"

"Time for bed, Serena." Her mother carried her upstairs and tucked her in. "You must be careful," her mother whispered.

"You always say that, Mummy."

"I mean it, darling. Now close your eyes."

It was a mantra her mother kept repeating: you must be careful. Every time Serena strayed anywhere near a family snapshot, a graduation photo, or a portrait hanging on a neighbour's wall: you must be careful. How many times had she heard that same warning, over and over?

After that night with George, her mother stopped taking pictures of people. She stuck to scenic images. Serena could never hear the buzzing bees or the lapping waves. But if a person snuck into the background, she could trace their voice if she stared hard enough. The same way she stared at the paper in the developing bath now.

Blotches darkened the sheet. Jason Green's smug outline filled the page. Serena snatched her tweezers and transferred the photo into the next solution, the stop bath. And then into a fixer, before finally washing it in water and pinning it on the line.

While water dripped into a puddle on the floor beneath the photograph, Serena grabbed her phone and sat on the cold concrete, crossing her legs. She hooked wires to new suction pads, attaching electrodes to feed the wires. She stuck the pads to her forehead and plugged the wires into an old Casio cassette recorder. Not just any recorder. This was the only machine in the world that she could use with her gifts. She handled it with a level of care reserved for ancient artefacts and sacred talismans. It took her forever to get it working. She probably couldn't make another one if she tried.

Then she dialled Julian.

"Hello?" he answered.

"Julian, is Mr Green still in the interrogation room?"

"You're not dragging me into this. I don't want Smith on my back."

"Look, will you just do me a favour and release him?" she asked.

"You mean, you're not asking me to stall for you?"

"No, Julian. Just process the release and I'll owe you. Deal?"

"Okay. Sure. Will do."

She hung up and reached for the tape recorder. The record button clunked as she pressed it and the cassette rolled out a static hiss. Then she stared at the photograph of Green and waited.

"Where's the lady?" Green's voice crept through the room, crawling over her skin, into her ears. Julian was probably in the room, but without a picture she couldn't hear his side of the conversation. Only Green.

"That's a shame. I was looking forward to telling her how wrong she was for bringing me in," Green said.

Serena's lip curled upward. If only he knew. "Fine. Goodbye, Sergeant." Green's voice scratched its way from Serena's head, down the wires, and onto the cassette, overwriting the blank tape with his guilt.

She listened to him now, guessing his movements from the timbre of his breathing. The rhythm gained tempo. Faster. Faster. He was running, but where? Then the pattern broke. He paused, panting, his breath snatching at the air. The back of his throat rasped.

"You told me it wouldn't be a problem. Do you know how long I've been sitting in that room, accused of killing that girl?" Where Green's tone had brimmed with arrogance before, now it was replaced with urgency. Fear. Who was he talking to?

"No, I don't know how she knew. All the evidence she had was circumstantial. I have no idea how she found out it was me. But she didn't want me. She wanted the person who hired me. She wanted you."

There was something muffled about the way Green spoke. The way his vowels flattened and his whispers strained her ear. She knew by instinct that he was in an alley. Over the years, she'd listened to voices in every environment, from open fields and amphitheatres to box rooms and closets.

"Of course I didn't tell her anything. But I want my money. You said the other half would be paid after I killed the girl."

Serena adjusted the electrode on her head, cleaning the quality of the recording. *You're going down, Green,* she thought. *And so is the guy who hired you.*

"You want me to do what? Get rid of the cop?" Green said, sounding shocked.

Serena scowled through the red haze between her and the photograph. Killing a helpless girl was one thing. But nobody brought the heat of disappearing a cop unless they had a wild enough reason. *What have I stumbled into?*

"Taking out a cop has its risks," Green whispered. "The fee will have to compensate. And I'll need a clean weapon." Despite the shock, there was no hesitation in his voice. The only way he'd be whispering in public, and not stuttering like a schoolboy, is if he were on the phone. "I can't meet you there. It's a crime scene. If I go back there, and someone spots me, they'll lock me up for sure."

Gotcha, Serena thought. Now all she had to do was follow him there to get the evidence prosecution needed.

"Okay, I'll meet you. One hour."

Serena stopped the tape and removed the electrodes from her forehead. She snatched the photograph from the line and dabbed it dry, stuffing it into her back pocket. She threw her leather jacket back on, removed the cassette from the recorder, and grabbed her phone. She smiled to herself as she rushed out the door. *You should have taken the deal, Green.*

She straddled her Ducati and roared across the city. High-rises crammed around her, pressing in with a claustrophobic unease. Shadows chased her as she sped between crowded streets.

The crime scene where that poor girl had been blown to bits was an apartment block on the shadier side of the river. Whoever wanted the girl dead had lured her there, baited her with promises or threats. But why? What reason would anyone have for snuffing out the life of someone so young? Naivety painted a target on your back, but not for murder. She opened the throttle, and the city blurred past her in silver streaks. All the while, her mind reviewed the details. The girl. Green. His employer. And her mother's voice tore across it all.

"You must be careful."

Serena shook off the doubt and rolled to a stop outside the apartment block. She parked across the street, left the bike, and hid in the shadows of a seedy club entrance. From the corner opposite, she watched Green approach. Right on time. He glanced around while she hugged the wall, out of sight. He vanished into the lobby.

Serena opened up the folded photograph from her back pocket, uncrumpled the creases, and glared at the pixels of Green's silhouette. His voice drifted into her ears.

"Do you know how dangerous it is to be meeting like this?" He was there. Room 542. And so was his employer.

Serena reached for her phone to call in backup, but stopped. If Smith knew where she was, it would be her badge on the line. Then how many more scumbags like Green would be left to get away with murder? She clasped the handle of her gun in its holster and hurried across the road, dodging traffic.

The apartment's lobby swallowed her in its gloom. Hairs on the nape of her neck prickled as she drew her pistol and moved through the darkness. She held the photo aloft, catching glimpses of it in the shards of light that streamed through broken windows.

"You got the cash?" she heard Green ask. "And the gun?"

Her footsteps haunted the stairs as she climbed. She pointed her weapon up, glancing to the winding labyrinth above.

"So are we going to do the handover or not?" Green's voice echoed in her ears, from both the photograph and the door to the fifth floor right ahead of her. She pocketed the photograph and entered the hallway. Through an open doorway, she saw Green with his hands raised.

"Wait a minute. This is a joke, right?" Green said. Then his smile morphed into terror. "No!"

Bullets ripped through Green's chest, splattering the wall behind him with blood. Serena launched herself through the door.

"Police! Nobody move!" she screamed. Then her jaw dropped. Before her, Andrew stood, aiming a pistol between her eyes.

Her prosecutor ex-boyfriend smiled. "Won't you come in, Serena? I've been expecting you."

She froze in the doorway. "It was you? You're the one who ordered the kill?"

"Not exactly." The barrel of his gun drew her vision like a magnet. Serena forced herself to meet his grey eyes.

"I just witnessed you kill a man, Andrew. Why should I believe you?"

"That was just to get your attention, Serena. Don't worry. You've got nothing to fear from me."

"Then you won't mind dropping the gun."

He tutted, shaking his head. "Can't do that just yet. I've got a message I have to give you first."

"What message?"

Andrew stepped towards her. "All those cases brought to trial, all those murders solved, and you had recordings of every single killer admitting their crimes. But the funny thing is, we checked the precinct's surveillance equipment, and there's nothing signed out to you. You never sought permission to use listening devices in an investigation. So how'd you do it?"

Serena scowled. "I have my methods."

"Exactly. That's what I was sent to find out. Your methods."

"You've been spying on me? Our whole relationship?"

"I'll admit, you were very good at hiding the truth. I puzzled over how you did it for months. The way you made connections out of nowhere and pulled in suspects without a shred of evidence. No one's that lucky."

Serena growled, growing impatient. "What are you getting at, Andrew?"

"And then I stumbled into your darkroom. You remember? That night I was 'sleep-walking.' You had a picture of every single person you interrogated, but not for any official precinct business. Why is that, Serena?"

Serena's eyes widened and her heart stopped. She had been in the middle of making a recording when he stumbled in that night.

"We knew you were listening in. We just didn't know how. And then I caught you staring at that photograph and making the same face you do when you're on the phone. Listening. And suddenly, everything that didn't make sense just clicked." Andrew's neck tightened and his fingers strengthened their grip on the gun. "You've caught the eye of a very powerful person. If I had a picture of them, of course, I wouldn't even need to be here. You could hear them yourself."

Serena paused, and shuffled back towards the door, speechless.

"That's how you traced Green here, isn't that right? A photograph?"

"Who else knows?" she asked.

"Don't worry, Serena. You passed the test. Your secret's safe with us."

"Test? What test?"

"The person I represent devised a little experiment to ensure their suspicions about you weren't misplaced. That's why the girl had to die."

Serena winced. "You killed her to test me?"

"How else could we be sure? But with you following Green, there's no doubt of it. And I'll bet you've got a recording stashed somewhere of that conversation I had with him earlier, don't you?"

The cassette burned a hole through her heart. It weighed on her soul, heavy as an anchor. She thought she'd nail a murderer with it. Instead, it had brought her here, straight into this trap. "Why go to all this effort? Who are you working for?"

Andrew dropped his arm. "My employer isn't easy to impress. You've done well. They want to give you the chance to keep impressing them. There's a lot at stake,

Serena. More than you know. They'd like to offer you the opportunity to do some real good in this city."

"How? By killing people?" She gestured to Green's body on the floor. "That's all you seem to be able to do."

"Think about it. How many low-level thugs have you put away for crimes they should never have been allowed to commit in the first place? You want to stop that? Now's your chance."

Serena shook her head. "There are laws for that. You, of all people, should understand that nobody is above the law."

Andrew laughed. "That's rich coming from you. How many people's privacy have you invaded without them even knowing?"

"That's different."

Andrew cocked an eyebrow. "Is it? Isn't everyone entitled to their privacy, Serena? The same way everyone's entitled to a fair trial. We're the same, you and I."

"No." She shook off the foul taste that filled her mouth. "We're nothing alike."

"Don't kid yourself. People like you, people like my employer, they make their own rules. No need to do things by the book as long as you get results, right? You serve the greater good, the same as me."

"What I do puts bad people away."

"But by what means? How many principles have you had to bend so you can sleep at night? Principles are like those handcuffs you carry. They limit you, stop you from reaching your potential. Don't you want to be free, Serena?"

"Free to do what? To stop criminals by becoming one? Where's the freedom in that?" But it was already too late. All those whispers she'd stolen in the dead of night became accusations against her. And no reassurance of the good she'd used them for would lift the weight he'd strapped to her with his words.

Andrew's grey eyes steeled over. "Offers like this only come once. Refuse, and you'll be taking on a fight you can't win."

Serena tightened her grip, focussing her aim on his heart. "I won't be a puppet. Not for anyone. Now, it's about time you dropped your weapon, put your hands behind your head, and stepped away from the door."

Andrew let the gun slip from his fingers, but he remained where he stood, inches from an open doorway that led deeper into the apartment. "You don't know who you're dealing with. Last chance, Serena."

"Andrew Simmonds, I'm placing you under arrest for the murder of—"

Andrew turned and disappeared through the doorway. Serena bolted across the floorboards. She followed him into the room beyond.

Hundreds of photographs littered the walls. Lines of string hung across the room, and reams of pictures dangled from it, all around her. And with every photograph, came a voice.

An avalanche of noise crashed against Serena. Every-where she looked, dozens of voices invaded her mind, too many to isolate. She covered her ears, but couldn't stop them. Louder and louder they grew. Her eyes scanned wildly for Andrew but they could not follow him in the sea of photos. Her head swam. She staggered forwards, wading through the quagmire of noise. The voices swallowed her, and she dropped to her knees. She couldn't let him escape, but she couldn't move.

"Andrew!" she called out. A shadow moved across the room, but she couldn't trace it. The overwhelming cacophony paralysed her, left her incapable of thought. She fought the swell, until it crashed over her, drowning her in sound. She thought of her mother, of that night when the police had come for George. The first night someone else had understood her gift. Serena recalled the tremble in her mother's fingers as she'd tucked her in that night: "Close your eyes."

The words hit Serena like a thunderclap. She squeezed her eyes shut, blocking out the voices, plunging into darkness, into silence. Across from her, towards the windows, she traced the creak of a floorboard and the scratching of fingertips on wood. The window to the fire escape must have jammed. She yelled for Andrew. The scratching quickened. And then the sound of shattering glass rang out.

Serena lifted her pistol and aimed towards the sound. She kept her gun low; her goal was to incapacitate, not kill. Bullets sliced through the air. A scream was followed by a thud on the floor a few feet ahead of her. Only one voice filled the apartment—Andrew's.

"My leg!" he howled. "You shot me!"

"Consider yourself lucky it wasn't your head." Serena kept one hand on her weapon while the other started pulling the strings of photographs down. Once she was confident most were destroyed, she was able to open her eyes and make her way to Andrew, being very careful where to look. She cuffed him and dragged him from the accursed room. Once she was assured he was not going to escape or bleed out, she took her phone from her pocket and dialled the precinct.

After hanging up, knowing reinforcements were on the way, she stared at Green's body. It lay in the same spot that poor girl had been found. Two dead. And why? Because some psycho had learned of her ability. It was her fault they were dead.

You must be careful.

In that moment, she realised what all those warnings meant. She understood what her mother had tried to tell her so many times. But it was too late.

Uniformed officers poured through the doorway, securing the apartment, and dragging Andrew out in cuffs. They would take him to the hospital to bandage his leg up,

then to the station, where she would interrogate him, find
out who he was working for. All in good time. She
stumbled down the stairs and rode her Ducati home. From
her pocket, she removed the tape of Jason Green admitting
to the girl's murder, not that it did much good now. She
toyed with the cassette.

"You must be careful," she whispered to herself. She'd
heard it so many times, but only now did she truly listen.

Serena entered the darkroom. She locked the tape inside
the desk. She reached for the cassette recorder and picked it
up. It weighed her palms down as she stared at its plastic
casing. How many criminals had she put away with this
thing? How many more could she stop with it? But what
price had she paid to get all those killers off the streets?
Two lives had been taken. How many more would be lost if
more people found out?

No recording was worth that.

She lifted her hands and smashed the recorder on her
desk, shredding plastic pieces across the room.

YOU LOOK FAMILIAR
By Paul D. Nolan

When the elevator reached the ground floor, the doors opened. Mike entered and pressed the button for the thirty-fifth floor.

Adjusting his black tie in the mirror on the side wall, he noticed a red splodge on his otherwise pristine, white silk shirt. After a tut, Mike tried to rub the stain off but it wouldn't budge. He knew exactly what it was; it was blood. He also knew it wasn't his, but looking through the elevator doors as they began to shut, he wondered which of the seven dead bodies scattered about the large lobby area could have splattered him. Seeing one guy with the handle of his favourite Bowie knife sticking out from his chin, Mike remembered the blood dripping onto his hand. He was sure he had wiped it off on the guy's suit. He must have missed a little.

The elevator was slow, which gave him time to think about what he was doing. A couple of months earlier and not a single person Mike had ever met in his life would have said he was capable of killing anyone; never mind the seven below him and who knows how many more to come on the thirty-fifth floor.

Everything changed one Tuesday night a few months ago.

He was on a second date with Jen, a waitress from his favourite diner. Mike had started going there after seeing Jen through the window and he couldn't help but go in. He spoke to Jen—well, made pleasantries—twice a week for a month before she asked him out.

"Nobody likes the food enough to come this often, and you are clearly too sweet," said Jen while Mike's face became blushed. "So, do you want to go out sometime?"

That first date was fantastic. Jen wanted to go bowling. He could tell she took it easy on him. They got on so well that the second date was arranged by the middle of the game. Mike let out a little laugh at the thought before the elevator doors opened, snapping him back to his present situation.

"You going down?" asked a woman holding an armful of files.

"No," replied Mike. "Going up this time."

"Ok. I'll wait for the next one," she said before standing back.

Mike gave her a little nod as the doors closed. He started thinking back to the second date while the elevator began to ascend floors again. Jen had asked him if he wanted to go see a new superhero movie with her on her next night off, which was midweek. He really wanted to, so he didn't mention that he was going to see it with some friends the weekend before. Deciding to go for a drink afterwards, they were discussing their favourite scenes of the movie when they turned a corner and Mike accidentally bumped into someone.

"Sorry, mate," Mike said instantly, raising a hand in apology. He carried on walking with Jen before someone pulled his shoulder back and punched him directly in the nose. Instantly, blood began pouring out and his eyes watered, blurring his vision. The next punch knocked him to the ground, where the kicking and stamping began. Mike could hear Jen scream but the blows to his head and ribcage made it impossible for him to get up. It was then that he passed out, waking up in a hospital bed a few days later.

Mike's attention was snapped back to the present when he heard voices through the closed elevator doors as it slowed to a stop well below where he was headed. Two men stepped in and carried on without acknowledging Mike at all.

Mike stood behind the two men in the back corner. There wasn't anywhere else for him to stand due to the size of them. The shorter of the two was at least seven inches taller than him, and since he was a little over six feet, that made these men intimidating by itself. Their bulking size extended outwards, shown by the stitches in their suit jackets fighting to hold together as they held their hands in front, a stance every person that size takes. They also had folds of neck fat spill over their shirt collars that made them look uncomfortable as hell. Mike thought about how every bouncer he had ever seen at a club took that stance. With the limited space Mike found himself in, he was glad that these men hadn't been made aware of the situation in the lobby yet. He wondered if he would be able to fight both of them off in that confined space. Relief filled him as the lift stopped again and both men got off, still not acknowledging him.

Only when he was alone again was he able to think back. He had another set of memories from that night; they weren't his own, but felt as real as if they were. He was hanging with his friends and was trying to show off. "Oi, where the fuck are our drinks," he shouted to a waiter who was walking past.

"I will be with you in one minute, sir," replied the waiter.

"He's taking the piss out of you, Connor," said Dean, one of the friends. "You gonna let him get away with making you wait like some punk?"

A man in a spotless suit walked over to their table. "I'm sorry, gentlemen, but it's time you left."

"Is that so?" said Connor without even turning around. "Do you know who I am?"

"I do, sir," he replied. "I also know your father very well. He comes here often and I'm sure he would be very disappointed by your actions."

"Aw, fuck this. Place is fucking boring anyway," said Connor. "Come on guys, let's get out of this dump and go somewhere with some fucking atmosphere."

Walking to the next bar, Connor was getting angrier by the minute. It didn't help that his friends kept telling him that he would never amount to much.

"How are you supposed to take on the family business when you let dicks like that talk to you like that?" Dillon, one of his other friends said.

As they turned the corner, some guy bumped into Connor. The guy apologised, but his friends were having none of it.

"See? Another dick taking the piss and you just let him walk away."

"Bloody hell. You would have me kill someone for bumping into me?" said Connor.

"No, holy shit. No one said anything about killing the guy," Dean continued, "but it's about respect. It's about not letting people push you around. Now, don't let that prick walk away thinking he got one over on you."

Even though it wasn't Mike's memories, he knew that Connor was more pissed off with Dean and Dillon but, to save face, took it out on him. The next part was the strangest of all. The memory that was on the forefront of his mind. He could remember both being Mike and Connor at once, but the perspective of Connor was strongest. He saw things through Connor's eyes, beating the shit out of this guy with Mike's face. He moved with Connor's body but felt every blow to his chest, face, arms, and legs. Suddenly, the pain stopped, even when Connor kept going. Mike realised his past-self had fallen unconscious from a final kick to the head by one of Connor's friends.

Now all of Mike's memories were fully Connor's. He was overwhelmed with rage and blind fury and something else. Something that felt very similar to fear. He could tell his friends were trying to talk to him, but he barely heard them. He caught a few words but did not comprehend them. Words like "stop" and "already dead." Then out of nowhere, a gunshot stopped him. He looked around and saw the woman drop to the ground.

"Floor thirty-five," announced the elevator as the doors began to open.

Mike knew where the six guards would be positioned so, withdrawing two pistols from holsters under his suit jacket, he took them out first. The next guarantee was the secretary. He had memories of her recruiting kids into drug pushing within schools. Some of the memories even showed her stab some of those kids who wanted out, so shooting her was just as easy as shooting the goons.

There was a young couple sat in chairs across from the reception desk. The man—who could only have been in his late-twenties to early-thirties—held his wife close and tucked her head into his chest. Mike pointed the gun towards them before realising they were just there to ask for help. A memory of people in the midst of desperation, pleading for loans, followed by other memories of smashing equipment and breaking the bones of those who couldn't keep up with repayments. Mike put the gun down. He walked over to one of the dead guards on the floor. Raiding his pockets, Mike pulled out the man's wallet. Opening it and taking a key card out, he then threw the wallet to the couple.

"There will be enough cash in the pockets of these scumbags to get you out of any situation you have found yourself in. Take what you can 'cause this loan department is about to be shut down," Mike told the couple. They quickly jumped up and grabbed everyone's wallets. They also took watches and whatever jewellery they could pull off quickly.

Mike continued farther into the thirty-fifth floor. From what he could see when the elevator stopped on his way up, the other floors were room after room of offices, but this level was set up differently: there was a reception desk, two offices to the left, plus the small waiting area that the couple had been sat before taking the dead people's money and jumping into the elevator. Walking past those, he found what he was looking for—a set of dark wood double doors. Even if Mike didn't have memories of being beyond those doors, he would have known it was going to be a large room by how much floor space was on the other side. What the memories did tell him was that the room had been soundproofed so as long as the doors were shut and the occupant wasn't sitting watching the CCTV, which he very rarely did, then Mike was going to give him quite a surprise.

Using the key card, he went in.

The room was more like an apartment than an office with its large sofa in the middle, facing a huge TV that was hanging on the wall. There was a bar to the left that looked extremely well-stocked. At the far right end was a beautiful desk that had a huge leather chair and a wall of windows overlooking the city behind it. The chair turned to reveal a familiar man Mike had never met.

"I don't know who the fuck you are or what kind of death wish you got going on, but you've got to be fucking crazy or fucking stupid if you think you're getting out of here alive," said the man at the desk.

"I'm not here for you, Val. I'm here for your son," said Mike as he stared, not taking his eyes or two pistols off the man in front of him.

"For fuck's sake," said the man in despair. "What has he done now? And you are not allowed to call me that. Nobody calls me that, you piece of shit. You call me Sir or Mr McBride, you hear me!"

"He tried to kill me. Now it's my turn."

"Jesus, what has gotten into that boy? Twenty years of letting me down, of being pampered by his mother so much that he's basically useless, and now he is trying to pop off people all over."

Val, which was short for Valentine and what only his close friends and associates were allowed to call him, walked across the room to behind the bar and grabbed two glasses.

"Drink?" he asked Mike, who shook his head while Val poured himself a drink. "This is the finest Irish single malt you will ever try. I insist."

"Leave the gun in the ice bucket," said Mike as Val dropped a lump in each glass.

"No worries," laughed Val. "How did you know?"

"I remember where every weapon is hidden in this room."

"Remember? You've been here before then?"

"I haven't," began Mike, "but the memories you planted in my head were from people who knew every inch of this office and every part of your business. I know all your little secrets."

Two months earlier, Murph and Dallas were listening to their boss complain.

"Why is he walking around, muttering shit to himself and fucking crying all the time?" Val shouted to the two older men, his closest associates and the most-feared men in his company. Their endeavours were still regular topics of conversation among the younger members of the organisation.

The stories of how vicious the two men could be, even in their senior years of life, was only equalled by the skills they had at their disposal. Murph was an explosives expert; known for never leaving any trace of his target whilst disintegrating all evidence in the process. Dallas was the complete opposite. A dedication earned him a 5th dan black belt in Taekwondo and he prided himself on his reputation as a silent assassin. Both were accomplished marksmen and trained to use a vast array of weaponry. Both men had served Val from the beginning as they worked for his father before him. Now they were old and knew Val had been expecting their retirement. Though he never brought it up, they knew he had even been searching for their replacements for when that day came.

"Apparently," said Murph, "he got into an incident last night."

"Killed a guy, they said," added Dallas. "With his bare hands as well. One of his buddies shot the guy's girlfriend as she was the only witness."

Val rolled his eyes. "Him? Really? I didn't think he had the balls. Looks like I was kinda right, as he is fucking losing his shit in the other room." Val rubbed his face as he went to pour himself a much-needed glass of his favourite single malt. "We can't let his mother see him like this. She will do her fucking nut."

Hours later, Murph returned to the office with Dallas. Val was standing by the bar, leaning on the counter and pouring himself another drink. Connor was pacing up and down in a separate room, still muttering to himself as he did.

"Boss! Boss!" they both said at exactly the same time.

"Don't give me any more bad news. The kid has drained me today," said Val, spinning his drink to allow the ice cube to infuse its coldness into every drop of his drink.

"Boss, he ain't dead," said Dallas.

"Who?" Val returned lazily.

"The guy your kid thinks he killed," added Dallas.

"Great, let's tell him so he can stop that fucking mumbling," said Val, pushing away from the bar, revitalised by the news.

"The guy's in a very bad way. He is not going to last much longer, but right now he is alive," Dallas said with a hint of excitement.

"So he will die later instead of last night? What's the fucking difference?" an exhausted Val asked while pinching the bridge of his nose.

"While he still breathes, there is a chance we can help him. Connor, that is," said Murph.

"Do you have a way of getting rid of his grief? Murph, please enlighten me on how you can subdue his conscience," said Val with a tone of sarcasm hidden under sheer annoyance.

"I think so, boss," added Murph with a touch less confidence than he had a moment earlier. "A buddy of mine, Bobby—a real clever ballox—he has this son, Gary—who is an even cleverer ballox—well, he told me about this doctor guy his son has been working with lately. Anyway, the doctor is trying to get this invention accepted by the government. Get this, he can take the memories and fears associated with a violent crime out of the victim and put them into the perp. Meant to end the vic's suffering and add to the perp's repercussions or some shit like that."

Val thought about this for a moment. "So you're thinking this doctor can do it with this guy and Connor?"

"According to my buddy, it's a possibility," added Murph.

"Interesting," said Val.

"We plant the memories and trauma and shit Connor's going through into this dying guy," explained Murph, "and since he ain't gonna make it, the guilt dies with him."

"That's the kind of shit those politicians have been trying to get for years," said Val. He hated to admit it—and in no way did he want it done to him—but it was an interesting scientific discovery. "Why haven't they started doing it to convicts already?"

"Those bloody human rights groups. A sniff of a cause and one of them will be all over it," added Dallas. "Strange to think of someone protecting us and not the victims."

"There are those who like a challenge over the results," laughed Val.

"Anyways, boss," Murph began again, "my buddy says Gary and the doc are working late tonight, preparing a speech about it or something. If we get the guy and Connor there, he will get his boy to point us in the right direction."

"What the fuck are we waiting for?"

They went to the other room and Val shouted, "Connor, come on. We're going out."

Connor followed behind as the four of them started towards the elevator. Murph could see that this lad was just following along and didn't really know what was happening. Connor continued to mutter to himself, the others unable to make out a word. In the car, Connor just stared out the window. After riding in silence, Val spoke to his goons, "If it is possible, I think you two should use this opportunity to retire. Remove the memories of our dealings and set up new lives where you can live a happy, normal life."

"What? You sure, boss?" asked Dallas, who was sitting in the back with Connor.

"We have enjoyed our lives," said Murph, not looking around as he spoke, since he was driving. "Both working for you and your father before you."

"I might regret this decision when some of my enemies come after me, sure, but you both have earned it ten times over," said Val. "I've set up a retirement fund and you can live out the rest of your days on the golf course or whatever you want."

The two older gentlemen had talked about this very thing for a while. They both knew that they couldn't work forever, but were afraid of not having excitement in their lives afterwards. Murph knew Dallas was a keen golfer who had a plan to play on every course used for PGA tours around the world. Murph had kept a log of all the little things he had never quite gotten round to doing while he worked, like eating at a certain restaurant or catching an old movie in a cinema that showed classics from time to time. Murph's wife, however, had always wanted to travel, which meant he would be visiting art museums, tourist attractions and various architecture around the world. He didn't mind because it made her happy, and after all these years putting up with his shit, she deserved some happiness.

When they arrived, Gary waited by the entrance and informed them that the victim was already inside. Having men planted everywhere—from doctors, nurses, and police—it was easy to get the barely-alive man out of the hospital and to the scientist.

Despite some initial reluctance, the operation went well, as the scientist realised he had no choice. He removed the targeted memories of all three men and planted them into the dying man before returning him to the hospital.

The same dying man who now stood pointing two guns at the biggest crime boss the city had ever known.

"I thought you were dead," said Val as he moved away from the bar and over to the sofa, checking his watch as he sat near the edge. He took a sip of his whiskey before placing the glass on a small round table next to him.

"You can leave the gun taped to the bottom of that table, like you left me in that bed to die," said Mike. "Where is Connor?"

"We both know that I'm not going to give him to you. Hell, I haven't even decided what to do to you for asking for him yet," said Val as he leaned back in his seat, holding up his hands to show they were empty.

"How about we make a deal?" Mike said, still holding a gun in each hand, but allowing them to hang down to his sides.

"Oh! You want to negotiate," laughed Val. "What the fuck do you have that I would want?"

"Memories," Mike replied softly. "Two old guys' memories in a young body. Skills they possessed in a vessel that is physically adept enough to perform the tasks."

"You want to join my organisation," Val burst out laughing before leaning forward and taking another sip of whisky. "It takes more than memories to survive in this business."

"Between the two of them, I know everything I need to know about everyone I need to know. That and I'm sick of getting by," explained Mike. "And I don't just want to work for you. No, I want your position in the business."

Mike had known how Val was going to react, through the memories he had a good sense of who the boss was.

The laughing stopped after a few moments, then Val stood up and took another sip of his drink

"Do you actually think I'm gonna step down and hand control over to you?" Val said as he put the glass down onto the counter, making sure to put a coaster underneath.

"Not at all," replied Mike. "I believe the memories that you put in my head advances me through the ranks to the position held by the previous owners of them. That's where I will start, eventually taking over for you when you retire."

"How do you know you could deal with certain aspects of the job?" questioned Val. He looked curious and Mike knew that by asking this, he was interested in hearing him out.

"I remember every feeling they had after everything they had to do. Desensitised to all the aspects you are talking about and I know their replacement isn't up to scratch," Mike replied confidently.

"What makes you say that?" quizzed Val.

"Because I killed everyone in the lobby before taking the lift up here. Not to mention killing everyone outside," said Mike, holding his confidence and doubling it down with old-fashioned eye contact. "So he was either already killed or you sent him off on a shitty task just to get him away from you. Otherwise, I would have had to kill him the moment I entered this room."

Val looked impressed, showing this with a slight nod. "But how do I know I can trust you? That my son will be safe with you around?"

"You won't trust me at first," agreed Mike. "You will carry a weapon at all times and demand I don't carry when I'm with you in here. You will also keep your son away from me 'till I've proven myself."

"Got it all figured out, don't ya?" Val said, picking up his whiskey and taking a larger swig.

"I also know that he is due here any minute now," Mike announced. "My only stipulation is that he doesn't know about this conversation. He is constantly going to try to prove himself to be the next boss, but he will never get that title." Mike changed his demeanour and his voice lowered with a snarl. "I want him pissed as you announce me as your successor. I want his entitled ass shattered as he is overlooked for the role he believed to be his birthright. I already know he's not cut out for it. Your men knew it. Hell, I'd be doing you a favour, really. But I also intend to earn it for myself. This is the only time I'm going to offer the deal." Mike shrugged. "I could just go ahead and kill him. Not only do I know where he and his mother live, but I know the location of every safe house in your organisation. The choice is yours, Val. And it sounds like you don't have much time to decide."

As if rehearsed, the door opened at the back of the room and in walked Connor. "Hey, dad. Oh sorry, I didn't realise you had company.

The door came from a separate lift that was accessed from a side alley and led directly into the office. Mike knew about the lift but didn't have a key to use it. The only people his memories ever showed using that lift were Val and his family.

"Hey, Son. Listen, go out the back there and I will be over to you soon."

"Do we have a deal?" asked Mike through gritted teeth. He came to kill Connor if he didn't get what he wanted, but would let it go for a new life. Hearing Connor's voice brought a rage to the surface that he was struggling to hold at bay, but he never took his eyes away from Val.

Val finished his whiskey and stood up, looked to his son, then back to Mike. "I believe we do. When can you start?" he asked as he held out his hand.

Mike put his guns away. "Thank you, sir. Is Monday okay?" he replied as they shook hands.

"That will be fine. See you then," Val ushered Mike towards the lift at the back. He wanted Mike out of the building and was going to make damn sure Connor was safe from this experienced newbie before letting them be in the same room again.

Connor walked back to shake the guy's hand. He couldn't place him, but he looked familiar. "I'm sorry, but do I know you?"

Val didn't see his son coming closer, but Mike did. He put his hand out to shake Connor's hand but instead pulled him in and slammed his forehead into Connor's nose. Conner pulled back and instantly pinched the bridge of his nose and shouted, "Argh, What the fuck?"

Val went to see to Connor while Mike got into the lift and—with the calmness of man assured of himself—said, "I think that was the least I should get." He pushed the button to send the elevator down. "See you Monday, Boss."

FORESEEABLE HARM
By C. Vandyke

Katrina jumped up from the couch to answer the door as soon as the bell rang. Her food was almost half an hour late—again. When she opened the door, she expected to see the delivery guy from Bombay Heights with her order of chicken tikka masala, so she was confused when, instead of a skinny Indian man wearing an oversized motorcycle helmet holding a bag of takeout, there was a tall white guy wearing a camel hair jacket over an expensive black suit. He was impeccably clean-shaven, with a strong jawline and pronounced cheekbones, his hair parted so neatly that it looked as if he had come directly from the barbers. *Since when did the Jehovah Witnesses come around at night?* she thought, but what she said was, "Can I help you?"

The man's finger still hovered over the bell, but as soon as he saw Katrina his lips moved into a slight, professional smile.

"Katrina? Katrina Freeman?" It was more of a statement than a question.

"Yes?"

Instead of answering, the man reached inside of his coat, pulled out a manila envelope, and held it towards her.

"My name is Jonathan Gottlieb. He/his. I'm here to serve you the official notice that your legal appeal in the case of Freeman versus Freeman has been denied." She stared at the envelope, then back at him. Jonathan's smile faltered slightly and he smacked himself on his forehead with his free hand. "Aw, man! I did it again. I'm supposed to give you the envelope *before* I tell you what it is. Sorry,

I'm still pretty new at this. It's my first internship." With a bit of effort, he plastered his smile back in place. "Still, I suggest you take it. If you don't take it, I'll just have to send it via certified chrono-mail, and the result will be the same regardless." He thrust the envelope towards her, then cocked his head to the side. "Hold up. Have we met before?"

Katrina folded her arms across her chest, highly self-conscious of the fact she was talking to a strange man while dressed in flannel Wonder Woman pyjamas. "What the hell are you talking about? 'My appeal'? I'm not in a lawsuit."

The man's smile flickered, then transformed into a frown. "You don't know about the lawsuit?"

"No, I don't know about any lawsuit!" Her heart sped up slightly. "Is this a scam? Some door-to-door con?" She wished her girlfriend, Rashida, was here. Rashida was never phased by weird things like this. A small part of Katrina wondered if someone *could* actually be suing her and she didn't know about it, but that seemed impossible. Who the hell would be suing *her*? Whether it was a con or not, she really wished she wasn't wearing adult PJs and T. rex socks when dealing with a strange white guy at her door; it made it hard to project the "I'm not someone you can fuck with" attitude she was hoping came across in her glare.

"You *are* Katrina Freeman, aged twenty-four, of 157 Madison Street, correct?" He glanced down at the name and address on the envelope.

"Yes, but—"

"And this *is* September 19th, 2021, correct?"

"What? 2021? No! Are you high?" Drugs would explain it, but the dude on the steps really didn't look like a tweaker. Not that preppy white boys didn't do their share of drugs, of course (if nothing else, that was one thing she'd learned as an undergrad at Bard College), but in her experience the white guys who *did* do drugs didn't then put on business suits and wander around Bed-Stuy trying to serve legal papers to random black women at night. Suddenly, she was very conscious of the fact that she was home alone and that Rashida wouldn't be back from her shift at the bar for hours. She started to ease the door shut.

"Listen, dude, I don't know what the fuck your deal is, but you need to leave now."

"Wait, I'm sorry!" His calm, legal veneer was gone, and he stuck his foot in the door to keep it from closing completely. "What year is it?"

Katrina rolled her eyes and pushed the door hard against his shiny black loafer. "It's 2019, asshole. Now if you don't leave right the fuck now I'm calling the cops."

He pulled his foot back and before he could stutter out an apology, she slammed the door and latched the deadbolt. She knelt on the couch and pulled up one of the vinyl slats of her blinds to make sure he actually left. For a moment the man stood on the top of her stoop, muttering under his breath, then he reached up and tapped his left temple. "Someone at dispatch screwed up the Freeman case. Yeah, yeah, I know." He continued to talk to himself as he took the steps on her stoop two at a time, then strode off down the block. She didn't see a Bluetooth earpiece, so definitely on drugs. Or mentally ill. That thought caused her a momentary pang of guilt, but she was home alone and wasn't taking any chances with a strange man who talked to himself. If he needed help someone else would have to take care of it. She watched until he turned the corner on to Bedford Avenue. Just as he did, a moped pulled up outside on the sidewalk with her Indian takeout. Late as usual—so just on time.

* * *

When the alarm on her phone went off the next morning, Katrina woke up to discover Rashida fast asleep in bed next to her. Katrina hit the snooze button on the alarm and buried her nose in her girlfriend's hair. Rashida had just done her braids the day before, and her long tresses were thick with the scent of shea butter and this new vanilla bean conditioner Rashida had recently started using that smelled like you could eat it with a spoon. Katrina snuggled up to her and ran one finger along Rashida's dark brown side until it teased the edge of her bra.

"Ungh. Let me sleep." Rashida's muffled voice came from under her pillow. Katrina draped her arm over her barely conscious girlfriend and let her hand rest on top of her breast. She burrowed her face deeper into Rashida's braids.

"Babe, I got to tell you about this weird-ass white dude that stopped by last night."

"What you gotta do is let me sleep." Rashida twisted her shoulders so that Katrina's hand slipped off her breast, then pulled the covers up over her body like a soft wall between them. "Reggie didn't show last night, so I got stuck with a double shift and had to close. Fucking hipster motherfuckers don't even know what the words 'last call' mean. I didn't even lock up until three in the goddamn morning."

Katrina's jaw tightened as she drew back her hand. Since Rashida had worked the closing shift she *did* need sleep, but Katrina couldn't help but resent the fact that they barely spent time together these days. When she *was* home, Rashida was so tired that all she wanted to do was sleep or stare at her phone. A part of her knew her girlfriend loved her, but every time she tried to touch Rashida and she pulled away, Katrina couldn't help but take it personally. Rashida fumbled one hand out from under the duvet and patted lazily at Katrina's leg in a half-conscious attempt at reconciliation.

"Sorry, sweetie. I'm just so tired. You can tell me all about the crazy white boy later. Promise."

"Okay," Katrina said. Rashida was too out of it to hear how leaden her voice was. The alarm on her phone went off again, and Katrina silenced it before it could wake up Rashida more than it already had. She leaned over to kiss her girlfriend on the neck and felt the other woman's body move slightly in response.

"I love you, Shida," she whispered against her skin. But Rashida was already out, the duvet rising and falling slowly as she slept.

Katrina was half-dressed and smearing lotion on her legs when her phone vibrated. It was a text from Jessica, a girl from her Figure Drawing class at Pratt.

U wanna grab coffee b 4 class?

Her stomach did a little flip-flop, and she glanced guiltily through the open bathroom door to the pile of covers that was her sleeping girlfriend. Not that she had a thing going with Jessica—nothing that she had any reason to feel guilty about—but she *did* have a bit of a crush on her classmate. Jessica was everything that Rashida wasn't: sarcastic, outgoing, tattooed. She had piercings in about everywhere it was possible to attach a piece of jewellery, she always stepped outside of their three-hour drawing sessions to smoke a cigarette, she changed her hair colour almost weekly, and she used the word "pussy" casually in conversation. In other words, Jessica was exactly the sort of "bad girl" that Katrina had always let herself pine over from a distance but would never in a thousand years try to hook up with. That didn't change the fact that every time she saw Jessica her palms got sweaty and she had a hard time stringing together a coherent sentence.

Whenever she met Jessica for coffee before or after class, Katrina wondered if she was doing something wrong, but she also knew she'd never *actually* cross that line of low-level flirting over lattes. She was way too shy—and besides, she loved Rashida. She'd never do that to her. Rashida was the best thing that had ever happened to her.

She wiped the excess lotion on her thighs, then tapped out a quick response.

Ok. 11:30 at the bean?

Her screen showed the repeating ellipses of Jessica responding. As she slid on the second-hand jeans and stained flannel shirt that made up her art-class uniform, she kept one eye on the phone, waiting for the message to finish.

Her phone buzzed.

Sure thing. See u there. And a winking emoji. A slight smile tugged at the edges of Katrina's lips as she put on her eyeliner, then pulled her twists back into a loose ponytail and secured it with a scrunchie. Nothing to feel guilty about; Rashida was busy and distant these days, and it wouldn't hurt if she found someone to flirt with just a little in the meantime. The fact that she decided at the last minute to wear perfume and freshen her lip gloss didn't mean anything. Of course not.

* * *

When she finally made it outside it was a beautiful spring day, the sort of weather that balanced perfectly on the edge between cool and warm, the first buds on the magnolia trees peeping out as the early April leaves rustled in a soft breeze. One of those picture-perfect, Brooklyn-in-Spring days, when even the cracked sidewalk and discarded coffee cups in the gutter seemed to glow with the promise of new growth and a boundless future. As Katrina waited for the B52 bus, she queued up a playlist of Nina Simone as the soundtrack for her commute. She was so busy humming along to the *High Priestess of Soul* and staring at the perfectly feathered clouds that she jumped when she felt a tap on her shoulder.

"Oh, shit! I'm sorry—" she started to say, then caught her breath as she realised she was staring at the white guy who had rung her doorbell the night before.

"Katrina? Katrina Freeman?" He was wearing the same camel hair jacket over the same black suit as he had when she'd seen him on her stoop last evening, and his thin lips were drawn in the same obsequious smile.

"Dude, what the fuck!" She stepped back, bumping up against the glass wall of the bus stop.

"I'm sorry, I didn't mean to startle you, Miss Freeman. My name is Jonathan Gottlieb. He/his. I'm here to serve you the official notice that—"

"I know who you are, asshole." An older black woman and a twenty-something Asian man dressed like a bicycle courier, both also waiting for the bus, looked up from their phones at the sound of her raised voice. "I don't know why the hell you are bothering me, but—"

He cut her off. "You *are* Katrina Freeman, aged twenty-four in 2019, of 157 Madison Street, yes?"

"My age and date aren't the issue, dude. Why are you harassing me?"

A pained expression flashed across his face. Looking at him now, she realised he looked young—younger than her, probably just out of college. In the clear light of day, it was also obvious that his suit, while expensive, barely fit him, as if he'd bought it the day before and was in too much of a rush to make sure it was the right size. It also seemed to be made of some bizarre, almost metallic fabric.

"Miss Freeman, I can see why this would seem like harassment, but as a legal intern at Fitzgerald & Cruz, it's my job to deliver this." Just like the night before, he pulled out a manila envelope from inside his coat. He noticed her glare at the envelope, and his face fell. "Ah, man! I'm supposed to have you take the envelope *before* I tell you I'm from a law firm. Crap. Sorry, I'm pretty new at this." He looked sheepish and blushed slightly. "You might as well take it since it doesn't matter whether you do or not. It's a notice of—"

"Yeah, yeah, I know. That I've lost some sort of appeal in some lawsuit I've never heard of."

Jonathan frowned. "Appeal? No. This is the initial notice that you are being sued in Temporal Court."

"Temporal Court?" The two other bus riders went back to their phones, though the old lady kept peering over the screen at Jonathan suspiciously. Katrina didn't want to keep a conversation with a creepy stranger going longer than necessary, but she was also determined to make sense of this bizarre interaction. "I've never even heard of 'Temporal Court.' And last night, you *distinctly* said something about my losing an appeal."

"Wait, last night? I didn't see you—" Jonathan's eyes widened. "Oh. Oh crap." The blush from his cheeks spread, and he ran his fingers through his pale brown hair. "Crap, crap, crap. Someone at dispatch must have screwed up big-time. Or, rather, they will screw up big-time. Or . . ." He trailed off, tapping the envelope against his leg nervously, then began pacing back and forth. "Janice, someone at dispatch screwed up the Freeman summons. Or rather the appeal. Wait? What was that?" He cocked his head to one side, his blue eyes staring through Katrina as he listened to a voice that wasn't there. Katrina stared at him warily. There was definitely no Bluetooth earpiece. He seemed harmless enough, more of a lost prep school kid than an actual threat, but she didn't want to take any chances. She started to edge away from the bus stop. She could walk to Pratt in twenty minutes, and the weather was nice…

"Please, take the envelope. I could lose my internship." Jonathan thrust the envelope at her, and the look in his eyes was so panicked and pathetic that she reached out and took it without even thinking. The second her fingers closed on the envelope he let go, and the relief on his face was so stark that she felt embarrassed for him. "Thanks. I've got to check back in at the office, see if they can clear this up. The summons should explain everything, and if you have any questions, there's a number to call." With that, he turned and walked quickly down the sidewalk, muttering to himself again.

* * *

Thirty minutes later, Katrina sat at a table in the corner of The Bean Cafe, a cup of coffee and the manila envelope sitting in front of her. She had originally planned to stop in to Open Studio time to get in some drawing before meeting Jessica at 11:30, but she'd been too frazzled from her bizarre run-in with Jonathan to focus on art. After he'd left, she decided to walk off her nervous energy, but she'd spent the half-hour walk to campus focused on the envelope in her backpack. So here she was, thirty minutes before her date—friend date, not *date* date, of course. She took a tentative sip of coffee and stared at the envelope.

It was a plain, legal-size manila envelope. Her name and address were clearly visible through a little plastic window on the front, with a return address sticker reading "Fitzgerald & Cruz, Attorney at Law: 550 Fulton Street, Brooklyn, NY 11217." She turned it over. On the reverse of the envelope the firm's name was printed again, this time next to an icon of a set of scales superimposed over a clock, under which were the words "Specializing in Temporal Torts: Holding the Past Accountable to the Present Future."

Weird, but everything about this was weird. A twist had worked its way free from the rest of her hair, and she tucked it back into place under the scrunchie. She hesitated, then slit the envelope open with one fingernail and pulled out the contents.

There were two sheets of paper. The one on top looked like a business letter, with letterhead matching the name and logo from the envelope.

April 15th 2035
Katrina Freeman c. 2019
157 Madison St.
Brooklyn, NY 11232

Temporal Court of Brooklyn, New York

Katrina Freeman, aged 40, Plaintiff vs. Katrina Freeman, aged 24, Defendant
Summons, Case No. 52345-1923

Dear Ms Freeman:

A lawsuit has been commenced against you in the above titled Court by the Plaintiff. Plaintiff's case is stated in the Complaint served with this Summons. In order to defend against this lawsuit, you must respond to the Complaint by filing your Answer stating your Defense in writing and serving a copy to the Plaintiff's undersigned attorney within 20 days of service of this Summons, excluding the day of service. If you have been served outside of the Decade in which the Complaint is Lodged, you have 40 days to send your Answer back to the appropriate Decade via courier, certified chrono-mail, or similar method.

Dated this 15th day of April 2035
Matthew Peabody, Esq.
Fitzgerald & Cruz, Attorneys at Law

"This has to be a joke," she muttered as she read the letter. One of her friends, a classmate maybe? As a grad student at an art school, she did know a bunch of creative types with *way* too much time on their hands, so maybe one of them? Jacob, in Oil Painting, was into improv and weird live-action role-playing shit. She flipped to the second page.

April 15th 2035
Katrina Freeman c. 2019
157 Madison St.
Brooklyn, NY 11232

Temporal Court of Brooklyn, New York

Katrina Freeman, aged 40, Plaintiff vs. Katrina Freeman, aged 24, Defendant
Complaint, Case No. 52345-1923

Plaintiff Katrina Freeman, aged 41, brings forth the following cause of action against her earlier self, Katrina Freeman, aged 24, and alleges that:

1. On or about May 4th 2019, the Defendant did get drunk at a party and then leave said party with one Jessica Melendez.

2. On or about May 5th 2019, the Defendant did return with Ms Melendez to Ms Melendez's apartment and engage in sexual intercourse.

3. That, following this initial sexual contact, Defendant did proceed to enter into an illicit relationship with Ms Melendez, and that over the next two years Defendant and Ms Melendez did exchange numerous texts of a sexual nature, and did meet on multiple occasions to engage in further acts of carnal pleasure, both at Ms Melendez's residence, and at the Defendant's, even in the <u>very bed</u> she and the Defendant's girlfriend had picked out at Ikea together, which was particularly low.

4. On or about April 31st 2021, the Defendant's girlfriend at the time, Rashida Robinson, did discover the existence of the above aforementioned texts between the Defendant and Ms Melendez.

5. On or about May 1st 2021, Ms Robinson confronted the Defendant about said texts and the existence of her two-year relationship with Ms Melendez, and that, following a verbal altercation that lasted for hours, Ms Robinson did end her Relationship with the Defendant, calling the Defendant a slut and a cheating whore, both of which were somewhat true, thus ending <u>the best thing that had ever happened</u> to the Plaintiff.

6. That, following the break-up with Ms Robinson, the Defendant did make a series of terrible life choices, including: moving in with Ms Melendez, who then

cheated on her multiple times, which really served her right; dropping out of art school, thus effectively ending Plaintiff's dream of becoming an artist; and moving back to New Jersey to live in her parent's house, like a <u>complete loser</u>.

WHEREFORE, Plaintiff seeks compensatory damages from the Defendant in the amount of $500,000, to cover the cost of her getting the hell out of her parent's house and going back to school to finally finish her degree, together with attorney fees and court costs.

Dated this 15th day of April 2035
Matthew Peabody, Esq.
Fitzgerald & Cruz, Attorneys at Law

"Hey, cute thing—this seat taken?" She looked up from the letter to see a flash of bright blue hair as Jessica slid into the seat across from her. Katrina looked down at the letter in her hand, her head swimming, the taste of bile rising in her throat.

"Is this your sick idea of a joke?" She waved the letters at Jessica. "Because if it is, it isn't fucking funny, Jess."

Jessica's brow furrowed, the line of silver hoop piercings over each eye catching the light as she frowned. "Joke? Trina, I don't know what—"

"Don't call me that! No one but my *girlfriend* calls me Trina!"

"Hey, you just called me Jess!" Jessica retorted, her smirk caught as if she was trying to figure out whether Katrina was actually mad or not. She cocked her head to one side, her neon blue hair veiling half her face but not hiding the real concern and confusion in her wide, brown eyes. "Seriously though Katrina, you good? Everything okay? 'Cause you aren't normally a raging bitch monster."

Katrina stared at the name 'Jessica Melendez' on the sheet of paper in her hand, then back at the woman sitting across from her. Jessica's lips, which today were painted black, were pursed as she watched Katrina.

"I'm... I'm sorry Jessica. I'm having a really weird morning. I just need... I can't be here right now. Sorry." She stuffed the papers in her bag, swung the backpack over her shoulder, and stumbled past Jessica out of the coffee shop.

Back outside, she took a few deep breaths, then started walking blindly down the sidewalk without a destination in mind. Someone was clearly messing with her, but who? Jessica? She didn't seem the type to do something this creepy. Could Rashida have sensed something and gotten jealous? But she hadn't done anything with Jessica! Besides, Shida wasn't the overly jealous type, and certainly not the type to pull some weird, elaborate stunt like this. As she walked across the wide, grassy field that ran the length of campus, she pulled out her phone and dialled Rashida.

"Yo, this is Rashida. Leave a message or don't, all the same to me. I'll try to—"

She hung up before the message ended. Rashida never listened to her voicemail. She slumped onto a bench at the edge of the field under a towering oak tree and tapped out a text.

Morning bae I Really want 2 hear ur voice.
Call me when you can. Luv u.

One of her twists had broken free again, and she absentmindedly twined it around her index finger. The breeze, which had seemed so warm and comforting when she'd stepped out the door this morning, now was cold on her neck.

Last night had been weird. Her run-in with Jonathan at the bus stop had been weirder. The letters he'd given her—suggesting a future affair with Jessica—were beyond weird, they were scary. What creepy weirdo not only knew that she had a crush on Jessica but was a big enough of an asshole to think sending her that letter was funny?

She pulled out the envelope again to see if there was some clue that she had missed, something to help her figure out who was behind it, when a small sheet of paper slid out and fluttered to the ground. She leaned over and picked it up. The insert was printed on glossy paper stock and about the size of a postcard. In the upper left-hand corner was the seal of the City of New York and, in a bold sans serif font, the heading declared: *You have rights!*

Beneath those words, it continued in smaller type:

> *According to New York State Law, all defendants have legal rights when subject to a Temporal Tort suit. As your knowledge of these rights may vary depending on what era you receive notice of a lawsuit, Municipal Code 27B-6 guarantees all defendants in such cases access to legal counsel, provided free of charge by the City of New York's Citizen Space-Time Advocate's office. If you wish to avail yourself of this service or have any questions regarding your legal case or the CSTA, please call 01-99-212-877-9999.*

Katrina's phone vibrated in her pocket. She pulled it out, hoping Rashida had texted her back. It was from Jessica.

If you need 2 talk, I'm around. C u in class?

She swiped 'dismiss' on Jessica's message. Jessica deserved a response after the way Katrina stormed out on her—assuming she *wasn't* involved in this nonsense—but she'd deal with her later. Right now she was going to call the number on the paper. She doubted the number was even real, but if it did work maybe she could figure out who was behind this. At the very least, if someone answered she could give them a piece of her mind.

After two rings, an automated system picked up.

"Thank you for calling the Citizen Space-Time Advocate's Temporal Tort Hotline. Para Español pulse uno. For English, press two. Putonghua, qing an san—"

She pressed two. "If you are a defendant and have questions about a summons you have received to Temporal

Court, please press one. If you are a representative of a legal services provider please—" She pressed one. If this was a prank, it was the most elaborate one she'd ever heard of.

"We at the CSTA understand that receiving a summons can be a distressing experience, and we are here to help. We know your time is valuable to you and our time is limitless, so please stay on the line and an operator will be with you in just a moment." There was a brief burst of music, some upbeat, electronic tune with a woman singing in something that sounded like Chinese, then it cut off as a voice came on the line.

"CSTA Defendant Hotline, this is Agent Alpha-Three-Aught-Seven speaking. What's your name and case number?" The speaker spoke quickly and with a flat affect, neither identifiably male or female, clearly reading from a script.

"Who the hell is this?" Katrina snapped. "This isn't funny, okay? Joke's over. I really need you to tell me what the hell is going on."

"Ma'am, we at the CSTA understand that receiving a summons can be a distressing experience, but please try not to—"

"Seriously, cut it out! I get that you're playing a joke, but I'm not laughing. Whoever you are or whoever put you up to this, this is some stalker level shit and if you don't leave me alone I'm going to call the cops."

There was a long pause, and through the phone she heard the sound of typing on a keyboard. "Ma'am, are you familiar with the Temporal Court System?"

"No, listen, I—"

The voice cut her off. "Ma'am, may I ask what year you are calling from?"

"What year?" Katrina's voice rose. "What year? It's 2019, jerkwad. I'm not playing with you! I am going to call the—"

The person on the other end of the line let out a deep, exasperated sigh. "Oh, you're an Old. That explains it." There was a flurry of typing. "Ma'am, I understand you are distressed and confused. As a citizen from before the passage of the Santos-Hwang Current Person Protection Act, you are provided extra legal services under New York City Law. I'm tracing this call to your temporal and spatial location and dispatching a public defender to provide you free legal counsel immediately. For your record, your reference number is 807364K, and I am Agent Alpha-Three-Aught-Seven. Thank you for calling the Citizen Space-Time Advocate's Temporal Tort Hotline, have a nice day."

"What do you mean, tracing—" But the line was dead. Katrina stared at her phone. The lock screen was a selfie she'd taken of her and Rashida this past New Year's Eve. She was sitting in Rashida's lap on their couch, both of them still wearing those ridiculous 2019 glasses and cheap paper top hats, glasses of champagne raised in a toast to the future. Here, in the present moment, a small, sad smile pulled at the edges of her lips. Whatever the idiots behind this prank had intended, it had reminded her how much she loved her girlfriend and how much she didn't want to do anything to mess up the good thing she had. That was the one thing that letter got right—Rashida *was* the best thing that had ever happened to her.

"Ms Freeman?" She looked up from her phone. In front of her was a person of indeterminate gender. Their head was shaved, with an intricate series of tattoos along their left scalp that almost looked like circuitry, and their light brown skin made their race as equally impossible to guess as their sex. They were dressed in a suit made from a strange, metallic silver fabric that shimmered with slight rainbows in the sunlight. The person looked down at a small cellphone that seemed to be strapped to their left forearm.

"Ms Freeman, age twenty-four in 2019, residing at 157 Madison Street?"

Katrina was too tired and confused to argue this time.

"Yes. Yes, that's me."

"Hi, my name is Toni Marcos-Nguen. They/Them. Wait, do you people do pronouns in 2019?"

"Um, some of us do, yeah. Who are—"

"Ms Freeman, I've been assigned your case," they looked back down at their screen, "number 52345-1923, Freeman versus Freeman, in which you are the named Defendant." They paused at Katrina's blank look. "I'm a public defender. I'm here to help you with your defence, and—since you date from before the Santos-Hwang Current Person Protection Act—I'm here to fill you in on the working of the Temporal Court. May I sit?"

Wordlessly, Katrina patted the seat next to her in a resigned invitation, and Toni sat down next to her. Katrina eyed them suspiciously.

"Temporal Court? Santos-what's-it Act? Listen, I'm still convinced this is some sort of elaborate joke, but I'm too tired to argue right now. So tell me all about it."

"Ms Freeman, can I call you Katrina?" She nodded. "Katrina, I assure you this is not a joke. The Santos-Hwang Current Person Protection Act, passed in 2030, allows an individual to sue their past selves for decisions or actions that have resulted in harm to that individual at the time of the lawsuit." Katrina stared at them. "In your case, in the year 2035 your future self, who at the time is forty, is suing you—her past self—for making her present—your future—unhappy in some way." Toni looked at their screen and scrolled through a document with their fingertip. "Looks like she is citing an affair you began with one Jessica Melendez on May 4th of this year as causing considerable emotional pain and suffering, as well as damaging her—that is your—prospects." They looked back up and gave Katrina a pained half-smile. "Pretty standard, really. Things like this make up the bulk of my caseload: affairs, unprotected sex resulting in an STD or unwanted pregnancy, dropping out of school, quitting a good job to chase a crazy dream, taking a boring job and giving up on a dream. Anyway, there are a few basic facts I'll need from you to plan our defence, starting with—"

"Wait, wait, wait." Katrina held up her hand to cut Toni off, then ran her hand over her twists. "You want me to believe you're from the future?"

Toni closed their eyes and took a deep breath. "I know that, given when you are from, that seems hard to believe, but the sooner you can accept it the sooner we can move on to responding to this complaint. In your case, the Plaintiff will have to prove that you acted in full knowledge of the possible consequences of your actions—namely that you knew or had reason to know that your having sex with Ms Melendez on May 4th would start a series of events that would result in your girlfriend leaving you. It's a basic reasonable person standard, similar to—"

"But I've never had sex with Jessica! Hell, I haven't even kissed her! We've had coffee a few times and, yeah, I think she's cute, but that's it."

Toni frowned and tapped the screen on their arm. "So you're fully denying the allegations? That's a different matter entirely and will require an affirmative defence. Can you tell me where you were on or about the evening of May 4th, 2019?"

"May 4th? It's only April! May 4th hasn't even happened yet!"

Toni's eyes went wide. "Are you certain?"

"Yes, I'm certain!" Katrina was waving both hands now. "It's only April! April 9th!" She shoved her phone in Toni's face. "See for yourself!"

Toni squinted at Katrina's phone, then looked down at the screen on their arm. "Well, that certainly changes everything!" They tapped rapidly on their forearm. "I can file a motion to dismiss based on lack of temporal-jurisdiction. In the meantime, I'll request a stay in your case while a judge rules on my motion."

Katrina stared at the screen Toni was using. "Is that... Is that part of your arm?"

Toni waved dismissively. "Subdermal implant. Pretty standard since 2028. In fact, this is a pretty old model." Katrina swallowed. For the first time, she began to wonder if this wasn't actually a hoax at all. "I'm due for an upgrade. If I wasn't a public defender and instead worked at one of the big law firms, I'd have one of those new Samsung-Xiang chips right in my head." Toni tapped at their temple. "Even the interns at those places have them. My parents think I'm wasting my law degree by not making buckets of cash, but I'd rather do something meaningful with my life, you know? Just hope my future self doesn't agree with my dads." Toni flashed her a quick smile. They tapped a few more times. "There. I've filed for a temporary stay. Since the incident cited in the complaint hasn't happened yet, this should be a pretty open and shut case. Assuming…"

"Assuming what?"

"Well, assuming that in twenty-five days you don't have sex with this Jessica Melendez. If you *do*, the case would reopen. In that event, the temporal-jurisdiction would apply."

Katrina laughed. "There is no way I'm fucking Jessica, not now. I really don't think I would have, but as weird as this has been, the one good thing about this whole mess is that it's made me realise how much I love Rashida."

Toni grinned. "Good. Not that I'm here as a relationship counsellor, but it's nice when it turns out that way. Most of my cases don't resolve themselves so easily." They stood up, straightened their shiny suit, and held out their hand. Katrina shook it.

"Well, Toni, I still think this is a super-detailed practical joke, but for what it's worth, you can tell whoever's behind it that I'm not angry at them anymore. This has helped me put a few priorities straight."

Someone coughed. A new voice said, "Excuse me?" Katrina and Toni both looked over to see a tall Asian man in a nicely-tailored pinstripe suit standing expectantly nearby. "Which one of you is Katrina Freeman?"

Katrina and Toni exchanged a look, and Katrina sighed. "I'm Katrina Freeman, aged twenty-four in 2019, of 157 Madison Street. That's me. What is it this time?"

The man held out a Manila envelope. "My name is Jia Bao Teng. He/his. Please take this."

"What is it?"

"Ms Freeman, please take the envelope." The man pushed the envelope towards her.

Katrina crossed her arms. "I'm not taking anything unless you tell me what it is."

Jia Bao frowned. "Listen, I'm not supposed to—"

Katrina glared and hoped she was pulling off the "don't fuck with me" look she hadn't quite managed the night before. After the morning she'd had, it must have been easier for her to do, because the man blanched slightly and took a half step back. Katrina sighed.

"Dude, I appreciate that you've learned your job better than the intern I ran into earlier, and I promise to take your stupid envelope. Just tell me what it is."

Jia Bao glanced at Toni, who reached out and shook his hand. "Toni Marcos-Nguyen. They/Them. I'm Ms Freeman's attorney from 2035 so you can speak freely."

After a brief pause, the man nodded. "Ms Freeman, I'm here to serve you a summons and complaint that names you as a defendant in the case of Freeman versus Freeman."

Katrina grabbed the envelope out of his hand, tore it open, and practically flung the contents at Toni. "What the hell! I thought you said you'd solved this! I haven't slept with Jessica. I haven't ruined my relationship with Rashida. I haven't done anything. This is all bullshit!"

"Hold on." Toni skimmed over the letter. "This says that your future self is suing you for *not* sleeping with Jessica." They looked up from the letter. "You said today was April 9th, right?" Katrina nodded. "And did you just walk out on having coffee with Jessica?" Katrina nodded again. "Read this. Starting here." Toni held out the complaint and pointed to an itemized list in the middle of the page.

1. *On or about April 9th 2019, the Defendant did walk out on a coffee date with Jessica Melendez at The Bean Cafe, resulting in Ms Melendez deciding to cease socializing with the Defendant.*

2. *On about May 4th 2019, the Defendant attended a party where Ms Melendez was present. The Defendant became intoxicated and told Ms Melendez she had a huge crush on her and that the Defendant was tired of her girlfriend, one Rashida Robinson, never paying attention to her, and attempted to kiss Ms Melendez. At the time, Ms Melendez told the Defendant that she had, at one point, thought the Defendant was cute and maybe something could have happened between them, but after the incident at the Bean on April 9th, Ms Melendez had decided the Defendant would be "too high maintenance" and she "didn't need that sort of drama in her life."*

3. *Subsequently, the Defendant and Ms Robinson decided to take things to the next level and make things permanent and got married, had two kids, and then bought a house near the Defendant's parent's place in New Jersey, where Defendant stopped working on her art and became a middle school teacher. Having recently turned 40, the Plaintiff asserts that, had the Defendant just followed her gut for once in her life and perused Ms Melendez when she had a chance, that she wouldn't have ended up the Sad, Middle-Aged Disappointment she is today.*

As Katrina finished reading, Toni rolled their eyes. "Purely speculative. There's no way to prove the theoretical repercussions from a hypothetical alternative course of action. That's standard case law. I'm surprised she even found a lawyer to write this nonsense up. I'll just need to file—"

"Hold up!" Katrina looked back and forth between Jia Bao and Toni. "How can I be sued both for sleeping with Jessica and for *not* sleeping with Jessica? For staying with Rashida and *not* staying with Rashida? That doesn't make any sense!"

The two lawyers looked at each other. Toni's eyes widened at the same time Jia Bao grimaced.

"You don't think—" Jia Bao began.

"It's got to be," Toni replied.

"But that almost never—"

"Almost never isn't the same as *never* never."

"But the odds of—"

"What else could it be?" Toni cried, throwing up their hands. "This is gonna be a royal shit show, pardon my Neo-French. We'll need to contact the attorneys handling the initial case and your firm will need to file a notice of a 6-16 Violation."

"What the hell are you two talking about!" shouted Katrina. A flock of pigeons roosting in the oak tree above them startled and took wing in a flurry of feathers.

Toni sighed and ran one hand over their bare skull. "We're dealing with an alternate timeline conjunction. A cross-parallel-reality lawsuit. It brings up a whole slew of jurisdictional issues that will take forever to sort out."

Katrina slumped back onto the bench. "What?"

Jia Bao tapped on his temple, then stepped a few feet away and began muttering furiously to some unseen other party, punctuating his words with angry jabs of his finger. Toni started typing furiously on their forearm, talking to Katrina without looking up. "I can never keep my Old Decades straight. In 2019 are people aware of the multiverse theory? It says that there are an infinite number of—"

"I know what the multiverse theory is, okay." Katrina glared at them. "I've read Hawkings and Sagan and I watch

Doctor Who. Just because I'm an art student doesn't mean I'm illiterate."

"Then you know that every choice you make results in a splitting off of a different reality, an alternate universe where you made a different decision." Toni gesticulated with their right hand, then went back to tapping rapidly at their implanted screen. "Typically, when a lawyer files a temporal tort, the summons is served on an earlier iteration of the Plaintiff but within the same version of reality. But time travel is more of an art than a science, ironically enough, so there's always a possibility that the summons will be served to a *different* iteration in a parallel past reality. This sort of thing used to happen all the time in the early days of the practice, but it's become vanishingly rare. There are supposed to be safeguards in place, regulations and federal oversight to keep it from happening. It pretty much only occurs in cases like yours, when the Plaintiff's attorney messes up and serves the summons to a time *before* the inciting incident has actually occurred."

Toni finally stopped typing and looked up from their screen. "When it does happen, though, it's a bureaucratic nightmare. Both attorneys of record will be investigated not only by the Citizen Space-Time Advocate's Office but the State Temporal Paradox Division. There will be internal reviews. I'll file a Motion to Dismiss in the Local Temporal Courts of both alternative futures, then an M-616 with the Standardized Existential Bureau to have the record of these filings expunged from the Cross-Reality Public Archives. There's a very good chance someone—or several someones, across various realities—will lose their jobs."

Toni paced back and forth anxiously. A moment later their forearm chimed. They glanced at the screen, then up at Katrina. "Sorry, but I've got to get on this right away. Mr Teng?" Jia Bao held up one finger, then pressed the side of his head.

"Yes?"

"I'll need your contact information."

"Of course." He bent his head down, and Toni pressed their forearm to his temple. There was a soft, electronic tone. Toni glanced at the screen and nodded. Toni held out their hand to Katrina, who shook it, still dazed.

"Ms Freeman, good luck."

"Wait! What's going to happen to me now?"

Toni raised their eyebrows and smiled. "You? Most likely you're getting off easy. In cases like this, both suits are almost always thrown out by a judge. This might be confusing and disorienting, but once I'm done drowning these firm-jockeys in motions, these lawsuits are just going to disappear. In fact, they will never have been filed in the first place. All this will have literally never happened."

"How will I know if things work out?"

"If things go the way I expect, you'll never hear from me, or any of these other suits again. If things don't go the way they should, well, time will tell." Toni smiled and their eyes sparkled in the sun. "I hope things work out with you and your girlfriend. If your future self isn't too upset about all this, I hope she looks me up in 2035." Toni held their forearm up to their mouth and spoke into it. "Toni to dispatch. Prep the chrono-pad for incoming." With one last smile and nod, they pressed a button on their forearm and vanished.

Katrina looked around. Jia Bao was gone, too. She was all alone, standing on the edge of the field outside of Tubman Hall, under an oak tree, its leaves rustling gently in the spring breeze. Overhead, a sparrow wheeled and bobbed in the perfectly blue sky.

"Katrina?"

At the sound of her name, Katrina flinched. She looked up, resigned to finding herself staring at yet another besuited lawyer from the future brandishing an envelope, but instead Jessica slid onto the bench next to her. Her bright blue hair fell in a curtain over one eye, the sunlight catching streaks of darker purple from an old dye job and glinting off the silver studs that ran along the rim of her ear.

Her light brown skin glowed bronze where the sun made it through the oak leaves overhead: the ridge of her small, cute nose; one bare shoulder; the soft curve where her breasts peeked out from her tank top. Jessica *was* gorgeous.

"Hey, you okay?" Jessica's hand rested on Katrina's thigh. "'Cause I'm worried about you. Back there, in the coffee shop?"

Katrina looked at where the other woman's fingers touched her jeans, shook her head to clear her mind, then gave a rueful smile. "Yeah. Yeah, I'm fine, Jessica. Thanks. I was feeling off, but now I'm fine." She stood up. "Can I get a raincheck on that coffee? I think I'm not going to be in class today. I've really got to check in on my girlfriend."

Jessica smiled back. "Of course. Gotta take care of the home front first. Text me later and let me know when you're free?"

"Will do. I don't know if I'll be free for a while, but I'll text."

Katrina cut through the grass field, heading back towards her and Rashida's place. She barely noticed that the dew was soaking through her Converse. She dialled Rashida's number as she walked and was surprised when her girlfriend picked up on the first ring.

"Trina, what's up? Sorry I was so out of it this morning. Something wrong?"

Katrina grinned. "No, nothing's wrong. In fact, I'm great."

She could hear the frown on the other end of the line. "Wait. It's Tuesday. Don't you have class right now?"

"I'm skipping class today, and I'm on my way back home right now. I think we need to make some time just for us. And I think we need to talk about our future."

WORK FOR HIRE
By D. W. Howard

Darkness—ebon, heavy, and pervasive—was the extent of his world. As his senses began to orient themselves, pain came rushing in to join the stygian blackness behind his eyes. With throbbing tenacity, the pain centred itself on an area slightly above his left eye. It lurked there, a dire warning if he should choose to do anything rash in the next moment. He groaned and rolled to his side. He curled into a fetal position as he gingerly felt for his forehead and located the egg-sized protrusion. The protuberance lurked in mute testimony to the as yet to be remembered trauma which had left him in this state.

Slowly he opened one eye, winced with the harsh light, and closed the eye again as he fought back the urge to vomit. He positioned himself on all fours and prepared to try again. His head hung low as he balanced himself on hands and knees. He noticed the cloying smell of organic decay and tried to reach into his memories to determine where he was. He found nothing.

He stayed there for a few moments and swayed slightly as his body attempted to steady itself. Satisfied, he opened his eyes. The light assaulted him, but he was prepared this time. He fought back waves of radiating pain and focused on the floor he was kneeling on. It was undressed concrete, roughly finished with what appeared to be copper wire threading its way through it. The wires formed roughly fifteen-centimetre squares in a grid pattern. That struck him as important, but his mind was still not cooperating.

Growing in confidence, he shifted his focus away from a single spot on the floor and slowly raised his eyes. At first he encountered nothing but more floor and the enigmatic copper wire. Occasionally, the square pattern was interrupted by piles of refuse and puddles of liquid. He paid these no heed as he had other things to consider.

He continued to raise his head. Approximately five metres away his gaze fell upon a concrete wall. No squares here. His vision moved along the wall incrementally before it came to a plexiglass window. Louvred shutters ran the length of the window. He noted that those shutters were currently open and that a face was staring back at him from behind the window. That face was outlined but barely visible in the dim light from the room beyond. It was hard to focus. He struggled for a moment, squinting his eyes and attempting to make out the features of the person opposite him as they blended into the shadowed interior. A fleeting glimpse of a gold chain at the person's throat struck a chord. A flash of light off that chain illuminated the weathered features of an older man. The man's skin would have been a rich light brown but for the ravages of time that had dulled its sheen. Time had also greyed the close-cropped hair upon his head. His mouth was drawn and determined while keen, vibrant eyes shone from the shadows. Those piercing eyes, those were impossible to forget. Konrad Graf rode a wave of memories as he met the gaze of his employer... Neema Taylor Ojukwu.

Olimpicon Limited HQ, Province of West Africa, Terran Federation - Terran Federation Year 2316

Olimpicon Limited's global headquarters was an impressive building in the sprawling city centre of Lagos. Rising 160 stories above the beating heart of the Province of West Africa, Olimpicon's reach extended from this edifice throughout Africa and The Middle East.

Konrad Graf felt the small scar on his wrist. It was ironic that Olimpicon was responsible for its being there, at a discounted price no less. The com implant embedded in his wrist, roughly the size of a grain of rice and working in tandem with other implants throughout his body, was a marvel of modern technology. By rights, he should never have been able to afford such a system. It was still new technology. Though Africa had done much to bridge the economic divide, labour on the continent was still cheaper than most other places. However, the quality of the product was second to none. When the Olimpicon 6200 system had come on the market, for half the price of its competitors, he had taken the leap. Norge Chemplex—nominally his employer—paid well, but not well enough to afford the "best." Graf was not one to be frivolous with his money.

Graf had never been to Africa and, truth be told, he was slightly nervous. He felt out of place and self-conscious at the obvious displays of wealth and power in this corporate enclave. Graf stepped out of the technologically impressive elevator and emerged onto the 158th floor, the executive suite. A tingling buzz at his wrist was followed by a message on his retinal display. It was time for his daily dose of Precosyn B, a tissue restorative which was his penance for kidney damage done during his incautious youth. A nonchalant mental nudge authorized his pharmaceutical implant to inject the drug. He grimaced slightly at the familiar chemical taste in the back of his throat. The medical techs assured him it was psychosomatic, but he never believed them.

Graf looked around the mostly deserted reception area as a man emerged from behind a desk at the end of the room. He was impressive. He estimated the man's height at nearly two metres and his body was long and muscular. Graf straightened his significantly smaller frame and began striding towards the man, intent on meeting him in the centre of the room. As they approached each other, Graf noted that neuropathic implants were obvious on the man's exposed skin. The small metal circles dotted his forehead. Small blue lights blinked occasionally, signalling when they triggered pain-blocking stimulators connected to the nerves below.

The two reached each other in the centre of the lobby and the man extended his hand. "A pleasure to meet you, Mr Graf. I am Moduope Pearce, Mr Ojukwu's secretary."

His hand remained between the two men, frozen in space as a blue light on a wrist-mounted implant blinked with more frequency.

"Sorry, I never shake hands, you know. Can't be too careful, with more and more people carrying remnants these days. I'm sure you understand." Graf held up his hands as he explained himself. He looked decidedly uncomfortable as he stared at the hand in front of him.

"Indeed," Mr Pearce said evenly. He looked at his hand as he lowered it. "A tad dramatic, but technically correct. Even if you had not commented, I am obliged under section 10.34.a of the Remnant Covenant to inform you I have contracted variant DZA-006. It is not contagious through casual contact. Right this way, sir." Pearce gestured towards a large set of clouded-glass double doors at the end of the lobby.

Graf recoiled in spite of himself and unconsciously kept his distance. Pearce turned and led him towards the double doors. Graf chose to study the doors so as to avoid staring at the living petri dish in front of him. The doors and attendant glass walls were completely clouded. The corporate symbol of Olimpicon adorned each door, a wireframe globe emblazoned with a stylized O in a font that evoked West African art. Graf smirked inwardly, assuming that the O could easily mean Ojukwu as he straddled the world.

Graf reminded himself to be cautious and suppress his natural tendency to speak out. The man he was about to meet was one of the titans of the world. He was a man to be respected if nothing else. Regardless, his "other" employer would most certainly want to hear about this meeting in his next report. It wasn't every day the head of a Terra level corporation asked to see the security director of a small petrochemical division. It was noteworthy, even if Ojukwu didn't know that Graf served in his current position at the behest of the Albion Clandestine Service, as one of many agents who helped the ACS and their desire to track the disappearance of various resources and commodities around the world.

Pearce held open the door, and Graf entered the office. He was careful to avoid Pearce as he did so. The interior was dimly lit, a table lamp on an enormous mahogany desk was the sole artificial light source in the room. To Graf's left, the entire wall was a series of windows. The light was partially dimmed because the glass was tinted, though it was clear enough to see the sprawling city outside and the glimmering azure of the Atlantic Ocean beyond. A loud squawk interrupted his staring and he turned his head quickly. A pristinely white cockatoo spread its wings leisurely and stared at him before tucking its head under its wing, preening itself nonchalantly.

"There, there, Razor. Fiat lux," a soft voice whispered from the shadowy space behind the desk. The tinting on the windows disappeared as the desk lamp increased in illumination. Evenly spaced lights along the ceiling also came to life. "My apologies. I sometimes lose track of time during my meditation periods. I find it helps me centre myself and focus for the rest of the day. Please come in."

"Mr Graf. Konrad Graf, sir." Pearce interjected while holding open the door. "He is the securities manager for Norge Chemplex in Trondheim. You wanted to see him on a matter of personal business."

An elderly man stood from a richly finished leather chair. He made a dismissive gesture with his hand as he moved to come around the desk. He moved easily, with a grace that belied the apparent age on his face. He was dressed in a professionally tailored dark tan suit, a glint of gold at his throat and hands as an accent. Far from being ostentatious, his appearance was refined; he was the perfect image of power and aristocracy. "You'll have to forgive my son, Mr Graf. He is overly conscientious in his duties at times and he has a preternatural talent for remembering information."

"I'm not surprised given...well, I'm not surprised. Mr Ojukwu?" Graf asked quickly to avoid his momentary lapse.

"Not surprised given his condition, you mean? Yes, that is one of his 'gifts.' Nature's little joke, I'm afraid. That will be all, Mo. I shall be a few minutes or so depending on how Mr Graf and I get on." Ojukwu smiled at Graf before continuing. "Can you please inform the chef that I shall take lunch on the rooftop solarium when I am finished? Thank you."

Ojukwu stretched out his hand. "It is a pleasure to meet you, Mr Graf. But where are my manners?" Ojukwu withdrew his hand and slid around the desk as he returned to his seat of power. "You prefer not to shake hands. Understandable. Can I offer you any refreshment?"

Graf stood still. He was confused and it showed on his face.

"Some time ago, as a safety precaution, I had an A/V transmitter installed in Mr Pearce as a result of his condition. I must admit I was eavesdropping." Neema Ojukwu chuckled and allowed himself a rare sigh that signalled his age even if his movements did not. He eased into his chair and settled himself before continuing. "What do you think of my haven? I find it is the little things that can sometimes bring the greatest comfort, don't you? My friend Razor, immaculate pieces of art, these little things give me peace and aid me immeasurably in my work."

As Ojukwu spoke, he blew a loving kiss towards the cockatoo who then bobbed up and down in approval. Ojukwu then gestured towards the wall behind him. An impressive collection of antique pistols was mounted expertly on the wall. Graf recognised some of them: a sixteenth-century Spanish flintlock, a seventeenth-century

Dutch wheellock, and an American nineteenth-century revolver.

"Mr Graf, I am not a man to mince words. Before we get started, may I offer you a chair?" Ojukwu stretched out his arm, his palm up, as he gestured towards the chair. His palm was decidedly lighter in tone than the rest of his skin, but no less aged. A web of wrinkles and scars gave testament to a long life that had not always been one of luxury. He watched Graf intently, a slightly raised eyebrow and disguised smile the only trace of emotion on his face. His eyes, bright and discerning, observed Graf closely as he waited.

Graf obliged and slid into the chair, easing himself into the richly upholstered leather before crossing his right leg over his left. He felt exposed and vulnerable; he wasn't sure how and when he had been put into a subordinate position. Nevertheless, he recognised that Ojukwu was not a man to be trifled with. Once again, he wondered why he had been summoned. "I appreciate that, Mr Ojukwu. I am also not one to mince words. I like to know who I'm dealing with and why. Forgive me if that is a little blunt, but I get the feeling you understand."

"Indeed, Mr Graf. Indeed. You see, I am in need of your rather…unique services." Ojukwu leaned back in his chair and folded his hands in front of him. "Services I am prepared to reward you rather handsomely for."

"I'm not sure what you think I do, Mr Ojukwu, or what services you think I can provide for you. I'm a security manager for a moderately sized chemical division. I'm sure you can find any number of people like me, probably some on your own payroll." Graf leaned back in his chair and studied Ojukwu. Something was amiss here.

"I thought we were being frank, Mr Graf? I see we must establish parameters. Very well." Ojukwu pressed a heretofore unseen button on the side of his chair and the door behind his guest opened. Graf tensed and turned his head, sensing danger before he saw that Mr Pearce had entered. Pearce closed the doors behind himand walked to the desk. Standing straight and unmoving, Ojukwu looked at Pearce and addressed him in a steady low voice: "Mr Pearce, please give me data on Mr Graf."

Pearce stiffened slightly, his eyes going distant before he began speaking in an even, monotone voice. "Konrad Graf. Born Lillehammer, Norway, 27 February TFY 2280. Parents Tomas and Brigitte Graf, deceased TFY 3010 in a train accident. One sister, Ortona Graf, born Lillehammer, Norway, 19 June TFY 2289. Mr Graf finished top ten per cent of his class in secondary school and was accepted into the University of Bergen TFY 2298. He then transferred to Eton University, Albion, TFY 2300 on a cultural exchange program. Expelled from Eton University TFY 2301 for repeated misdemeanour charges of battery and disturbing the peace, resulting in two months jail time. Hospitalized six months at Royal Hospital London, Albion TFY 2302. Kidney damage as a result of—"

"That's enough. I get the point." Graf sat forward in his chair wondering what exactly was going on here and not liking what he was coming up with. "You seem to know a lot about me, but you still haven't told me what you want."

Ojukwu gestured to Pearce who had stopped mid-sentence, his mouth still hanging open. Pearce continued, "Damage as a result of extensive steroid use. Debt at present 687,000 Terramarks owed to various creditors as a result of health care treatment in the former Pan Pacific Republic. This treatment was for Ortana Graf to combat aggressive tumours in the liver, colon, and ovaries. The cause is unknown and the tumours were removed with no new growths for two years. Mr Graf is currently employed by Norge Chemplex, a division of Thienyth Industries. He has also been employed as a human intelligence asset for the Albion Clandestine Service since TFY 2306."

"That is all, Mr Pearce. Thank you." Ojukwu placed his hand on Pearce's arm and a look of sadness and pride crossed his face. The light returned to Pearce's eyes and his posture relaxed as he walked to the doors and showed himself out of the room. A silence hung in the room between Graf and Ojukwu, neither one willing to utter the next word.

Finally, Graf decided to speak. He struggled to keep his voice even as he did so. "That's ridiculous, of course. I'm a security manager, nothing more, nothing less. I've had to work hard for that, first in Albion and now in Norge. Spy? Please. As you heard, I never finished school. No, I'm afraid your information is incorrect. It's ludicrous actually. I'm not sure where you would come up with something like that? Thank you for the trip to Nigeria all the same if that is what this is all about."

Ojukwu leaned forward, placing his hands on the table. The gleam in his eyes had become a smouldering fire. Graf found it difficult to look away. "Humor me for a moment, Mr Graf. For the sake of argument, let's say my information is correct." Ojukwu paused and let that statement of fact hang in the air a moment before he continued. "What then would you say if I told you I had an employment proposition for you? One that would help you and your sister disappear once it was complete. One that would pay you fifty million Terramarks. What would you say to that?"

Graf sat silent for several moments, blinking three times as he did so. He weighed several options in his mind while hoping nothing was betrayed by his face. He uncrossed his legs and cleared his throat before he spoke. "Well...only for the sake of argument, of course...I would say that I'm listening."

Present - Location: Unknown - Year: Unknown

Graf kept his eyes locked on Ojukwu's as he gathered himself. For the second time in the last few moments, he felt for his weapons. The Glock 322 he always carried in a shoulder holster was gone. The extra magazines, which carried the precious rounds he hoarded, were also missing. Each of his two knives, with their diamond-tipped blades of carbon steel, were missing as well. The empty sheaths on either side of his waist felt like missing limbs. He shifted slightly and adjusted his belt. He realised that the garrote that was hidden there had been overlooked and he felt a slight glimmer of hope as he moved to get to his feet. He grimaced, his right knee locked as he shifted his weight and pushed himself into a standing position.

That was a grim memory, the night he had hurt that knee. He had accepted Ojukwu's money. He had accepted Ojukwu's job. It should have been clean and easy. A simple matter to sabotage a computer system and cause a fire. Konrad Graf and his loving sister Ortona, who had signed in to visit and bring him dinner, would tragically "die" in the accident. They would disappear and be free to live a private life elsewhere. He had sent his men on break, putting them safely out of harm's way. Ortona had already been on the boat waiting for him. A second craft was set to meet them off the coast. Imagine his surprise when three of his men walked in on him as he manipulated the tank controls to cause the explosion. The technicians had already been killed. That had been unavoidable. However, Graf felt loyalty to the men who had worked for him. They fought like lions…he had to give them that. The memories of that confrontation overwhelmed him

Norge Petrochemical Plant, Province of Scandinavia, Terran Federation - Terran Federation Year 2316

Three guards shouted as they entered the control room. It took them a moment to come to grips with the fact that their superior was sabotaging the company. To their credit, they recovered quickly and charged forward as a unit.

The first guard died instantly. A silenced .40 calibre round to the head usually had that effect. The other two rushed Graf with their batons out. A lucky strike knocked the gun out of Graf's hand and he swore to himself. They grappled with him, each of them struggling to subdue him as Graf attempted to improve his position and end the fight quickly. One of the guards, Olag, stomped on the inside of his knee as Graf moved to get behind his partner. The ligaments in the knee tore and Graf stifled a scream as waves of pain radiated from his crippled limb. He put aside the pain and rewarded his attacker with a powerful blow to the throat. The open V between his thumb and index finger pushed the man's Adam's apple back into his airway, causing him to suffocate.

The third guard, Sven, screamed in fury and attacked with wild abandon. That was his undoing. Even hobbled, Graf easily pushed the furious attack aside with an open palm. As Sven ran past, Graf's hand went to his waist, drew a dagger, and sliced it across the man's abdomen in one smooth motion. Sven dropped his baton, the sound reverberating through the room. Several metres away Olag gasped for breath as he tried to stave off death.

Sven dropped to his knees, clutching at his wound. The knife had bit deep. Sven was already doomed, though he would never know it. Limping painfully, Graf had come up behind him. With practised nonchalance, he placed the knife at Sven's throat and pulled it from left to right. Graf justified the killing by telling himself that he was sparing Sven from the fire which would soon engulf the room.

Walking out of the room that night, he hadn't realised that his actions had just successfully hidden the theft of five hundred metric tons of liquid oxygen. Those realizations and what they portended would come later.

Present - Location: Unknown - Year: Unknown

Returning to the present, something broke inside Graf. Those calculating eyes held his, and it enraged him. Throwing decorum aside, the veins in his neck strained as he suddenly exploded. "Let me out of here, Ojukwu! God damn it, you treacherous bastard! I swear to God if you don't let me the fuck out of here, I'm going to kill you! I'm going to wring your damn neck, but not before I roast that fucking bird of yours and make you watch me eat it!"

Ojukwu shook his head and extended his hand to the window before turning aside. He moved to Graf's left, ignoring his epithets. Graf sprung forward and began pounding on the window. "Honour your bargain, Ojukwu! Honour the fucking bargain!"

The SS Pinnacle, somewhere in the Mediterranean Sea - Terran Federation Year 2319

The sun shone with blazing intensity on the brilliant cerulean surface of the Mediterranean Sea. The SS Pinnacle sat upon this dazzling canvas, lying at anchor some twenty miles off an anonymous shore. Graf stepped off the small powerboat and onto the floating platform at the side of the Pinnacle. His leg locked slightly as his weight shifted onto his bad knee. He steadied himself on the rocking platform, which moved at the whim of the Mediterranean. Graf understood how it felt. Awoken by a phone call in the middle of the night, he had been summoned forth by Neema Taylor Ojukwu. Ojukwu had helped arrange an escape for him and his sister; that had been three safehouses and two continents ago. Graf thought their bungalow in Curacao to be safely hidden away. Somehow Ojukwu had found them. One agonizingly long private flight later, and here he was. He had been met in Athens and shuttled by car and boat to present himself once more before his one-time employer.

Graf supposed he shouldn't complain. His life these past few years had been good. Ojukwu had delivered on his promises. Money and anonymity were both his and—save for the occasional change of address for the sake of security—he was content. In the past few years, Graf had done some research, curious to know the purpose of the "accident" he had orchestrated. Graf eventually pieced it together and traced the disappearance of several large shipments. What he had never got his mind around was the why of the matter. However, his new life offered tantalizing diversions and he let the matter lie.

A white-uniformed yeoman escorted him up the platform's steps and showed him into a canopied lounge on the second deck of the yacht. It overlooked the ship's pool and was relatively large. It had room for several tables, chairs, and a full bar. The yeoman went around the bar. "Can I get you something to drink, sir?"

"A whisky sour with pineapple instead of orange, please. Where is Mr Ojukwu?" Graf sat down in one of the lounge chairs, placing his sunglasses on the table next to him as he took in the sights. His vision narrowed as he noticed several young women sunbathing topless next to the sparkling pool in the deck below. He let out a low whistle and accepted the drink from the yeoman without removing his gaze.

"Perkins, I will have whatever Mr Graf is having, please. Then, if you would be so kind as to leave us." Ojukwu stepped out of the darkness of the yacht's interior. He was dressed in a white bathing suit with a black robe that he left open. His feet were bare and Graf was surprised to see that Ojukwu still looked fit and toned. In fact, Ojukwu looked much the same as he had three years ago. Graf made to rise and Ojukwu waved him back into his chair as he took his drink from the retreating yeoman. "I see you also have an eye for beautiful women. Man is truly blessed to walk this planet with the female of the species."

Graf laughed. "Obviously you've never seen my sister when she wakes up in the morning." He took a sip of his drink before setting it down on the table. Ojukwu had sat in the lounge chair next to him, reclining as he watched the women below languidly. Graf shifted his legs and sat on the edge of the recliner. "I never thought I'd see you again, Ojukwu. As beautiful as the view is, I can't imagine you've flown me halfway around the world for this."

"No, no indeed Mr Graf. You see, I have a little problem. It's a problem I think you can help me with." Ojukwu sipped at his drink, holding it loosely in his hand while his eyes never strayed from the deck below.

"I'm retired. You made that possible, so thank you," Graf picked up his glass and raised it in Ojukwu's direction before taking another drink, deeper this time, "but I'm afraid I have many millions of reasons to stay retired. Though I sympathize with your problem, whatever it is." Graf looked around quickly before returning his gaze to Ojukwu. "By the way, I'm surprised to see that Pearce isn't here. He doesn't enjoy the ladies?" Graf chuckled and took another drink before setting it back down again.

"No. Mr Pearce is with his mother." Ojukwu took another drink and sat silent for several moments. Graf shifted uncomfortably and was prepared to rise before Ojukwu spoke again, his tone low and inquisitive. "Indulge me for a moment, Mr Graf. What do you know of 'Remnant' and what followed?"

"Not much, I suppose. Only what I've read or seen on documentaries and the news. It led to the collapse of the American Confederation and eventually the formation of the Terran Federatin… Either way, I know enough not to shake hands if I can avoid it. While I enjoy the ladies, I'm cautious, you know what I mean?"

Graf leaned forward, unsure where this conversation was going. "Why do you ask?"

"It's a fascinating subject. Remnant has been with us for nearly 200 years. In that time, it has spread around the globe. We, the collective we, study it on Io and Ganymede, before we lost contact with them. It has helped some and ruined many. It has taken and it has given. It continues to evolve as it rewrites our species genetic code. It's theorized that it was a bioweapon unleashed by the Pan Pacific Republic during the Wasteland War. Regardless, it has changed us and shattered every system on this fragile planet. I have had five children who were born with gifts like Mr Pearce's. As you know, mothers of children with Remnant gifts never survive childbirth. That is one price for…genius. It is a terrible thing to watch someone or something you love die, don't you think?"

"I'm so sorry, Mr Ojukwu. No, I was not aware." Graf paused uncomfortably before continuing. "I'm still not sure what this has to do with me. You'll excuse me for being blunt, but that has been the nature of our relationship up 'till now."

Ojukwu took another drink and set the empty glass down next to him on the deck. "Yes, it has."

Ojukwu sat silent and then spoke suddenly. "Mr Graf, there is an Indian advanced research and manufacturing facility I very much want to buy. They are in financial straits and—until last week—I thought my purchase was fait accompli."

Ojukwu wrapped the robe around himself, chilled from the shade of the canopy. "It has come to my attention that a Greek billionaire, a man who lives thirty miles east of here, intends to retain the services of this facility. If he is successful in retaining their services, his contract will most assuredly lift them out of their financial difficulties. I have spoken to Mr Kazidies, but he is most insistent and refuses to cancel or delay his contract so that I might make my purchase. I need you to eradicate Mr Kazidies as a problem."

Silence hung between the two men, and Graf blinked in anticipation of Ojukwu's next words. Finally, Graf could stand the silence no longer. "And?"

"And what Mr Graf?" Ojukwu answered calmly.

"Well, usually at this point you would mention some sort of payment. I would then demure and we'd either agree on a price or I'd go on my way. You know you have my silence since I'm already in debt to you. So what's the catch, if you'll excuse the colloquialism?" Graf reached for his drink again, genuinely curious now.

"Price is not a concern this time, Mr Graf. The stakes are too high. As we speak, I have six separate wire transfers ready to process. They will pay you in excess of 1.5 billion Terramarks if that is what you wish."

Graf choked on his drink and dropped his glass. It clattered on the deck without breaking, the ice already beginning to melt in the radiant heat. "What? You must be joking."

"No joke, Mr Graf. I can offer you more if you wish. However, there is a second option I'd like to offer, if you would care to listen. One with more long-term prospects. One that will assure your future." Ojukwu reached down casually and picked up the dropped glass, placing it next to his, and met Graf's eyes for the first time. The same intensity was there from their first meeting. However, that intensity had been joined by something else that Graf had never seen there: desperation.

An unbidden shiver ran down Graf's spine, defying the heat outside. He was tempted to take the money and do the job. However, something in Ojukwu's eyes told him he wanted—needed—to hear the second option. Whatever had shaken this man was something worth knowing. "Go on," Graf said softly.

"That research firm I intend to purchase, the one Achilles Kazidies must die for so that I may acquire it, is going to cement my position on Io. It will lead to the formation of a new order away from the madness that is now Earth. This firm has perfected the final technologies I need for my own outpost. An outpost independent of the Terran Federation science station that may or may not still exist. I intend to relocate there. You have already aided me in my dream. The 'accident' you arranged provided a portion of the fuel I will begin using to transport materials into high Earth orbit. Now you can provide another service that will aid me in making this dream a reality. This will happen." Ojukwu paused and gazed evenly at Graf.

Graf looked nonplussed as he took a moment to digest this new information. He had only had the one interaction with Ojukwu, but he had never struck him as the type of man for jokes. His intensity eliminated that idea as well. "Io? You're serious? What does this have to do with me? Tell me why I shouldn't take your money and buy an island somewhere?"

Ojukwu sat up and mirrored Graf's pose, holding his gaze as he folded his hands in front of his chest. "I want you to know I'm deadly serious when I tell you this." The old man paused for effect. "You could accept my first offer, complete this task, and live a good life for a time. However, I believe I could use a man of your nature where I am going. It is why I have chosen to give you this second choice."

Ojukwu leaned in closer, his voice lowering to barely more than a whisper. "The fact is that life, all life, as we know it has a limited amount of time to exist on this planet. Within the next decade, give or take a few years, complications and deviations of Remnant will begin having permanent and devastating effects on this planet. Rampant and uncontrollable mutation will overcome this fragile blue marble. I have seen the calculations and the computer projections. Earth will become something…different. I do not want to be here when that happens. You've seen the Terran Federation in action; do you think they have the ability to control the problem?"

Graf shook his head and Ojukwu nodded his approval. "I intend to start over somewhere new. Others share my concerns and my vision. If you wish it…I would have you be one of a select few, globally speaking, to accompany me."

Graf sat back stunned, unable to wrap his mind around what he had just heard as he stared pensively at his empty glass. Ojukwu obliged and rose from his recliner, pouring both Graf and himself a double dose of scotch. He handed Graf his glass and sat back down before taking a drink. Ojukwu spoke again, "As you can see Mr Graf...nothing can stop me from achieving my goals."

Graf took a drink and looked at Ojukwu with an unasked question. "Yes, I am serious," Ojukwu answered.

"If this is real, and I want to see the information for myself, is there a place for me?" Graf took another drink and thought for a moment. "I'd also want my sister along. That's non-negotiable."

"I anticipated as much," Ojukwu answered with a low purr. He sat back knowing that he had gotten his man, despite Graf not acknowledging it yet. Graf was not unintelligent, even if he was just a blunt instrument.

Ojukwu raised a finger. "I have one little side job that will pay for her passage."

Present - Ojukwu Enclave, Io Dome 616e - Terran Federation Year 2323

Graf could see the back of Ojukwu's head. He had stopped and stood impassively still in view. Graf banged on the window once more. He screamed in rage. He stood there panting as Ojukwu tilted his head to one side. It was a curious pose, one that brought Graf back to that one little side job. The side job had been Leslie McAfferty, a journalist for The Defender, a media conglomerate out of London. Her sin had been one of curiosity. Her investigations had put her on the trail of a number of different resources and technologies disappearing around the globe. Some of those had belonged to Neema Ojukwu and his vision. So, to protect his vision, she was sentenced to death.

Graf had hidden in her flat, waiting for her to return home. Right before she died, she had cocked her head to the side—somehow sensing a foreign presence in her home, something out of place. She had ignored that sixth sense. Graf had come up behind her silently, snapping her neck with one clean motion. He had arranged her body so that it appeared to be an accidental fall. He had read about the "tragedy" on the net.

Kazidies had died just as suddenly, albeit more publicly. A Cypriot terrorist cell, eager for funds, had been only too willing to plant the bomb that took the life of Achilles Kazidies. The fact that that same bomb took the life of Kazidies' young wife and two daughters kept Graf awake some nights. However, it had been necessary, and so he absolved himself of the blame. That's what he told himself.

Ojukwu turned to him and Graf came back to the present. He leaned down and placed his hands on his knees, catching his breath. It was hard to breathe in here; the decaying waste around the room was overpowering. There was also a hint of something else in the air. He looked closer at the purple liquid puddled on the ground, a wire transecting the puddle in front of him. A dawning horror crossed his face. Terrified, he looked up into the passive indifference of Ojukwu's face.

Two Hours Ago - Executive Wing, Ojukwu Enclave, Io Dome 616e - Terran Federation Year 2323

The door smashed open; its top hinge pulling off the wall as the doorjamb was launched into the room. Konrad Graf stormed in, the lead-lined grav boots that helped alleviate the lessened gravity aiding him as he recovered from his assault on the door. His face was a crimson mask of anger as he flew halfway across the room in an instant. He landed

with his hands on the back of a chair, a chair familiar to him
from his first meeting with Neema Ojukwu. "You
motherfucker! You couldn't keep your cock in your pants
even with my own fucking sister! She hasn't had her period
for two months and you've been screwing her since we got
here. Screwing my sister, you piece of shit! So now what?
You'll kill her with another Remnant progeny, you piece of
crap?! Deny it, I dare you! I swear to God I'll slit your
throat if you do." Graf tensed, ready to spring again.

"Sit down!" Ojukwu snapped. Ojukwu slapped the back
of his chair as he turned to face Graf. His tone brooked no
disobedience and there was anger in his eyes.

"Mr Graf, you disgrace yourself! Again I say, sit down!"
Ojukwu waited, his body rigid and partially hidden behind
his elegant chair and large mahogany desk. He held a thick
cane of acacia wood, its knobbed end worn from years of
handling. Graf paused and took the measure of Ojukwu
before sitting in the chair he had grabbed. His face was
slowly returning to its normal colour, though his breathing
was still deep and ragged from anger.

Ojukwu waited a moment more, taking the time to
assure himself that Graf's rage had subsided. He continued;
"I deny nothing. I have loved and made love to my dear
Ortona, as well as others, since shortly after our arrival
here."

Graf tensed at Ojukwu's words and prepared to rise
again. With a glance, Ojukwu held him in place. "I did not
force myself on her, as I am sure she has told you.
However!"

Ojukwu paused, taking a deep breath to centre himself
and retreat from the anger he had let come into his voice in
that last word. "However, she is not pregnant. It is with
deep sorrow that I must reveal that her tumours have
returned. They are now in both of her ovaries. I just learned
of this news today. I have not had the heart to share this
with her yet. My medical professionals are not certain they

can help her." Ojukwu remained standing and studied Graf. He wondered what reaction this news would receive.

Graf sat back in his chair and exhaled sharply. He felt as if he had been punched in the gut. The colour had completely drained from his face. His eyes had lost much of their anger and were now mirrors of desperation and grief. Graf shook his head from side-to-side, muttering to himself softly as Ojukwu's posture relaxed slightly. Suddenly, Graf's muttering stopped and his head rose quickly. His eyes gleamed with a glimmer of hope. "The Remnant derivative I stole from dome 823a last month. The one you sent me after. They were researching restoratives there, correct? Their gene splice is potentially miraculous. You said so yourself. Give it to me. Give it to her! You owe me. I'll get more, but use that one on her. I beg you."

Ojukwu took a deep breath and resigned himself to the word he was about to utter: "No."

Graf sat stunned, unsure of what he had just heard. "What do you mean?"

"I mean what I said. No." Ojukwu said with quiet determination. His face betrayed grief and resolve in equal measure as he stood there impassively.

"What do you mean 'no?!'" Graf rose from his chair as his voice increased in volume. His face had become a crimson mask again. "You cold-hearted, merciless, son of a bitch! What do you mean 'no!' You will give it to me and you will cure my sister, or I will end you and take it for myself!"

"No! No you will not, Mr Graf. You will sit down and think about the greater good. The things we are attempting to accomplish here that go beyond you and your sister." Ojukwu had straightened again as he slammed his cane on the ground. The cane, so similar to the weapons of his ancestors, was ever-present now as the ravages of time took their toll on him. The force of the blow propelled Ojukwu a few inches off the floor and his heavy grav shoes brought him back to the floor with a soft thud.

The force of Ojukwu's will was not enough to sate Graf's anger. "Yes! I've seen your 'greater good.' I've been the instrument of that good, you bastard. I delivered that good to three security guards, Achilles Kazidies and his family, that journalist, and countless others on two different planetary bodies! You left them all behind. You left your son behind. You left Earth behind! I think it's time you tasted some of that good yourself, you black-hearted piece of crap!" With that Graf launched himself into the air and across the table.

Ojukwu moved more quickly than Graf had anticipated. Launching himself up and to one side, Ojukwu evaded Graf's initial launch. Graf reached the far wall and tucked his knees into his chest. He thrust his feet in front of him to rebound off the wall and launched himself again at Ojukwu. Ojukwu flipped open a cleverly hidden latch in the top of his cane and depressed a concealed button. Graf was confused as he felt his com implant vibrate. His optical implants flared to life and random images began blitzing his brain as his cochlear implant relayed tones at various frequencies and volumes. Graf screamed as nausea overtook him. He clutched at his head, his body falling slowly to the floor as consciousness began fading away. The final thing he saw before he lost consciousness was Ojukwu standing over him, the cane held firmly in one hand as he raised it over his head.

Present - Molecular Decombinator Waste Reclamation Room, Ojukwu Enclave, Io Dome 616e - Terran Federation Year 2323

Graf forced himself to straighten up and slammed his fist into the window once more. An inch of plexiglass separated him from Ojukwu. He pressed against it, hoping to reach the man whose face was practically, if not physically, miles away from his. "Please, Neema. Please. Kill me if you must, but save her. I could have used that serum on myself, you know I could have. You know I need to. I could have told you I never found it, but I didn't. I gave it to you. I got you here, damn it. Help her for God's sake."

Ojukwu watched Graf dispassionately. He considered for a moment before extending his hand to the side of the window. A slight buzz resonated through the chamber Graf occupied. Ojukwu cleared his throat before his voice resonated through the room. "No, Mr Graf."

Ojukwu paused, unsure if he wanted to elaborate. He considered and then continued, "I have sacrificed more than you can possibly imagine. You are correct. I have left many people behind. Those you mentioned: my son, countless other children I have sired, my people, my continent, and yes, even Earth. I've left fragments of my soul behind in every instance. Each one gnaws at me, Mr Graf. However, I cling to one undeniable fact as I progress forward. I am uniquely positioned to accomplish a greater good. I have the means and the power to establish something new here. I have the means and the power to research and develop new technologies and new medical advances that will save our species. Perhaps, I may even be able to save Earth in time."

Ojukwu paused for a moment and collected himself. "What are those I've lost compared to that? What is my soul compared to that? I have a duty. A damned duty, sir!"

Ojukwu took a breath and calmed himself. "I will not jeopardize that duty for you or for anyone, Mr Graf," Ojukwu stated with some finality. "I thank you for your service. You are correct. You did, indeed, help me greatly in my journey thus far. If I am successful, I will ensure that your name is always remembered as a part of our great work. I'm afraid we must part ways here. It seems our paths have now diverged."

Ojukwu stared at Graf for a long moment. "Farewell, Mr Graf."

He reached out and toggled the switch on the intercom before turning sharply on his heel. As he began to walk away, Graf banged on the window, his voice reverberating through the room. "Come back! Come back and honour our bargain! Come back, damn you!" Purple liquid began pouring from the nozzles in the ceiling. Graf's legs tingled as a low current began flowing through the copper wires crisscrossing the room. Graf knew that the electric current would activate the bacteria in the liquid. That bacteria would then dismantle the molecular structure of any organic material it came in contact with. He looked around in desperation. A primal scream was all he could conjure.

The shutters on the window closed, and Ojukwu walked to his office, mentally preparing himself for his next meeting of the day.

THE SURPRISES NEVER END
By Tim Davis

Foosh! The sound of the arrow hitting the scarecrow had become almost comforting. He had been training all day; intentionally trying to work himself to the bone. The Trial tomorrow had three possible challenges, and you never knew which one you would get until you stood before the village Triumvirate. Sam never took his eyes off the target as he pulled back the arrow. He focused on where he wanted to strike, felt his muscles strain, and finally loosed his shot. *Foosh*! He couldn't help but smirk when the arrow landed exactly where he wanted it to. But it was still his last arrow, so he had to walk over—slight limp still in his gait—to retrieve his shots, and begin again. Aunt Dana came by as it got dark.

"I thought you said you knew you would pass the Trial, kid."

Sam shrugged. "Yeah."

"Then why are you training so hard?"

Samson did his best not to get annoyed. "I only know that I pass the Trial. I don't have any memory of the Trial itself. Just after it."

Dana scoffed. "Some gift."

Sam grimaced as his aunt walked back to the farmhouse. Mathis had gone back to his little house on the outskirts of Victor's Circle for the week due to "pressing business," but Sam suspected that just meant he planned on getting drunker and louder than Dana tolerated around her own house. Sam loosed the arrows quicker than he had before. Even someone like Aunt Dana, who understood how much he hated the Knowing, could make him angry. This gift had cost Sam so much that he would have given almost anything not to know the things he did. Of course he had to train harder not knowing how he got through the Trial; the trouble with knowing some of the future was always going to be the parts that you didn't know. The surprises are what hurt the most...

There were memories that Sam had that went so far back he couldn't remember not remembering them. Like seeing The Wizard of Oz in the Town Hall on an old projector when the generator still worked; he must've been four then. Sam supposed everyone had memories like that. What made him different were that some of his memories were of things that hadn't happened yet. He remembered his friend Louie and his family leaving town when they were both nine-year-old kids. He remembered it all before it happened—that Louie and his father would leave Victor's Circle when they found out his mother had been unfaithful and that it would have been Sam's fault because he would be the one to let it slip. Louie's mother Georgia had been rather thorough in covering up her affair with one of the town elders. If Sam had never said anything, Louie's father never would have known. And even though Sam remembered letting it slip, he still tried never to tell. That's why I let it slip rather than outright told it, Sam thought bitterly. Even trying to stop it, it just meant that it happened a particular way rather than another. Knowing Louie would leave was troubling before, but after it happened, it was devastating. I may know how some things will happen, but I never know how I'll feel until I'm there. Why is there such a difference between knowing and feeling?

Louie was a quiet, kind boy; he had heart and humour and he never seemed to mind that Sam was clumsy, strange, and bad at school. Sam knew Louie would leave, but he didn't know how much it would hurt until after the fact. He hadn't realised how much that friendship mattered until it was gone. Worst of all, Sam didn't have any memories of

Louie after his family left. I never see him again. Sam supposed he knew that all along, but it hurt much more going through it than knowing he would go through it. He didn't have any friends his age for some time after that since everyone in town began whispering about Sam's "gift" when Louie and his family left town. The Knowing was tricky.

Four years ago, when he was twelve, he got beaten to a pulp by a trio of other boys who liked to joke about how he was a witch: Spencer, Barney, and Torvald. Sam didn't even put up a fight—he knew he was going to get the scar which turned out to be from Torvald when his knife almost took out Sam's eye. The broken leg he got was a surprise from Spencer. Pain didn't bother Sam the way it did other children his age, but even he couldn't help screaming in agony when the other boy broke the bone. The leg would never heal quite right and he'd be limping the rest of his days, but he still refused to struggle back. He didn't remember the fight—just that it would happen. It was his Aunt Dana's silent heartbreak as he healed and what the town doctor told him after that made him regret not standing up for himself.

"But it was three against one!"

"Boy, they damn near killed you! Three against one is bad odds, but they aren't such bad odds!"

"Easy for you to say."

The Doc gave him a hard look. "You were bigger than the biggest of them. And they were afraid of you at that— you'd be surprised how much of a difference that could've made."

The surprises are what hurt the most.

Sam didn't have foreknowledge of the beating itself, or the talk he had with the Doc, but he did remember being different after then without knowing why. The change was simple—he was done letting himself be the victim; he wasn't going to let himself get dragged along and call it fate. He was going to take a stand and be the leader of his own life, even if he knew how things would turn out. It may have meant that his only real choice in the matter was being afraid or being angry his whole life, but it was still a choice. I'd take anger over fear any day. The Doctor was also the one who first suggested to Dana that she take Sam to see Mathis. Sam didn't remember what spurred Mathis into his life, he just remembered that eventually the strange old man came to live with them after he got his limp. It was one of the few pleasant surprises in his life.

Old Man Mathis—the strange elderly dandy living on the edge of Victor's Circle. He was the only other person in the territory the townspeople were aware of who was afflicted with the Knowing, and his presence in the town was tolerated because he lived on the outskirts and kept mostly to himself. The first meeting between Sam and Mathis was a mystery to Sam, but something Sam remembered well, even before it happened. As soon as Sam was able to walk at all after Barney, Spencer, and Torvald gifted him with the limp, Dana loaded them into the cart and they rode down to the lonely house on the desert road. Dana wanted to send Sam by himself (because God willing, she was going to raise him tough), but it was too far, he was on crutches, and she wanted to get the scope of the old man herself.

Sam's knock on the door was greeted by an old man in a light blue suit, with wild hair, and a walrus-y moustache.

"You're late, boy."

Not only was their visit unexpected and unplanned, but it was also impossible to contact the old man without walking down the long desert road. The only other person who knew it would happen, outside of Sam and Dana, was the Doc, and he was too important to leave his clinic on a weekday. Before either of them could respond, the old man broke out into hysterics with a deafening donkey cackle that shuddered Sam and his Aunt.

"Bahahahaha! Come in, come in!"

Dana gave Sam a worried look, to which the boy replied: "I forgot the Old Man likes to laugh at his own jokes."

Samson remembered Dana telling him that Mathis rubbed her the wrong way at first, and watching them talk over their pipes, Sam saw himself how much the Old Man grated his aunt's nerves. Mathis was expecting the two of them, so he showed Sam to a desk to tinker with a typewriter (the antique being something Sam had a surprisingly dim memory of), while the two adults smoked their pipes. Dana was mistrustful of dandies in the first place, and she guessed from the wrinkles in Mathis's suit that he dressed himself in such a manner regularly, and not just when he was expecting visitors. Dana may have been old and small, but she was tough, wearing overalls more often than dresses, to hell with what anyone said. Sam's aunt was also too serious to suffer fools or to tolerate mockery, and the Old Man's boisterous laughter at the door set her on edge immediately. Worst of all, tobacco was a scarce luxury crop those days, and when the Old Man imposed himself on her tobacco pouch, fury began to boil under the old woman's surface. Sam was fascinated by the typewriter, but he seemed to recall he had more time with it in the future, so he merely pretended to fiddle with it while he eavesdropped on the adults' conversation.

It turned out that Samson's clumsiness, his panic with crowds, and his trouble with pen and paper were part of his affliction. "Or at the very least, if it isn't part of the Knowing, it's an affliction that goes hand-in-hand with it," explained Mathis. When Mathis told Dana that Sam had more smarts than he knew what to do with, Dana was dumbfounded—she worked on the boy every night with his writing and she was quick to flick his wrist with a ruler whenever he made a mistake. Mathis asked Dana how long she intended to abuse Sam in such a manner, and she said, "Until he gets it." When Mathis cheerfully pointed out that Dana's insistence on "beating a dead horse" had to be one of the worst jokes he had ever heard, he tipped her over the edge and she gathered up her nephew to leave. "Don't forget the typewriter!" Mathis laughed as they left.

Dana could be a proud woman at times, but that didn't mean she couldn't admit when she was wrong. When Sam told Dana that Mathis would be coming to the house to live later that week, she said she'd never allow it. And when Sam told her that it would be her idea, it was her turn to laugh for once. It was when they sat down to Sam's studies that she realised how much the boy would need the Old Man. She long worried that Sam might grow into a functional illiterate, he had such trouble writing. When she saw the pages he produced with the typewriter, she was flummoxed. Even figuring that Sam probably remembered how the damned machine worked from the future, she knew that the Knowing didn't give the boy skills; he still had to practice like anyone else to do something with artfulness, and somehow the words and sentences he put on paper with those keys were as coherent and well-composed as the best work of the boys and girls his age who worked with pens.

Samson didn't have foreknowledge of the glossy-eyed look Dana gave him that day. Things hurt Dana so rarely that it often took Sam time to suss out why after the fact, even with the Knowing. It was oddly touching and somewhat unsettling when Sam realised later that the tears in Dana's eyes were because she finally saw that she had been failing her nephew in some ways. That night, Dana swallowed her pride and wrote a letter that she would have Sam run to a messenger at first light; it was an invitation to Mathis to stay with them. She wound up smoking two pouches of tobacco that night out of sheer paralyzing rage.

Even though Sam knew it would happen, it wasn't until he was actually living it and he felt Dana's agitation that he realised how much she loved him; she surely wouldn't have put up with the "old goat of a man" if she didn't. The Old Man usually woke up sometime in the afternoon, and he was usually good for a few hours to give Sam his lessons, but he typically spent his nights drinking himself into oblivion. Mathis said the drinking helped him forget some things and that made the Knowing more bearable. Dana bristled at the Old Man's drinking, and at first feared it was a bad habit he would pass onto Sam, but to her relief, it didn't catch. Sam had found the man passed out on the kitchen floor in a puddle of his own piss clutching a whisky bottle enough times, he vowed the weak beer that the town brewed with its excess grain would be the only alcohol he'd ever drink. The whisky was itself harder to come by, but Mathis received deliveries of it regularly from an anonymous Triumvirate member two towns over as a blackmail payment. Funnily enough, the Old Man didn't actually have anything on the politician, but the politician thought he did, and the fear of the Knowing in those who didn't have it turned out to be a powerful weapon.

As Sam's self-appointed tutor, Mathis gave the boy a schedule that he had to follow every day, even over the summer when he didn't have school and they worked at the harvest. Sam resented it at first, but eventually he embraced it, since the structure did help. Mathis also didn't just tutor Sam on writing composition and mathematics, but also on swordplay and other areas of what the Old Man called the "gentlemanly arts." Mathis even managed to help Sam learn to walk again, even though Dana thought it would be a lost cause since the boy used to trip himself mid-step even before the trio of other boys broke his leg. He never quite got rid of the limp, but Mathis was relentless about Sam's "rehabilitation," and with enough work, Sam could walk unaided. Though sometimes Sam walked with one of Mathis's old canes (made more to be a gaudy decoration than a walking aid) when he wanted to show off, act fancy, or get on his aunt's nerves.

The Old Man's humour and flamboyance rubbed off on Sam more than his Aunt was sometimes comfortable with. Sam still missed Louie, and he still craved a bond with someone his own age, but Mathis brought humour back to Sam's life, and that was something a boy like him sorely needed. Sam always said Mathis was a friend more than anything else, but that was only because he never wanted to admit that deep down he knew the Old Man was the closest thing he'd ever have to a father. Probably the best thing about Mathis coming to live with them was that it gave Sam a figure in his life who not only understood the Knowing, but also how to live with it. As a rule, Mathis tried not to discuss the future too much with Sam, since they both had memories the other didn't about what was to come. Mathis maintained that even though they knew the future, they couldn't actually change how things occurred, so sometimes it was best to stay in the dark about the grim things fate had in store. But all the same, they were two people with the Knowing whose lives overlapped for several years, and that made it unavoidable that they would have certain foreknowledge in common. Dana was often lost with the conversations the boy and the Old Man would have—and that was by design—since they spoke just vaguely enough for the other to understand the future event they referred to, but to leave Dana in the dark lest they spoil some surprises down the line.

While it would be years before she admitted it, Aunt Dana was secretly glad that Mathis and Sam had decided to keep their foreknowledge of the boy losing his virginity from her. Sam himself looked forward to his first taste of the sins of the flesh, but also found himself regretting it after the fact. The girl was Victoria Anabelle Darby (Belle for short), and all the adults knew she was trouble, but all the kids thought she was fun. She was the oldest child of the youngest generation of the family who ran the town; practically royalty in their little corner of the world. Being the oldest child, her father raised her much as another parent would have raised a male child, and she spent her younger years as a tomboy who shunned dolls and dresses. Sam was an overly timid child until the bullies broke his leg, so Belle never had time for him when they were in grammar school. Once, after Belle had stolen a pouch of Dana's tobacco from the house and outran Sam and Louie when they tried to chase her down, Sam had told Louie about how Belle would grow to be the prettiest girl their age. The other boy baulked at the foreknowledge.

But sure enough, after Belle developed a woman's body, after she grew her hair out, and after she started wearing skirts instead of trousers, the young men of Victor's Circle took notice and stopped thinking of her as another boy with a higher voice. At first, the Darby family was pleased with Belle's transformation, since they had often considered her tomboy phase embarrassing, but soon after they began to miss those days. Only Belle's presentation changed; she still had her wild streak. She cut school, she cursed like a soldier, drank and smoked whenever she got the chance, and worst of all, had developed the reputation of being fast with many of the boys considered to be bad seeds by the general populace of Victor's Circle. Once at a ball the Darbys had thrown to celebrate the visit of a prestigious family from another village, the head of the Triumvirate from Bronntown commented that Belle looked much lovelier in her gown than she did in the trousers she used to wear. She smiled politely and left everyone gasping when she replied: "I prefer my ball gowns and dresses as well; it gives the boys much easier access." Rumour had it that Belle left that ball early to wrinkle that lovely gown in a barn with one of the servers.

And so, Sam had gone off to the village tavern on a warm midsummer night rather looking forward to the encounter he knew he would have with Belle. Though he didn't yet know why, Sam knew that this would be the only occasion he got to lie with the wild member of the town's ruling family, and he couldn't help being excited by the prospect. The older folk of the town may have given her dirty looks, but the boy found Belle's bluntness and outrageousness rather endearing. Besides, she might have been the only person in town with as maligned a reputation as Sam himself; surely two outsiders would be able to find comfort with one another. It was almost perfunctory the week before when Mathis gave Sam the "supplies" he'd need for his night with Belle.

It was Belle who approached Sam that night, her eyes locked on him from the other end of the bar for the first few minutes he sat there. She approached him and they spent much of the night drinking and laughing. When the mistress of the tavern finally cut them off, Sam showed Belle the small bottle of whisky he had brought, and she led him to a cornfield just off the side of the road. There in the dirt between the cornstalks, under the Flower Moon, Belle took Sam's virginity. She giggled at first when she saw the strange sheepskin sheath Mathis had called a "rubber," but she accepted it easily enough (apparently it was a more common implement among the boys she had known than Sam realised). Afterwards, Belle adeptly rolled a pair of cigarettes with her rolling paper and the tobacco Sam had brought, while he laid watching her in the moonlight on the pile of their clothes. It was while they lay smoking in each other's arms that Belle laughed and surprised him: "I can't wait to see the look on my grandfather's face when I tell him about this." Sam's heart sank. He finally understood why he never laid with Belle again; she hadn't truly wanted him, she just wanted to infuriate her family by having one off with the town witch.

Belle rolled her eyes at the hurt in Sam's face as they put on their clothes, and they went their separate ways. As Sam walked back to the farmhouse, his clothes dishevelled, he realised the whisky Mathis supplied, which the pair of lovers left untouched, had been solely for him. Sam's anger abandoned him and he let his sadness consume him as he trudged home, the small bottle empty by the time he stumbled into the farmhouse. He had memories of Belle from the future. They became friends sometime after his Trial, but he failed to see how he could ever bring himself to be friends with someone so unkind. The next morning, a surprisingly sober and alert Mathis sat Sam down at the table. It was always disarming when the Old Man took on a more sombre tone since Mathis was ever the jester. Knowing the Old Man cared and that there was nothing Sam could have done to change the course of the night gave Sam little comfort, but it was still the best the boy could hope for.

Dana often bristled at Mathis, but all the same, she developed a begrudging respect for the old goat. He may have been a dandy who eschewed physical labour of any kind, but he was tough in his own way and, most importantly, he was the only other person in the town who came close to caring about Samson as much as Dana did. Mathis may have been a tired old drunk who laughed too much for his own good, but he also understood what it was like to be an outcast. And maybe best of all, he taught Sam that working hard to overshadow an affliction meant you knew how to work harder than the unafflicted.

That was why he toiled away with the bow and arrow now. The Trial consisted of three possible challenges: rifle, arrow, or short sword. It was a coming-of-age ordeal every boy in the territory had to pass when they turned sixteen in case another territory took up arms and decided to invade. Aunt Dana had one of the larger farms in the town and could still afford shells for her old bolt-action rifle, and even with his limp, Sam was quick with a short sword and his height gave him a better reach than most of the other boys his age. Best of all, because of his affliction, he had to work so hard with his movements that with enough training he was eventually able to use either hand in swordplay; giving him the advantage of being able to throw off the village's other children with an opponent who could mirror them. That made his weak point the bow and arrow. The combination of the distance of the target with having to measure the strength needed to hit it tripped Sam up in his head sometimes, but if he did it enough he could fall into a rhythm where the work with his hands soothed him and it came more naturally. If bow and arrow was the challenge he had to overcome for the Trial, Sam would be ready.

The Trial was always cruel, even if you passed. It wasn't just that they tested your skills, it was that they tested your skills against another person—boys exiled from other towns who failed their rites of passage were the enemy. You had to prove that you could shed blood for the safety of your town, and if you couldn't, they exiled you and you became an orphan. The orphans got sent to other towns to serve as arrow fodder for other Trials. The orphans always had the chance to redeem themselves in some other boy's Trial though—if two boys went into the ring with swords, the boy who came out alive would always be the one who had a place in the town afterwards, regardless of if it was his hometown. It never seemed right to Sam that blood made you a man. He sometimes wondered if it made it easier not knowing the other boy who you had to kill. But killing was still killing.

It hadn't always been like this. At least that was what his teachers said, though none of them remembered a time that was better. There were still the odd remnants of the old world here and there that spoke to a different time, like the guns and the motion pictures. It always struck Sam as a shame that people made new guns, but no one made new picture shows. He hadn't even seen a picture show since he was seven. A month after they showed The Day the Earth Stood Still, the town generator blew and nobody in Victor's Circle knew how to fix it. Even having seen all eight of the different stories they could project, it still felt like almost as big of a loss as when Louie moved away. Maybe it was because he knew the stories and how they turned out that he used to find them so comforting to revisit. Shame that knowing the future isn't as comforting.

Sam couldn't remember the world before. His memories were strictly limited to his life span—he only got glimpses of what he would personally see and hear between now and his death. His memory only went so far back as The Wizard of Oz; he couldn't remember his parents. The furthest he could remember forward was the forest and his bloody hand, wrinkled and old, reaching for a blue flower, but he always pushed that back down whenever it came up. Everyone else likes to walk around pretending they're never going to die. Why should I be any different?

Depending on who you asked, a Divine source might have been where Sam got the Knowing…or the radio waves from the old powerplant a few miles away. Or it was a gift from the Devil. It wasn't known when people afflicted with the Knowing started to appear. The people of ages passed were foolish enough to put their records on a great machine that ran electrically; when electricity became scarce it stopped working. No living person in Sam's time quite understood how that machine worked, where it went, or even what it was called, but somehow it linked the world. Now the world was unified under one regime, but somehow peace was still never guaranteed. The old empire that used to stand in Sam's community had stretched from one coast of the continent to another—the territories used to be states and they used to be united under one banner. The teachers said the problem was that every state was too different from the other to move as one, and eventually they tore their fragile alliance apart, but the teachers also told Sam he was wrong when he told them about the war that was coming. They only start listening to me when they have no other choice. Desperation makes strange allies.

Sam only had five arrows. As the sky grew darker, he stopped hitting the scarecrow with every one of them. The first time he missed three out of the five shots was when he decided to go to bed. Aunt Dana had left him a note saying she'd wake him at first light for breakfast. His aunt was a tough woman—losing a sister and a husband in the same Spring sickness probably hardened a person something fierce—but that somehow didn't make it harder to love her. Sam often wished he didn't love her at all; he knew she died in five years when he was twenty-one, and while he couldn't remember the pain, he did remember all the nights he'd spend crying for her. It's not fair. Worst of all, the first time

Dana let him try a drink of Mathis's whisky, they both got soused and she pried her death out of him. Yet she still carried on as if it were nothing but a bad dream. Sam didn't know how a person became so tough that they could shrug off their own death like that, but it helped him in some peculiar way he couldn't explain or admit out loud. But it still pissed him off that Dana knew it was cancer and still smoked that damned pipe of hers every damn day and night.

Dana woke him up earlier than he wanted, banging on his door at first light. For such a slight woman who had been whittled down as much as she had, she still knew how to make a noise. That used to be how Dana woke up Mathis, who preferred to sleep late, until that fateful morning when he opened the door to his room and splashed his tobacco spittoon across her face and screamed, "The Lord of Chew compels you, Devil Woman!" He laughed about as hard as he ever had in his braying jackass old man laugh, and she walloped him about as hard as she had ever walloped anyone, and with his own belt at that (his breeches slipping off his hips). It seemed Sam wasn't the only one who could be hurt by life's surprises. After that, there was an unspoken understanding between Aunt Dana and Old Man Mathis; she would never bang on his door again and he would keep her out of his strange japes.

Sam didn't have much of an appetite that morning, so he just drank half the pot of black coffee. Aunt Dana fussed just enough to get Sam to eat a few mouthfuls of the eggs she prepared.

"You're lucky that you've got yourself an aunt who can afford chickens, kid."

Sam rolled his eyes and Dana took out her tobacco pouch and began loading her pipe. Sam hated watching Dana smoke. For all the death Sam saw in his future, he hadn't touched it first hand, at least not yet. There were his parents of course, but he had no memory of them. His first real taste would be Aunt Dana five years later. Mathis disappeared a few years after that. Later still, there would be Mara. He'd marry Mara sometime in his late twenties and it would last almost two years. Almost. She would pass quietly of a stroke (or at least that would be the best the Doc could figure). It made Sam angry to think about, knowing he would love someone only to lose them almost as soon as they entered his life. *I'm angry at Dana for her death, but I'm angry at myself for Mara's.* He couldn't imagine why he would still marry her knowing she would die so young. Sometimes he could recall her face perfectly, other times not at all. When he thought on it long enough, he could almost make sense of it—he only had the knowledge, after all, not the feeling of what it would be like to love her. *From what I've seen, love is always part folly anyways. Why should I be any less of a fool than anyone else?* Sometimes Sam wanted to be just like everyone else so bad it hurt.

Aunt Dana wanted to take the cart to the Trial. Sam thought that was a fool's notion since they were close enough to walk. Other boys his age would shout something or occasionally throw a bit of food at him on the way there, but he remembered it was nothing serious enough to warrant a cart. Sam took a deep breath as they neared the town hall—going through the doors of that building was where this stretch of fog on his memory began and it didn't clear until he woke up tired the next day. *I guess the only way out is through…*

The Triumvirate were seated in the old courtroom: a younger man to Sam's left, a burly middle-aged woman to his right, and the old man who really ran the town in the centre. They wore plain grey robes and their faces masked any emotion, though Sam suspected they had the same contempt for him as anyone else in town. The woman, Gretel, was almost as tough as Aunt Dana—she wouldn't have been seated on that bench if she wasn't hard as nails. The old man was Victor Darby III—the grandson of the Victor who first founded the town. The younger man was

Victor Darby IV, who only sat at the bench because his father put him there. By all accounts he was weak, otherwise he wouldn't let Belle run as wild as she did. It's probably that weakness that's going to make him turn to me for advising when the other two are dead and he leads the Triumvirate.

Sam stood waiting and trying his best not to let his impatience show. Finally, Victor III spoke. "Your name is Samson Judah Clarkson." He looked expectantly at Sam.

"It is, Your Township," coughed Sam.

"Today is your sixteenth birthday. Correct?"

"It is, Your Township."

"Do you stand ready to face the Trial of manhood?"

"I do, Your Township."

"Very well. Bring forth his challenger!"

The boy the town guards dragged in was a little shorter than Sam, but skeletal in his starvation—there was hardly anything to him. When he saw Sam his eyes locked on him as if in great shock, but why? Had talk or rumours of Sam's gift reached other—

Aunt Dana gasped in the stands behind Sam. When he looked back and saw the shock of the boy mirrored in his aunt's face, that was when he recognised him. The boy who stood before him in shackles, staring at him, was Louie. Louie had been a little older than Sam; he must've failed his rite of passage in Franklinville, or Bronntown, or wherever he found himself when his father left Victor's Circle. And here he stood, a shrivelled young man where the boy Sam loved used to be. "Well…this is awkward," japed Louie with a weak smile.

Sam must have been wearing the shock on his face because Victor III broke the silence. "Is there a problem, young man?"

When Sam stammered, his aunt spoke for him.

"That boy was his friend in this village once! You can't expect him to—"

"He agreed to the Trial. If he backs out now he is an exile."

The crowd in the room murmured, but Sam's eyes were locked on Victor III. He understood it all instantly. They're doing this on purpose. They want to make an example of me because I laid with Belle.

Sam stared down Belle's grandfather and steeled his heart for what was to come.

"I accept the challenge."

The crowd erupted in shock, even Victor IV and Gretel, but Victor III's face was made of stone until he shouted: "Take them to the field of play!"

The noise of the crowd and the commotion around him made Sam lightheaded and he came close to fainting. The next thing he knew, Sam was standing in the dirt field with a short sword in hand, watching as the guards unshackled Louie. When Victor III commenced the fight, neither of the two boys moved. They just stared at each other. Louie sighed and threw his sword into the mud. Sam pointed his sword at Louie and looked to the Triumvirate.

"He yielded. I win."

Victor III grunted with cruel laughter. "If you don't swing that sword at a person, you don't pass the challenge. You must take his life or you both go into exile."

Louie looked at him with pleading eyes. "I guess I can't blame you, Sammy."

Sam wanted to throw down his sword and walk away, but that may well have meant death down the line. And besides, he didn't remember a future where he went into exile... He stayed in Victor's Circle all his days. And yet...

"I refuse to shed his blood. He was my friend. Send me into exile."

The crowd gasped again. Even Victor III finally showed an emotion: anger. Victor signalled the riflemen watching the perimeter and they pointed their guns at the two boys.

"Samson Clarkson! If you do not fight, you will both die."

A commotion arose from the audience as the guards had to restrain Aunt Dana.

"Victor, you pig! You're only doing this because my nephew bedded your grandchild!"

The crowd gasped in astonishment. Someone else threw in, "Why be angry!? It's not like he was the only one!"

The two Victors both turned red with anger. The mix of laughter and astonishment from the crowd made Sam's vision begin to tunnel, it was too overwhelming. Finally, the Third bellowed, "Fight or die, Sam. It is your choice."

Tears welled up in Louie's eyes. "It's alright, Sam."

Still, Sam couldn't move.

Victor yelled, "You have until the count of five."

The world grew hazy as the old bastard counted down. Things slowed down to the point that it felt like years between each number. Sam tried to resist the action he knew he was going to take, that he had to take, but then things disconnected and suddenly he was watching himself charge Louie. It has to happen this way. I don't remember Louie surviving or me going into exile…

Then Sam realised what a load of horseshit that sounded like and he stopped. The next thing he knew, he was kneeling in the mud, his sword thrown aside. The crowd gasped again, and Victor's count had stammered at number three. The wrinkled old bastard scoffed.

"Four!"

And then before he could shout "five," someone else was in the ring.

"Stop!" There stood Belle in front of the two boys.

"I won't have you make Sam my whipping boy, grandfather—if you want to shoot these two, then you have to shoot me as well."

The crowd was stunned. Aunt Dana took her chance and stole a pistol from the holster of one of the guards restraining her. Dana shot the one who was still armed in the foot, and fired two shots into the air as she made her way into the ring.

"Victor, you son of a bitch! You know damn well it's unlawful to execute a boy when he warrants an exile! Now call off your flunkies or I'll shoot you dead!"

Victor III stiffened at that. He gave a signal and all the riflemen took their sights off of the four people in the ring. But Dana wouldn't lower her pistol. A devious smile crossed Victor's lips.

"Torvald!"

Everything happened so fast it may as well have happened at once. A town guard jumped from the crowd, knife in hand, ready to stab his aunt in the back. Before he knew it, Sam was on his feet, sword in hand, and the sword itself was plunged into the guard's belly. The two of them stood together for a moment like that, and when the guard made to stab Sam instead, Sam knocked the knife from his hand and drove the blade deeper into him. Sam stood dazed as the guard fell dying into the mud. When his guard cap fell back and he lay there spitting up blood, Sam finally recognised the boy who had nearly taken his eye out only a few years before. Torvald had passed his own Trial with flying colours just a month earlier, and had taken up a new post with the town guard.

Dana looked to Victor. "Looks to me like the boy passed his Trial. If you come for him again, I swear by all that is holy that I'll burn that lofty estate of yours to the ground." Dana looked to the crowd. "You can all go home now."

As everyone dispersed, Dana turned to Sam and smiled. "This just had to be a day where I decided to look nice and wear a dress instead of my overalls."

Before Sam could laugh, his whole body clenched and he found himself thrashing in the mud next to Torvald's body. And then he wasn't in the mud looking up at Dana, Louie, and Belle anymore; he was almost in a dream, riding his flood of new memories of the things to come. The ongoing feud he'd have with the rest of the Darbys, the new times he, Louie, and Belle would enjoy together, his aunt living on to head the Triumvirate instead of dying of cancer, and so forth. New memories. Too many to remember at once.

Sam woke up in a bed in a room he didn't recognise right away, and then he realised he was in the Doc's clinic. When he tried to speak he couldn't. He reached into his mouth and felt that his tongue had stitches. The Doc said Sam was lucky that he hadn't bitten his tongue clean off. After the Doc shined a light in his eyes and made him nod yes or no to a few questions to make sure his head was okay, Samson was allowed to leave. Dana and Louie waited for him outside in the cart; apparently Louie had been granted permission to stay with them until he had to participate in some other boy's Trial a few weeks later.

Later that night, Sam walked all the way to Mathis's house with a bottle of wine. He expected the Old Man to be too drunk to answer the door right away, but to his surprise Mathis answered after two knocks. Even more surprising, Mathis wasn't drunk. Sam had typed up a letter explaining what happened and how he had beaten the odds and changed his future before making the journey to Mathis, since the bite in his tongue kept him from speaking. But, much to Sam's surprise, Mathis already knew what had happened. "That's why I couldn't be there for you, my boy." When Sam stared long enough into Mathis's sad grey eyes, he was hit with a strange revelation: the Old Man had been lying to him. Mathis had known all along that Sam had the power to change the future, and he had purposely kept it from him. The hard look Sam gave him was all that Mathis needed to confess the truth. The Old Man sighed…

"I'm sorry, boy. I should have told you outright long ago, but I couldn't. I had foreknowledge that you would discover it when you had to face your Trial, and I knew if I told you it might alter the course of things. You see… I haven't changed the future in years. The more you change the future, the less of it you can see. And you never know whether you're changing things for good or ill."

Tears welled in Mathis's eyes as he spoke.

"When I realised I could change my fate... I thought I could live a perfect life. A life without sorrow. A life with limitless booze and wealth where all my loved ones would be safe. It worked at first, but I reached too far... I lost everything that I held dear. I know I die alone, and that's better than some of the fates I almost had, and quite frankly better than I deserve given my great vainglorious folly."

It was then in the pale light of Mathis's fireplace that Sam finally understood the Old Man; he didn't drink because he mourned a future he couldn't escape, he drank for the mistakes of his past that he could never undo. Mathis wasn't trying to forget his foreknowledge, he was trying to forget his sins.

"Be careful, Sam. Be very careful. You never know how changing the future will turn out."

Of course you could never know, thought Sam bitterly...

The surprises are always what hurt the most.

BLOOD AND ASHES
By Steve Sellers

The corpse greeted Ashlyn Frost like a long-awaited friend.

She guessed that the boy had passed through Death's Gates perhaps two hours before. Certainly no more than three. The blood had barely dried around the gaping wounds in his throat and chest, and the colour was already starting to fade from his skin. He had fought bravely, at least if the nicks and cuts on his arms were any measure. His iron dagger, lying cruelly by the dead boy's side, had been no defence against the thing that slaughtered him in the dying embers of the sun. The land around him was dust, as dead as the child now decomposing on the ground before her.

Ashlyn cursed herself for being too late once again. Had she not been sidetracked by that foolish priest in Caladryn, by his lies and false leads, she might have arrived with time to spare. She hadn't known this child, but it mattered little. Ashlyn had failed the boy, and now he was dead. One of many who had passed the Gates because of her. Just like fallen Archadia and all the rest of them. His death was not her fault, but it was her responsibility.

"It was a scornbeast," Ashlyn said absently, approaching her horse along the left side. "Hades, my old friend, once more we rode too late."

Ashlyn began to mount Hades when a noise made her hesitate. A scrunching of the bushes around her, not far from the road. With a swift gesture of her slender hands, her blades slid free of their sheaths. The Crimson Sword burned in her right hand, glinting with unspoken fury. The longsword was slender, curving slightly towards the centre of the blade. The reddish metal glinted in the firelight blazing along the edge. Black runes crackled along the flat sides of the weapon. The Azure Dagger shone in her left, its blue mist hanging in the air around its razor-sharp tip. The dagger gleamed a soft silver, with blue runes etched along the flat sides. The jagged edge, lined with steel jaws, dripped with misty hunger. The last weapons of Archadia, earned by right of blood and valour.

A scrawny figure in brown, armed with a short sword, emerged from the brush along the path. He looked like he hadn't eaten in two days, but that made him more dangerous. A much larger man stood upon the other side of the road, slipping out from behind a massive rock formation. He held a double-bladed axe with both hands, dripping with blood and menace as he raised it.

These men had not murdered the child. Even vultures like these weren't so desperate or lacking in honour.

"See, now, how my plan paid off," the scrawny one said, gesturing at Ashlyn with his withered talon of a finger. "See who comes for the child. Now we take the girl and her beautiful horse."

"Ye always was the smart one," the ox replied, spinning the axe above his head.

Ashlyn merely sighed as she crouched into a battle stance. The Crimson Sword burst into song, its red flames scorching the air. The Azure Dagger spun into a frenzy in her left hand as the ox approached. Her gold-flecked eyes met her opponent's, knowing the outcome. She dashed forwards as the longsword sang its deadly song, the sharp edge slashing out in a single movement.

The ox lumbered to the ground behind her as Ashlyn passed, cleaving through his midsection. His lifeless face was empty and soulless; his eyes glassy as he stared upwards. His mouth hung open in disbelief, not reckoning against Ashlyn's swift strike. The scrawny one stepped backwards, gesturing wildly with his short sword as the axe crashed into the earth.

"Reaper, take the soul of this buffoon," Ashlyn said, pointing to the survivor with the tip of the silver dagger in her left hand. "Now, where is the beast who killed the boy?"

The scrawny attacker dropped his sword and raised both hands upwards.

"Bordertown!" he squeaked. "I saw the monster slink down the path that way. I swear that's all I know!"

Ashlyn hesitated, but only for a moment. The fool would say anything to keep her from killing him. But there was no reason for him not to speak the truth, especially as desperate as he was. And if he was lying, there was an answer for that too.

"I believe you," Ashlyn said, lurching forwards and piercing the man's eye with the Azure Dagger. "Burn in hell."

Ashlyn mounted on the back of Hades, weapons sheathed once more. Two more sent to the Gates. That would buy her a little more time, keep the Reaper at her back for a little longer. She had little sympathy for vultures who preyed off the weak, and little time to care about checking the validity of the fool's information. If he was right, he might buy a little peace beyond the Veil; and if he was wrong, he deserved to burn anyway.

The pale horse bounded towards the path to Bordertown. Pity was a luxury the world could ill afford.

* * *

The guards let Ashlyn through the gates of Bordertown with surprisingly little fuss. They merely waved her in with a shrug.

This was not common in her experience. In the first place, she wasn't exactly human. The gold eyes of her people typically gave her away. She was unnaturally pale, though not too much, with shimmering silver hair that ran straight down to her shoulders. The black dragonscale armour she wore also wasn't common, one of the last relics of Archadia that yet remained. And then there were the Crimson Sword and the Azure Dagger, stained with blood from her encounter on the roadway. Hades snorted as he trotted past the guards, but Ashlyn knew to be more cautious.

Most riders would simply think that the guards were ill-trained, but Ashlyn knew better. Their nonchalance was born of confidence rather than poor discipline. Their movements bore that out as Ashlyn observed the Bordertown guard. They were a well-oiled machine, no doubt used to dealing with armed ruffians.

"Ravinder should be expecting you at the Tower," the guard said as she passed. "He's sent out a call for the likes of you."

Ashlyn assumed that was the leader of this place, or at least, someone in authority. The guard had spoken with a hushed, almost reverent tone at the mention of his name. The mention of the Tower suggested an Artisan. She crinkled her nose in slight irritation. Magic always complicated things.

The streets of Bordertown were a different story. Ashlyn had heard the place spoken of as the City of Ships. The buildings sprawling around her had been towers built upon the decks of ancient boats, broken and tossed ashore during The Calamity. She supposed that in the days of Antiquity, these boats had once been seaworthy, back when there was a sea near this place. But the advent of gods and dragons had changed all that. Now the place was a ramshackle collection of buildings set upon a foundation of sunken ships.

If there was a previous city before Bordertown, it had been wiped away by dragonfire. Fires set by the previous rulers of Archadia. Ashlyn reminded herself to be cautious in this place. She knew not whether old grudges persisted here.

* * *

The Artisan's Tower opened itself to Ashlyn without even an ounce of effort. Her fingers, slender and bony, just lightly brushed the door handle when it moved. She scowled slightly as the door flew open, an invitation for her to walk inside.

She found herself in what she presumed was the Artisan's waiting room. There was a pomp sterility about the place that quietly offended her. Portraits that had survived the days of Antiquity, depictions of gods that had been dethroned with The Calamity. Marble statues, finely carved, though browned and chipped with the weight of centuries. Ravinder had gone to great effort to acquire these things, all to preen like a strutting rooster.

Ashlyn was not impressed with the display. She had seen such things back in her youth in Archadia, far more lavish than even this. The perfumed scent of the room, the soft pillows lining the chairs, more to impress guests than to offer comfort. Ashlyn did not take the seats that were offered. She had left comfort back in Archadia when she had lost all that had once mattered to her.

"Will you take a drink?" a serving girl asked, but Ashlyn refused with a wave of her hand. She knew all too well the tricks of Artisans. Ashlyn kept her left hand on the hilt of the Azure Dagger, though she smiled politely.

Ashlyn had not much longer to wait before the master of the house descended the stairs. His skin was scorched brown with the sun, with a carefully trimmed beard. He wore a green silk shirt, ornately decorated with gold runes, with brown breeches and a pair of black boots. A grin was plastered on his face, but her gaze was affixed to the gold flecks in his brown eyes. Golden flecks that matched Ashlyn's own.

"So the tales are true," Ravinder said with a fine bow. "A Drachenblood comes to visit my humble abode."

There were precious few of their kind left, and they both knew it. They had been hunted to the edges of the Earth, their numbers thinning with each day. Once, the Drachenblood had been gifted the world after the days of Antiquity. But their people had fallen prey to the curse of their blood, the weakness of arrogance that had toppled proud Archadia. Ashlyn saw that same pride in this man, the same folly.

"There seems very little humble about you," Ashlyn pointed out, flashing a look to one of the marble statues.

"I do not deny it." He shrugged. "Our kind once ruled the Earth. You have the look of Archadia about you. No doubt your people lived in similar comfort?"

"No longer." She turned away in disinterest, keeping her left hand at her dagger's hilt. "Not since the Isle of Dragons fell."

The blood of the Drachen ran through the reins of this Artisan, though he was not of Archadia. She would have known of such a man as this in her own kingdom. He probably belonged to another of the Great Clans, Cerulia or Adrastia, both no less prideful than her own. Their numbers were still dwindling, but all Drachen were born survivors.

"I've heard the tales." He laid a hand along an onyx statuette of a panther. "Which makes you the Pale Maiden, does it not? The warrior who follows the hand of Death?"

"And if it does?"

"Then I have a task that would reward you handsomely. I offer a gift worthy of the last Princess of Archadia."

"I'm listening."

"There is a monster roaming the edges of Bordertown. A thing of fire and hate. A thing I cannot kill."

"The scornbeast," Ashlyn nodded. "I'm aware."

"It took my apprentice," he said, his tone acidic. "Lazaria. I want this beast slain."

"Why?"

Ravindar's face twisted into a glare of fury. Up to that point, his expression showed only a slight smile, brimming with arrogance. The way of the Artisans, those who crafted Exceptions to the ancient laws that governed the world.

"Because I will not be made a fool of within my own walls!"

Ashlyn nearly pulled the dagger from her side, but she held firm. Ravinder's blood drained from his face, waving his previous outburst aside with a snap of his fingers. If she wanted, she could have stabbed him in the neck before he had a chance to chant a spell. But the smile returned to his face, and the Azure Dagger rested in its sheath.

"My apologies, kinswoman," Ravinder said, opening his palms towards her. "That was impertinent of me. The loss of Lazaria has been a weight upon this house."

"Did anyone see the abduction?"

"No," he said. "Though my last remaining apprentice had followed her trail until it grew cold. Alindra. In the morning, she will lead you to the monster's lair. I will compensate you fairly for its death."

"I haven't agreed to your quest, Master Artisan."

"I expect you will. Blood must be satisfied, Maiden. And your blades must be fed if the honour of Archadia is to be satisfied. Is that not so?"

Ashlyn could not deny the truth of this. For her to survive, she needed to claim the lives of others. She preferred to kill the corrupt, the venal, and the unworthy. It sat more easily upon her conscience that way. But sometimes she killed so that she could stay one step ahead of the Reaper.

"If you say so," she shrugged. She was too proud to admit that he'd cornered her into his game.

* * *

As the sun blazed over the red-orange skies, Ashlyn carved her way through tall blades of grass.

As she cut a path through the vegetation, she had time to reflect. Ravinder had been true to his word, at least so far as any Artisan could be trusted. He had provided Ashlyn all the lodgings that she needed for both her and Hades, away from people and in silence. He offered her the former room of Lazaria, who presently had no need for it.

This proved to be convenient. Ashlyn had spent most of the night studying the victim, trying to understand why she'd left the Artisan's Tower. Ravinder had said little when asked, and Ashlyn wasn't certain she believed anything he did have to say on the subject. The people of Bordertown shied away from the Tower, and it wasn't simply because he wielded the Art. She had caught a glimpse of the darkness inside the silver-tongued devil, and Ashlyn wondered whether Lazaria had seen it too.

Before bedding down for the night, Ashlyn caught a glimpse of a wooden box, the top lined with finely polished glass. Inside was blue cushioned padding, clearly meant for a small handheld item. The impression within the padding suggested some kind of rod-shaped object, with a handle protruding downwards. Ashlyn vaguely recalled the shape, something she had seen in the halls of Archadia, though she could not place exactly what it was.

"Ah, the Rod of Thunder," Ravinder said when she had asked him. His eyes shone when he laid his eyes upon the box. "A weapon of the ancient world. Broken when I found it, but I learned to make the Rod answer my call. Lazaria must have left to run tests with it."

This nearly made sense to Ashlyn when he had said it. Certainly, she did not contest the claim when he'd made it. But something had felt wrong to her. Ravinder's eyes were upon the box, not upon the portrait that hung above her bed, the one of the assistant he professed to be so distraught over losing.

Ashlyn returned to the here and now and glanced back at the apprentice behind her. Alindra was still a waif of a girl, perhaps around eighteen winters in age. Her hair was long, straight, and black, raining down her shoulders, concealed by blue silken robes. Her eyes were more haunted than they should be—distrustful.

This girl had seen more than she was telling.

* * *

"This is where I last saw Lazaria," Alindra said, the first words she'd uttered all morning. She pointed down to a clearing between bent blades of grass.

Ashlyn motioned to Alindra to keep hidden behind the undergrowth. The last thing she needed was to give the scornbeast a target if it was still lurking about. Ashlyn scurried through the brush, drawing the Azure Dagger with her left hand.

She kept a watch on the tracks, then she realised the indentations in the ground were familiar. Though the tracks were covered with a light layer of dust, she could still make out webbed feet with razor-sharp talons upon each toe. She then noticed the remains of a wild hog in the brush, though the blood was too dried to be recent.

"Old marks," Ashlyn said, beckoning the girl to reveal herself. "The scornbeast was here, but it has a lead on us. Several hours, at least, or I'm a jackrabbit."

"You plan to kill it?" Alindra asked.

"I must." She leaned forwards with a heavy heart. "Scornbeasts are ravenous things who know only hunger and rage. To spare one is to risk innocent blood. You're an Artisan's apprentice. Do you know how they are made?"

"No, Mistress."

"What do you know of Vows and Compacts?"

"First there was the Ancient World, governed by the Old Laws that ruled the universe. Then the Old Laws failed, brought about by the arrogance of man. They breached the Netherspace, where came the gods and the demons, and those who fathered the Drachen." Ashlyn bristled but remained silent. "That was the Calamity; the end of

Antiquity. To survive the coming age, humans struck deals with gods and demons for protection and survival."

"You didn't answer my question." Ashlyn's tone had the sharpness of her blade.

"Gods feed on faith, while demons feed on souls. Vows. Compacts. Power in exchange for sustenance."

"A Vow to a deity can be twisted," Ashlyn said, sliding the Azure Dagger back in her belt. "Sometimes gods demand a heavier price than any demon. At least with a demon, you can trust that they will honour their end of the bargain."

"And gods?"

"A god may revoke its gift for the slightest reason. Each god plays by its own rules, and their gifts carry a high price. But they all have one thing in common: they demand absolute fealty, and anything short of that is a breach of the Vow. Sometimes they even inflict terrible punishments upon Oathbreakers."

Ashlyn looked back for a moment, a painful reminder that she could not befriend this child. Death still lingered near, though, hopefully, far enough behind that Alindra might yet be safe. But the longer she went without shedding blood, without sending souls to the Reaper, the more she feared for the girl.

"Like turning them into scornbeasts?" the young apprentice asked quietly.

"Among else, yes." Ashlyn took the girl's hand. "You should go back, child. Where I go is no place for an apprentice."

"No," Alindra said, holding her right foot in place. "First answer me this: would my master know about Vows and Compacts?

"He is Drachenblood and a Master Artisan. He knows the Old Ways. He must."

"Then I'm safer travelling with you."

Ashlyn raised an eyebrow at this assertion, but then she wondered if there was more to the situation. The apprentice feared her master, that much was clear. Her task would be best done without the girl slowing her down. At the same time, her Arts might be useful. And if Ravinder truly deserved such terror, then sending the girl back could be returning her to greater peril.

"So be it," Ashlyn decided. "But on your own head be the risk."

Normally, she would feel inclined to pay Ravinder to her blood debt as well, but there were complications. One, he was one of the few remaining of their kind, and even the loss of one Drachenblood was a loss to the world. In addition, he maintained order within Bordertown, and the fear of him perhaps extended to the monsters outside their walls. Also, selfishly, she wondered whether she was better served with him as an ally to her cause.

She decided to table that question until her task was done. There were enough dark thoughts to occupy her mind already.

* * *

The cave of the scornbeast beckoned like a gaping maw.

Ashlyn immediately took point, motioning for the apprentice to stand behind her as she approached the entrance. She drew both the Crimson Sword and the Azure Dagger, keeping them steady as she moved into the opening. She willed the red blade alight, letting its soft flames light the way through the darkness.

The cave itself was part of a natural rock formation, red-orange and covered with dust. Few things grew near the scornbeast's lair, perhaps because even the plants themselves knew to avoid the thing that inhabited the place. Stalagmites jutted upwards from the cave floor on the inside, almost like jaws waiting to clamp shut on anyone who ventured in.

It was dank and moist inside, with the air growing damper the farther Ashlyn made her way down the rocky path. This must have been a natural water source at one point, although she couldn't be entirely certain of it.

"Is it just me, mistress," Alindra said, breaking the silence, "or are the walls too smooth to be natural?"

"Silence," Ashlyn hissed in a low voice, perhaps more harshly than intended.

The girl had more wits than actual sense as far as Ashlyn was concerned. Perhaps she was bookish enough—a lifetime spent with an Artisan would grant her a fine education—but she knew nothing of the world outside the city. Perhaps that was a reason she was so hesitant to return to the Tower.

Still, she'd had a point about one thing. The walls seemed too smooth to be formed by nature. This was not the doing of the beast; even a scornbeast wasn't so strong nor methodical. Ashlyn presumed that this hole was carved in the days before the Calamity, where steel beasts were said to dig with precision.

A scream pierced the dark. Two goblins, shrivelled and green, scurried in their direction, towards the entrance behind them. They withdrew daggers as they ran, looking towards the two women with bloodshot eyes.

Ashlyn sent her blades spinning. The goblin on the right was beheaded in a single motion, the Crimson Sword cleaving through its neck. The goblin's head rolled to the ground, its eyes wide in surprise as life faded from them. Ashlyn sidestepped the second goblin, swiftly moving behind it. The Azure Dagger caught the surviving goblin's neck at the tip, Ashlyn clutching the fiend from behind.

"What do you run from?" Ashlyn demanded, her tone venomous.

"The beastling," it said. "A thing of fire and hate. It took our scouting party."

"I am satisfied." She dug the blue-silver blade deep into the goblin's neck. "Join them in peace."

Alindra's eyes leapt open in shock, her hands clamping over her mouth as she looked at Ashlyn. Ashlyn merely shrugged and turned back to the path in front of them. These deaths would keep the Reaper sated for a little while longer.

"Why?" Alindra asked.

"They would have reported back to their tribe," Ashlyn said. "And then we'd have to fight a patrol of them on our way out. Safer this way."

"I see why your kind is feared, mistress."

"For good reason. We are monsters." She shrugged. "We have to be. The world makes monsters of us. Let this be your first lesson in survival."

Ashlyn slid the Azure Dagger out of the goblin's corpse and resumed her path.

* * *

Ashlyn's quarry awaited her deep within the cavernous maze. Whoever had carved out these tunnels had done so with care and design. The walls were smooth and polished as they reached the centre of the maze.

She motioned for Alindra to stop once they reached a polished steel ledge, no doubt some kind of lookout. However, the ledge was constrained by a wall of glass, though far more refined than anything that Ashlyn could recall even in the Silver Palace of Archadia. This enclosure must have been built in the days of Antiquity, though she could not recognise for what purpose.

A steel panel stood before the glass frame. Knobs and dials protruded from the top of the panel, made of some smooth material that Ashlyn couldn't recognise. Archaic devices from the ancient world, made before the days of sorcery. She brushed her hand in front of Alindra, who started to reach out to the machines.

"Leave these be," Ashlyn instructed. "We know not what these might do. It could alert the creature."

Alindra started to mouth a word of objection, but thought the better of it. The girl took a step back, folded her hands around her waist demurely, and allowed Ashlyn to take point.

"You know best, mistress. It's just… I think I know why Lazaria came this way."

"You think she knew of this place?"

"No, but there are rumours that could have led her here." Alindra leaned over the panel, taking care not to touch the implements. "She came to test an antiquated relic. If this place was built before the Calamity, it would suit her needs."

Ashlyn shot an interrogative glance back at the apprentice. There was more to this story. She didn't doubt the girl's theory, more that she had left gaping holes in her narrative, things that didn't completely ring true.

"Would Ravinder have truly allowed such an expedition?" Ashlyn asked.

"No, mistress. What the master told you was a lie," Alindra said. "Lazaria didn't come with his blessing. I think it is safe to tell you now."

"I thought as much. And the truth?"

"Lazaria left the master's service." She turned slightly away from Ashlyn as she spoke. "Ravinder is a harsh and cruel master. He uses us as little more than slaves. He delights in torture, in inflicting pain for his pleasure. Then, one night, Lazaria grew weary of being his toy. We both had. Except only she had the courage to do something about it."

Ashlyn permitted herself a cool, impassive nod. She allowed herself to feel nothing except for rage. There was little room in her heart for anything else. For she saw the girl she'd once been in the eyes of Alindra, and she saw truth in her eyes. For Ashlyn had sensed the cruelty beneath the eyes of Ravinder, the eyes of the ancient Drachenblood. The Clan of Cerulia was known for both magic and its capacity for needless cruelty. Ravinder acted as one of their kind.

"So she stole the relic from Ravinder," Ashlyn said. "No doubt, she came here searching for other antiquated weapons to protect herself from him."

"Not protect," Alindra said, shaking her head. "She hated him. She came to find a way to kill him."

It was well-known that weapons of Antiquity could pierce the veil of magic. They were made from the Old Laws, before the Calamity struck. But such weapons were rare, fading through rust and time, and they were difficult to maintain after so many centuries. Ravinder would have kept one for himself, to protect himself from rivals. But he was arrogant, no doubt thinking his power secure. It was the primary failing of their kind.

A dark thought popped into Ashlyn's mind as she peered through the lookout glass. The scornbeast paced at the very bottom of the catacombs, picking away at a goblin corpse. It was large and lean, with the sleekness of a panther and the armour of a tortoise. Smoke trained from its nostrils, and flame burned behind its mouth.

"Scornbeasts do not exist in nature," Ashlyn said. "They did not exist before the Calamity, and not for centuries after it. They are a product of either malefic sorcery or—" Ashlyn paused to look Alindra in the eyes, "or a Vow gone terribly awry. This is important. How much sorcery do you think Ravinder taught Lazaria?"

"Not enough to summon a fiend like this," Alindra said. "She knew more than I, but Ravinder would never teach her anything so dangerous. She would have used it to destroy him."

"As I thought, then. Which means she must have taken a Vow. The poor, desperate fool."

Alindra halted in her tracks. A tear fell from her right eye, trickling down the length of her cheek. Ashlyn did not know the depth of their relationship, but she supposed the two had been like sisters. They were bonded through hatred of the same master, through shared pain. They must have coped by turning to one another. Now the elder sister had become truly lost, leaving the younger one to survive alone.

Ashlyn was not without sympathy. She had suffered through a similar tragedy when Archadia fell. She admitted that she saw too much of her former self in this apprentice. She had seen too many horrid masters like Ravinder in the Drachen kingdoms.

"She hated him enough to do something that rash," the girl admitted.

"Then my course is clear. I must slay the scornbeast."

There was no other way, Ashlyn thought. A Vow to the wrong deity, or worse, a Broken Oath, often created these sorts of fiends. A Vow to gain the power to slay her tormentor would tempt Lazaria, but she was altogether too young to know how to parse the terms. A Vow made in desperation and hatred, made by a young sorceress with more knowledge than wisdom…if Ashlyn was right, this scornbeast would be unlike any she had encountered thus far.

Any humanity left in that girl would be the part of her filled with pain and hate, the part that wanted to rend her torturer limb from limb. Death would be mercy on the girl she used to be. It would also spare further innocent lives from being slain in its blind rage.

"Mistress? Do you believe that the scornbeast…"

"Is what is left of Lazaria? Yes." Ashlyn turned to the door, raising her palm towards the girl. "Your friend is gone. There is nothing left of her except hatred and malice. I am truly sorry."

Ashlyn left the apprentice to her tears. At least she would be alive long enough to mourn her friend.

* * *

Ashlyn scaled down the passages to the lowest level of the catacombs. She was swifter on her own, relying on her Drachenborn strength and speed to reach the bottom unimpeded. She kept the Crimson Sword in its sheath, dousing its magical flames. The fires were necessary only to navigate the catacombs, and the girl's presence added to that. But Ashlyn was perfectly capable of seeing even without them. Her night vision was keen enough to work in the dark, a gift from her predatory ancestors. Light was better for certain things, but she could hunt quite easily in the dark. She kept the Azure Dagger drawn, though she knew it wouldn't be sufficient defence unless she was able to get up close.

The scornbeast had fallen asleep at that point. The acrid stench of smoke filled the air, the breathing of the fiend spewing ash from its nostrils and mouth. The creature's head rested upon its front paws, which matched with the tracks they followed earlier, webbed with protruding talons. This was the same monster that had left its handiwork on the surface. The lingering thoughts of Lazaria had no doubt led the beast to hunt near Bordertown; her hatred of Ravinder keeping it nearby.

Ashlyn crept around the beast as it snored, hiding behind tall stalagmites at the edges of the cavern. She surveyed her surroundings carefully. The centre area was open and wide, giving plenty of room for the scornbeast to slumber in peace. She caught sight of the monster's hoard of bodies, piled in a heap of decaying flesh behind where it lay.

At the top of the heap, however, she caught a glimpse of something else. A rod of steel, encased in finely sanded wood, with a leather handle at the back end. A curved grip, no longer than a finger's length, ran between the handle and the length of the rod. This was no doubt the antiquated weapon that Ravinder and his apprentices valued so highly.

For a moment, she considered going for the relic. Even a scornbeast couldn't long stand against a weapon of the ancient world. However, Ashlyn thought the better of this. She knew some of the principles of these weapons, but she was no expert. Moreover, she had no guarantee that the instrument would even work.

Ashlyn reverted to her original plan. She crept from behind, keeping downwind of the scornbeast, her dagger drawn. If the beast awoke, the small silver blade could offer at least some defence against its flames. And if the beast remained asleep, the blade was sharp enough to pierce through its eye and into what remained of the fiend's brain.

Suddenly, the scornbeast startled, lashing out with its front claw. Ashlyn hopped back a few paces, falling into a defensive position, clutching her dagger. However, the beast simply rolled over, still slumbering. Dreaming of feasting on Ravinder's entrails, she supposed. At least it slept long enough to allow Ashlyn to creep a few paces forwards from where she was before.

Ashlyn edged in a foot closer, closing the gap between her and the sleeping face of the scornbeast. She ducked slightly, keeping her weapon aimed at the creature's eye. Her eyes narrowed as she dropped into a combat stance, preparing for the single fluid motion. If she missed, the monster would have her at its mercy. After steeling herself, she lunged forwards, Azure Dagger moving in for the kill.

Before the blade could hit its mark, the creature jumped to life, roaring angrily. A burst of flame shot forth from its open maw. Ashlyn barely dodged the full brunt of the strike, her black armour taking most of the damage. However, she felt a stabbing pain in her side where the flames hit. If she were anything less than a Drachenblood, the Reaper would have taken her already.

With her right hand, Ashlyn drew the Crimson Sword, its flames igniting at its mistress's call. The scornbeast charged forwards, slamming into Ashlyn's midsection before she could react. She crashed back-first into the stalagmites behind her, tangled up in the jutting stones. Both of her weapons clattered to the stone floor, with only the Azure Dagger within arm's length. Her now-extinguished red blade was near the monster's left paw, which threatened death with each step it took towards Ashlyn.

Ashlyn slipped through the stalagmites, allowing them to work as a natural barrier. The scornbeast lashed out with its front talons, slashing chunks of rock with each swipe. She tried to reach for the Azure Dagger but to no avail. The monster batted violently at her outstretched hand with its talons, forcing Ashlyn to retreat behind the stones once more.

The battle was swiftly becoming a stalemate. She couldn't hurt the creature without her weapons. But the scornbeast couldn't reach her behind the rock formations either, not without spending considerable hours slashing through them.

Then, suddenly, the sound of Alindra's voice echoed through the cavern.

"Lazaria?" she called. "It's me! Are you down here?"

Some part deep inside the scornbeast softened. Its eyes opened up wide, and something other than hatred flickered through the mind of the beast. It stopped where it stood, turned its head to the left, raised its jagged ears in interest.

Ashlyn did not know where the voice was coming from. It didn't seem like Alindra was in the catacombs. She had no light, no way of navigating through the dark crevices of the catacombs. The scornbeast seemed just as confused, sniffing the air and pacing in confusion.

Ashlyn did not hesitate. She reached forwards and grabbed the hilt of the Azure Dagger, gripping it with her right hand before passing it to her left. She withdrew softly, looking for just the right angle to strike the eye of the beast.

"Lazaria, don't hurt Lady Ashlyn," the voice of Alindra said. "She's my friend. You were too, once."

The scornbeast, or rather what remained of Lazaria within it, lowered itself to the ground. Its head lifted, trying to catch the words floating in the air. There was a small part that seemed to understand, but not entirely.

"Must…kill," the scornbeast growled. "Or die. Made…a vow."

Ashlyn was taken momentarily aback. She had never seen a scornbeast regain enough of its humanity to speak, much less remember its former life. She paused long enough to address the creature.

"Ravinder is my enemy as well," Ashlyn said. "I can take your revenge."

"Cannot hold…long," it said. "Kill him. End…curse."

"I so swear. Sleep in mercy."

Ashlyn barely heard Alindra's scream as she plunged her silver blade in the scornbeast's right eye. The monster made no cry of pain, no scream of death, as it met its end. The beast rolled over as it fell, its massive form slamming helplessly against the stone floor. A smile of peace formed on its face as its eyes closed slowly.

By the time the creature breathed its last, she was Lazaria again. Or what was left of her. She laid on her back, arms sprawled on the ground, palms facing the ceiling. The sapphire hilt of the Azure Dagger shed its frozen light as Ashlyn pulled it out of Lazaria's human-looking remains.

Ashlyn marched back to the room where she left Alindra. First, Lazaria must be buried and mourned. Afterwards, Ravinder would have much to answer for.

* * *

Ravinder of Cerulia preened in front of the mirror, staring at the one man he could ever trust.

He smiled at himself, lifting a wine goblet in his left hand, raising it in a mock toast. After all, there was much to celebrate as far as he was concerned. If the scornbeast Lazaria was dead, he knew Ashlyn could be relied upon to return the antiquated weapon and advance his interests. If the scornbeast survived, then Ashlyn was yet another boastful Drachenblood full of empty promises, and he would be rid of both her and another bothersome apprentice at the same time. He had played everything perfectly, and with none the wiser.

Or so he believed, until he felt the coolness of a silver blade at the side of his neck.

"I presume by your survival that the scornbeast is dead, and you have come to collect," Ravinder said, appearing unswayed by the implied threat. Ashlyn pressed the tip deeper into his flesh, enough to allow a single drop of blood to trickle down his collarbone. "Oh," he said flatly as he lowered his drink. "How much do you know, I wonder?"

Ashlyn moved in front of him, pulling the Azure Dagger away from his neck. If this was anyone else, she would simply have stabbed him and been done with it. But he was a kinsman, a Drachen of Cerulia, and this death was not worthy of one of their kind.

"I know enough," Ashlyn said, stepping forwards raising the Azure Dagger in a reverse grip. The blade was pointing directly towards Ravinder's heart. "Enough to call you a deceiver. And worse."

"So Alindra divulged her secrets to you." Ravinder's smile never once faded as he drew a golden sabre from his belt. "I will need to discipline her for that. For her own good, of course."

"It's time for the master to be on the receiving end." The Crimson Sword jumped into Ashlyn's right hand. "You have tormented your disciples long enough."

Ravinder struck first, slashing forwards with his sabre, now crackling with electricity. Ashlyn batted the strike aside with her flaming blade, fire pounding against thunder as the weapons connected. Ravinder darted to one side, lowering himself into a combat stance. Ashlyn did the same, sword and dagger sitting comfortably in her hand.

"You should have killed me immediately. I would have, in your place."

"And that is the difference between us," Ashlyn said, lunging forwards.

The blunt side of Ravinder's gold sword rapped Ashlyn's left hand. The Azure Dagger slid to the ground, allowing Ravinder to kick it away with a motion of his foot. Ashlyn wielded the Crimson Sword with both hands, bringing it down in an overhead strike at his skull. Ravinder barely caught the blow in time with his golden sabre. He was pressed back by her sheer ferocity. For all the strength afforded him by his Drachen-blood, he was a mage and not a warrior by trade.

Ashlyn dropped back a pace, bringing her sword up. She recognised the fighting style he used to block her attacks. He was a fencer, one who had studied in the courts of Cerulia. There were few remaining who knew that style, and it was one of the few effective against Archadian swordsmanship.

However, she knew one of the few weaknesses in the Cerulian style. But to exploit that weakness relied on Ashlyn's sword-and-dagger combination, one of the specialities of the School of Archadia. And her trustworthy dagger was out of reach. Her remaining blade clashed against the Artisan's golden sabre again and again, with neither finding a weakness the other could exploit.

Ashlyn finally noticed an opening. After a particularly frenzied blow, she broke away from Ravinder and rolled across the room in the direction of the Azure Dagger. She kicked the dagger up into the air, freed her left hand, and grasped the sapphire handle tightly in her palm. She smiled deliciously as she readied her stance.

"Why are you helping these humans? There's no need to side with the weak," Ravinder reminded her. "We could work together, become gods over these lowly humans as we were meant to be. Rebuild the Drachen Empire as it was in its former glory. Remake the civilization that was lost, make it greater! Why make a kinsman your enemy?"

Ashlyn for a moment almost hesitated. Together, they could achieve all that Ravinder promised and more. But at what cost? She had more than once wondered whether

Archadia deserved to fall. Ravinder gave her the answer she never wanted.

"Because they were once the dominant power over this world too," Ashlyn said. "They ruled for a time, grew arrogant, and then reached too far. Calamity struck, and then we had the audacity to topple them. Then we grew arrogant and rapacious and the same happened to us. The cycle must end."

"With my blood? What drivel. I offer glory, and all you see is death."

"You have no idea what I desire." She called to the door outside. "Alindra, now!"

A burst of thunder exploded from outside the room. Smoke blasted inwards, smashing through Ravinder's defences and pounding the Master Artisan backwards. A golden sphere shimmered briefly, then cracked into splinters. The runes he wore were Exceptions, spells that granted him advantages in combat that he could never achieve through training. Alindra stood in the doorway, wielding the Rod of Thunder, its barrel pointed towards where Ravinder's empty heart had been.

Ashlyn wasted no time, slashing through his barren defences with the Azure Dagger. The Crimson Sword found its mark at Ravinder's neck. The head of Ravinder rolled off helplessly, falling at the foot of the floor-length mirror, staring at itself.

She smiled in satisfaction. The Reaper would be sated for some time to come.

* * *

The next morning, Ashlyn stood outside the Artisan's Tower, prepping Hades for their next journey onwards.

No one in Bordertown had blinked an eye at the death of Ravinder. Everyone knew that it would have come soon enough. He had made too many enemies for him to live forever. Most of the city had either feared him or hated him. They only tolerated him because he protected them from greater monsters. When his death finally came, the bartender had offered Ashlyn a free night of lodgings and a pint of his best beer.

Only Alindra came to see the Pale Maiden off. In the eyes of many people in Bordertown, Ashlyn was as terrible as Ravinder. Ashlyn did not disagree with this. Best that people keep an appropriate distance from her. The Reaper would always follow.

"What now?" asked Alindra, wearing her master's former robes. She kept the golden sabre tucked into a gold sash at her waist.

"What indeed?" Ashlyn asked, looking back at Alindra. "There is no new Drachen Empire to come. There is no grand renewal, either for your people or mine. You have your time, and then it's over."

"I think you misunderstand, mistress," Alindra said, shaking her head. "We have overcome the evil of Ravinder because we stood together. Old and new. Magic, sword, and the Old Laws. Perhaps that is the next cycle."

"Perhaps." She allowed herself a slight hint of a smile. "But I must take my leave. I cannot tarry in any one place too long. I have a Vow of my own."

"A Death Vow, yes. I do not fear it." Alindra looked down where her fingers toyed with the sleeve of her garment. "I could come—"

"No." Ashlyn's tone felt like shattered glass. She attempted to soften her voice before continuing. "Bordertown needs an Artisan, especially now that we slew its last one. Continue your studies. Care for this city. Live your life in peace."

Alindra nodded in understanding, not saying a word. Instead, she took a package swaddled in cloth and handed it to Ashlyn. It felt hard and cool to the touch.

"Then take this," Alindra said. "I no longer have any need of it. And it could even be a hindrance if it fell into the wrong hands."

"The Rod of Thunder," Ashlyn realised, feeling the trigger against the cloth. "Child, you give a weapon to an instrument of death."

"The Pale Maiden. Yes, I know. I studied the legends last night. I know of the Vow you made with Death."

"Then why…?"

"Because you kill only those who deserve death," Alindra said, rubbing her hands together. "Or those who deserve mercy. I know you gave Lazaria peace."

"I wasn't able to save her."

"No. No one could. Only a god can break a Vow." She smiled at Ashlyn. "But you ended her pain. And mine. That was the best anyone could do."

Ashlyn found no argument in this, and nothing else to say. She threw herself atop her steed and marched Hades in the direction of the Bordertown gate. Alindra raised her hand and waved farewell.

As Ashlyn rode towards the sun, she did not look back. For once, she had a head start on the Reaper.

TRANSITIONING OF POWER
By Luis M. Cruz

As of twenty minutes ago, civilization had ended on Earth, caused by a nuclear war between the two largest factions in the world. However, the tragedy didn't prevent two of the most powerful beings from meeting once more. There wasn't a place on Earth that had not been affected by the war, except for one small area in Central Park, Manhattan. In that half-acre of the park, the temperature was 78°F and the sky was perfect, not a single cloud in the air. Sitting on a bench was a well-dressed young man, enjoying the sun's warmth, with his arms spread across the back. He sniffed at the air, catching an aroma he hadn't smelled in centuries.

"Well, well, well. Look what the cat dragged in," he said, as he stood up from the bench.

"Greetings, Satan."

"Now, now, Jesus. Let's not use titles. After all, you didn't hear me call you Messiah."

"Very well then, Lucifer."

"Please, call me Lou." He said as he sat back down and gestured for Jesus to have a seat beside him. "You must learn to keep up with the times. Speaking of such, why are you dressed like that time I tried tempting you in the desert?"

"Unlike you," Jesus replied as he sat down on the bench, "I am not deceitful when it comes to my appearance."

"Whatever," Lou said, looking away. "Let's get started with the reason we're here in the first place."

"Yes, let us begin with this transitioning of power."

"Speaking of which, what world am I to rule if everyone in this one is dead!" Lou yelled.

"That is of your doing," Jesus replied, sitting completely still.

"Yes," Lou said, once again feeling calm. "I am to blame whenever something cataclysmic happens, aren't I? However, when Father flooded the world, killing hundreds of thousands of his people, it was considered righteous."

Jesus turned to look at him, feeling sorry for this once proud angel. "Father is all-forgiving."

"We both know that's a lie." Lou looked Jesus in the eyes. "Do you know how many times I've asked for his forgiveness, only to find that the 'Almighty' knows how to hold a grudge? But you wouldn't know what that feels like. You're one of his favourites."

Jesus felt even more sorry. "You were once the most handsome of all angels. You were blessed with illumination. You were his favourite—"

"Favourite?" Lou interrupted. "Favourite till he created more advanced monkey-looking creatures."

Jesus smiled at him. "Oh, Lucifer, even after all this time, your jealousy still rules over you."

"Tell me, Jesus, on the night you were betrayed—by one of your own disciples, mind you—when you asked Father to let what was to be pass over you, did you not feel ignored when he did nothing to help you?"

"Enough!" Jesus's voice reverberated for several city blocks. He rose from the bench and stood directly in front of Lou.

Lou smirked. "Touched a nerve, did I?"

Jesus took a deep breath, regaining his composure. "Before we lose our senses, let us proceed with the reason we are both here," he said.

"Yes!" shouted Lucifer as he stood up from the bench, pushed past Jesus, and looked up towards the sky. "The transitioning of power."

"Let us be done with this."

"Transitioning of power over what, exactly?" Lucifer fumed, revealing his true form as a result of his anger. "There isn't a single living soul on this planet."

"This is true, but nonetheless, it is what you and Father agreed upon since the heavenly revolt you orchestrated a millennia ago."

"The agreement stated I would rule over every human."

"Again, you're correct," assured Jesus. "Every human *on Earth*."

Enraged and still in his true form, Lucifer yelled so loud that the buildings that remained standing crumbled. Three demons suddenly appeared from the ground. Jesus showed no fear. The archangels Michael and Gabriel flew down from the sky and stood beside him.

"I was hoping Father would send you to defend him, Michael. I have been wanting a rematch," said Lucifer, "because you got lucky the first time."

With a devilish grin, Michael replied, "I defeated you once. If need be, I will defeat you yet again."

"No!" Jesus yelled. "We are here for a purpose. Once it is done we will all go our separate ways."

However, Jesus's words went unheard. Suddenly a loud crash of thunder echoed through the sky, followed by a lightning strike between Michael and Lucifer, causing both of them to leap backwards.

"I see Father still watches over all of his creations," Lucifer said, as he looked up in discontent.

"Come, let us be done with this," said Jesus, as he extended his hand.

Lucifer followed by also extending his hand. "I agree."

A beautiful bright light emanated from their bodies as they shook hands and Jesus spoke the words: "As it was agreed upon by Father, prophesied and written by man, this world is now under your guidance to do as you desire."

"As I desire?" Lucifer asked in anger. "I desire for people to return."

"That will not happen. As you know, they have moved on to the stars and have colonized Mars. They are beyond your reach."

"You are mistaken, my Lord," Lucifer said with a smile on his face. "As long as they believe in and worship you and Father, they will know of me. And fear me. Therefore, bringing me into their existence no matter what planet they live on."

With that said, Lucifer and his demons faded away, followed by Jesus and his archangels.

APEX PREDATOR
By Micah Richards

Lieutenant Commander John Hennesey's breath caught.

As one of two tactical action officers aboard the Mud Dauber—the fastest naval vessel in the Galactic Federation of Stars fleet—it was his responsibility to monitor for threats and deploy weapons, if necessary, in defence of the vessel. His authority to defend the ship during his watch was second only to the captain's when he was not at the helm. Which he was not. The captain was currently sleeping one off in his stateroom. To prove there was no double standard on the ship, Commander Deland, assigned officer of the watch, had at least posted a marine guard to ensure the captain served his time properly.

Hennesey continued to stare disbelieving at his monitor. Moments before, the Dauber was the only ship traversing the Lyran system. Now it was being trailed by another vessel. Its sudden appearance meant that the pursuing ship must have only been light minutes away when it began its pursuit. It was also concerning that the ship was running dark, or rather, its universal identifier was either missing or destroyed. By design, they were not capable of being turned off. This meant the GFS Mud Dauber could not immediately identify the make or size of the ship.

Moments later, radiation and heat scans of the ship returned a profile three times the size of the Mud Dauber. Analysis of the heat signature from the pursuing ship indicated it had been at a dead stop before igniting its engines. This would have undoubtedly allowed it to evade passive scans from the Dauber as it passed by. The question was, why would anyone want to do that?

Hennesey hesitated a few more seconds before sounding the alarm. Warning klaxons cried their warning as the Dauber's ambient light changed from a dull yellow to an angry red. Deland called out sleepily to Hennesey from the captain's chair.

"What is it, Hennessy? I thought this was going to be an easy jump."

"Unidentified vessel two light-minutes on our six, Commander."

"Pirates?" asked the commanding officer, unsettled by the news.

"Could be. Their universal identifier is not broadcasting. They're big though," Hennesey hesitated for a moment, "and running fast."

Deland called for the communications watch officer to hail the pursuing ship.

"No response, Sir," replied Ensign Gupta.

Deland then called for the conning officer, or Conn, to increase the ship's speed from aughts one light (.001 light speed) to aughts one five (.0015 light speed). Deland ordered the increased speed to make it more difficult for the pursuing ship to accurately target the Mud Dauber. Relativistic distortion caused by travelling faster than point one the speed of light could cause targeting systems to degrade their normal pinpoint accuracy to something more akin to guessing blindly.

"The unidentified vessel is increasing its speed. Aughts one five light. Aughts two. Moment of intercept one minute fifty," replied the Conn, Ensign Burnette, whose large stature made him look like he'd be more comfortable as a marine instead of a naval officer.

"If that bastard thinks he can outrun a Peregrine-class naval ship with scramjet propulsion, he's sadly mistaken. Take her to aughts three and begin evasive manoeuvres."

The ship lurched slightly as it transitioned to a higher fraction of the speed of light and dove towards the celestial plane of the Lyran star system. The Mud Dauber had entered the Lyran system only five hours previous and was scheduled to travel to the system's exfiltration point at the far end of the star. At its current velocity, the Mud Dauber would be close enough to the gravitational pull of the Lyran star to attempt a jump in a little over two hours.

"Unidentified vessel is matching our speed," replied Burnette, with a hint of nervousness.

"Crazy. Ships that large shouldn't be able to move that quickly," replied Deland. "Hail it again."

It didn't take long for Gupta to report negative contact.

"Hennesey, give me a firing solution," barked Deland.

Hennesey keyed in the command to begin aiming the aft-facing gauss cannons at their pursuer. The light from the pursuing ship, now visible to their sensors, caused Hennesey to hesitate as he marvelled at the sleek design of the jet-black behemoth barreling down on the much smaller Mud Dauber.

Once the onboard computer had a possible lock, Hennesey thumbed the firing trigger and the ship shuddered as a tungsten carbide munition, roughly the size of Hennesey himself, magnetically accelerated at un-observable speeds towards the pursuing ship. Moments later an explosion of molten metal blossomed several kilometres off its port, friction and heat ripping the projectile to dust. The shot had gone wide, but not without some benefit.

"Unidentified ship has slowed to aughts two light, but is still in pursuit," replied Burnette.

"Hit her again," demanded Deland.

Hennesey punched in a few calculations he thought might zero in the gauss cannons and fired. The round again exploded into a brilliant flash, closer but still far from the hull of the incoming ship.

As the Mud Dauber burned towards the exfiltration point of the Lyran system, a verdant green world located in the Goldilocks zone of the star appeared on-screen. If they held their current course, they would pass within several hundred thousand kilometres of the planet, bypassing it entirely. Hennesey read its designation as the ship's onboard computer started populating information fields about the planet. Planet APX-137 held minimal settlements and was largely designated as a nature preserve, or so Hennesey reported as he prepared to send another round towards the enemy ship.

This time, through luck or expertise, Hennesey's round made direct contact with the phantom pursuer. The round blossomed into a brilliant cloud of dust and light as 90 kilograms of tungsten evaporated upon impact. A cheer rose among the several watchstanders on deck.

"Damage report," barked Deland.

Ensign Jones, stationed at long-range sensors, eagerly reported the Mud Dauber had appeared to score some damage along the port side of their pursuer's ship. Groups of armour plates weakened and began shearing off in brilliant droplets of molten slag as both ships pushed the limits of their ability.

The shared elation quickly returned to concern as warning indicators appeared on Hennesey's screen. The Dauber was detecting weapons ports being opened on the pursuing ship. Four sets of cylindrical pods appeared as armour plating slid away to reveal their deadly armaments.

"Sidewinders detected, Sir. Likely four volley capacity," reported Hennesey.

Deland took a minute to assess the situation. For a moment he appeared to be frozen with indecision. Hennesey, having already served a deployment under Deland, knew the commander was just careful and not prone to emotional outbursts under pressure. A decorated and skilled commander, Hennesey was not worried by his silence.

"Conn, take us on an orbit intercept course with that planet. Increase to aughts three five light, heading four four seven."

The operational maximum of a Peregrine-class vessel was aughts four light. Sustained velocity beyond this, even for mere minutes, risked the degradation of the ship's outer hull. Travelling at aughts three five light, however, posed no imminent risk and allowed for maximum sustained velocity.

"Yes sir," replied Burnette.

"I want to take the Dauber on a swing course around the planet and then burn like hell to the exfiltration point. We might not be able to take that thing in a fight, but we can beat it at a foot race," continued Deland.

"Yes, sir," replied Burnette a little more enthusiastically.

"Hennesey, what can you do to distract that ship while we make our escape?"

Hennesey thought for a moment. "Mines."

"Mines?"

"Mines," repeated Hennesey.

"Correct me if I'm wrong Hennesey, but aren't mines not normally deployed at aughts three-five light?" began Deland, but he was cut off by Ensign Jones.

"Missiles away. Tracking four on intercept. Time one minute thirty."

"What are the chances they'll hit us?" queried Deland.

"Depends on what the warheads are loaded with. If they're nuclear-tipped, I'm afraid we're already in their area of effect," replied Hennesey.

"You were saying something about mines?" said Deland.

"Anti-ship mines are normally armed with proximity fuses but can be programmed to engage with a timer. If we release the Dauber's entire payload, we can time them to explode when the enemy ship encounters them. They're almost directly behind us and likely to run into them."

"Do it," barked Deland.

As the two ships burned soundlessly through space, inching ever nearer to the surface of APX-137, four comets of light advanced towards the Dauber on a seemingly straight line from the phantom pursuer. The lights tracked the Dauber and for a moment looked as if they might overcome the smaller ship. Two CIWS cannons on the aft of the Dauber sprung to life, vomiting a cloud of tracers at the incoming missiles. Luckily, one of the missiles exploded, revealing a non-nuclear cloud of heat and debris. Moments later, two of the other remaining missiles lost their target lock and veered away from the slipstream of the Dauber, silently gliding to a halt somewhere in the darkness of space. Unluckily, one sidewinder performed admirably, enough to make any weapons engineer grin, and zeroed in on the exhaust of the Dauber and exploded.

Inside the ship, the personnel on duty rocked upwards in their safety restraints from the force of the explosion. Hennesey noticed one of the watchstanders failed to engage his neck restraint and the sudden jolt appeared to have snapped his neck.

Deland was the first to recover.

"Damage report," he barked.

Hennesey, not normally assigned to monitor damage, announced one engine was misfiring and the other appeared undamaged.

"What's our speed?" said Deland to no one in particular.

Burnette answered groggily and somewhat slurred.

"What was that, sailor?" yelled Deland.

"Aughts two light sir and steadily decreasing," choked Burnette a little more coherently. "Enemy intercept in three minutes thirty."

"Hennesey, release those mines. And Conn, get us around this planet," instructed Deland.

"Aye, aye, Sir," replied a now fully-recovered Burnette.

Three minutes later, miniature fusion explosions dotted the midnight black around the pursuing ship. Most exploded harmlessly, not in close enough proximity, but two capitalized on the Dauber's earlier strike, causing the ship to change course, pulling up and away from its pursuit of the Dauber.

At the same moment, APX-137 was growing large in the viewport of the Dauber's main screen. A few light seconds later, and the Dauber made a successful orbital rendezvous around the planet at aughts one seven five the speed of light, the most its dual scramjet engines could currently travel.

"Conn, reduce to a safe speed and start plotting our exit arch towards the Lyran exfiltration point."

"Yes, sir. Gravity assist is engaged. Engines are down to aughts one five light, but gravity assist has us back up to aughts two five light. Plotting exit. Burning engines in ten," replied Burnette.

Hennesey was just beginning to relax. The phantom ship was arching away from the planet, not willing to pursue the Dauber into an orbit around the scarcely populated APX-137.

"Enemy phantom breaking pursuit, Commander," stated Hennesey. "Looks like he's turning, EXFIL'ing the area."

"Excellent," breathed Deland. He quickly summoned a pair of marines to come and remove the unfortunate ensign who died as a result of the enemy salvo. None of the crew had been expecting such a vicious and sudden attack, especially while transitioning through the relatively calm Lyran system. Now that the danger had passed, a collective appreciation for the previously mundane system crossing was felt by all.

Hennesey, whose heart rate was rapidly returning to normal, let out a relieved sigh as he ran his hands through his hair, feeling lucky to be alive. He turned back to his workstation to determine the source of the remaining alerts on his screen.

Before the crew of the Dauber had time to react, a brilliant flash of light burst from the surface of planet APX-137. The bolt of crimson light instantaneously made contact with the Dauber, striking the bow of the ship. All lights on the command deck blinked into darkness. The initial shockwave from the impact tortured the limits of the safety restraints onboard, causing all but Hennesey to lose consciousness.

Bloody, and barely coherent, Hennesey could sense the sudden and immediate loss of velocity inside the ship. He blacked out several times during the Dauber's descent into the atmosphere of the planet. He semi-consciously noted his body floating upwards in his restraints as the ship lurched downwards. When APX-137's atmosphere ignited the ship's heat shield, his eyes fluttered open long enough to see a world of green rushing forward to envelope the ship.

The ship and crew of the Mud Dauber were reported MIA by GFS Central Command three standardized days later. All hands reported lost.

MURMURING JOHN AND THE RECORDING OF ALEXANDER A. WILLIAMS

By Christian Prosperie

My name is Alexander A. Williams, and I am an astronaut from the Sixth Division of Earth's Galactic Exploration Administration. To help you understand my state of being, my experience, I'm going to have to take my time. While my mere existence is brief among the infinity of the cosmos—I do understand that—I can't help but desire to extend these moments out. I do not wish to speak on what I'm about to say. Admittedly, I am terrified of it, but it is imperative I go on record.

To start, I must go back to a time of my more youthful days, when my more-eager heart yearned for these stars and my insatiable thirst for knowledge placed me nose-deep in my studies. As most know, it is here where every potential star jumper is required to learn about fellow and former GEA astronaut, John Cal Doughty. Morbid as it may seem to examine, at length, the final ramblings of a good man, untethered from his ship, sentenced to float away into nothing from a minor mistake, it was necessary. And practical. No one person, sane or unstable, should willfully dive into the universe's open mouth without a perspective on its potential destruction. John's final voyage was a glimpse of that.

It's slightly shameful to say, but during my childhood I had to be swayed over to science from mysticism at times, still clutching onto a belief of something *more* beyond this existence. I must also be open about how I studied John long before my days in graduate school. I was nearing sixteen when I first listened to his final transmission and I *believed* him my entire life. For weeks, months—no one truly knows—he jettisoned past nothing, emptied out and suspended, coming no closer to anything. The final five days he began muttering to himself. Never ceasing for a moment. No sleep, no pausing. He repeated many phrases, some incoherent, some were fabricated languages from his mind, somehow compartmentalizing his madness into an unrecognizable, yet structured speech. Other things came through clear as a star against space: "They are coming... They are everywhere... I am not alone."

And I believed.

I felt in his last blip of existence there was something there with him. That is until I went through Black Hole Week to train for those very situations myself. During the course, recruits are left to float for a week; alone in the cold, open vastness with only water and food-mash rations to suck meekly from a tube inside their custom-fashioned suit. It was meant for us to get to know the suit's functions, to be comfortable in the true three-dimensional vacuum, to prepare ourselves for a life-and-death scenario, but mostly to test our mental fortitude when time blends into a long, single moment.

In my group, many didn't last the entire week and called themselves in. Most don't last in any group. The majority decide against a career among the stars after it. But not me. Out there I stayed. After enduring my own week of absolute, mind-numbing solitude, I paid homage to a man who I now knew had merely lost his mind.

Psychologically, many would imagine that the reality of being stranded is vastly and horrifyingly different from these basic recreations. Not only were we recruits flown out to designated holes in space, but also—in the backs of our minds—we understood there was a way out, with nothing but a simple command typed into our omni-watch. Our mortality was never truly at stake. At the very least, our subconscious knew it.

Those who believe this are correct. Ten Earth-years later, I can confirm that the real thing is dimensions-upon-dimensions worse, as I have become untethered from my own ship. Dropped, a tiny spec, into the endless beyond.

How did this happen? People will study my history after my passing and will only find exemplary marks in all subjects, including field and maintenance work. They will see that I loved my family uncontrollably, as any father should, and when studying my career will see I have never made a single mistake in the dozens of interplanetary missions I have done prior to my last. Perhaps that's what brought me to this end? My one moment of over-confidence.

We were en route to the nearest jump station, just beyond the Vanadis system's outer rim, when we were hit by the residuals of a rogue solar flare. I was outside, clinging to the side of the ship on a maintenance walk. It took out my suit's power. No one answered my calls. I couldn't hear theirs. Protocol was to go in immediately; but to go in, just to have to put my suit on again moments later seemed tedious. Even for myself, after working the same droll for the past month. Only one more external draft head remained to tighten, twelve metres from me. So I climbed slowly, and carefully, around the cylindrical hull of the ship as we spun.

I'm unsure why the ship made such a drastic turn when it did. Their guidance systems were most likely rebooting along with my suit. Why would the crew yank it in such a violent way? I was not prepared for it. My grip slipped. Surely, they knew I was still out there. Or, perhaps they figured I was following protocol, as I always had, and was already inside the decompression bay. Whatever the case, they required an emergency turn, hoping I was inside or could hold, and if I didn't, that my tether would. When I reeled myself in with the long rope, the rope came to me, snapped at the insertion.

Sixty hours and they were still in view.

I watched my ship's light become no more than a pinprick, and every moment I went back and forth, not truly accepting the situation, seeking to blame anyone, anything. *Why, why, why did this have to happen?!* was a broken record in my head. A mistake, a piece of faulty equipment, a random breath of the universe out in the middle of nothing, all combining into one catastrophic moment set against me.

My crewmates continued onward, not turning around to look hopelessly for a man among a million oceans without scanners of their own. The chasm I was swept into wasn't a designated hole in space for me. There was no S.O.S. command to type into my watch. Once their tail finally dimmed away, I felt it creeping up. Higher and higher through my stomach and into my chest it built, as it always did.

As a child, my anxiety attacks came from situations out of my control. A sleepover at a friend's house or being confined in a long car ride with nowhere to go. It was my first taste of the existential elements affecting me, and the only way I knew how to cope was to lie awake, shaking as if I was freezing, or stick my head out of the window to gulp in fresh air. As I aged into early adulthood, the anxiety shifted towards the direction and point of my existence. How was I going to impact the world? The species? The universe? Those years were the worst of it. Some mornings I awoke in pure consternation. My heart pounded like I was running a marathon, and my jaw ached from my molars grinding throughout my dreams and into reality.

One of the most comforting pieces of advice about my attacks came, not from my therapist, but the physician prescribing my anti-anxiety stims. She told me, "The body can only be that wound up for so long before it simply crashes." Setting a limit on the suffering was a comfort indeed.

So, moving forward, I would fight the beasts away with my natural reaction to overwork. I'd let it hold me by the throat until I could take no more, until my mind was exhausted, and I'd fall violently to sleep. I'd wake, only to do it again. The cycle usually perpetuated until midafternoon, or later, but always until I had enough fortitude to face myself. When I found my calling in the stars, I found my serenity. The cosmos settled my restlessness. Perhaps from the idea that no matter what, I could always just *go*.

The stars have betrayed me. Floating helpless among them, they no longer warded off those chest-constricting thoughts, but brought them back a thousandfold. I coped the best way I knew how. I forced sleep through the brutal, crippling anxiety that came from the stars ceaselessly bearing down on me.

I did this for three, maybe four, days in total.

I barely ate. I only sipped liquids from my tube in my short bouts of consciousness. The only sound heard was my off-rhythm exhales from tight sucks of air. Most of the time, I didn't dream, only being able to stay asleep for an hour or two at a time. Blackness, into blackness, into blackness. I only knew I was awake from the tears on my cheeks.

At one point, between my fleeting moments of awareness, I had one of those awful Cosmic-Pop artists—if you could even call them artists—stuck on repeat in my head. The song was popular as a child, with my peers streaming it on their omni-watches at school, or at the mall, doing the dance in groups, while I sneered from afar: "Jump, jump, do the Klump. Take it, shake it, to the stars. Then bring it back, down to Mars!"

God, I *hate* that song; yet I sang it to myself. I sang it for thirty-seven hours in between sleep. It may seem depressingly comical—and I am laughing at myself, even now—but I appreciated that it focused me onto something, even if that something was anger. During that time was when I considered the fact that I may be losing my mind.

Rarely, though, I did dream. Grass between my toes, and a crisp spring breeze from the mountains on Earth, back home. I'd envision myself with my two little girls, Ayleah and Thea, at the park with our golden retriever. Or having a lazy Sunday with my lovely wife, Brellah, at my side, and a good book. Coming back from those beautiful, perfect fantasies into what was my unchanging, inevitable fate to be swallowed by the void is a hell I couldn't have fathomed if anyone begged me to try.

I am only speaking on these things because all evidence must be considered and accounted for, assuming my body is one day found and this recording preserved and retrieved from my suit. I want to be a reliable data point, as John Cal Doughty and I are the only two case studies on record of this extraordinarily frightening event. On record, at least. My early fascination with, and beliefs surrounding, John need to be taken into account, as well as my history with mental illness. Maybe I've lost it, and am not really seeing what I'm seeing now, as many believe was the case with John. Maybe we both coped with death in a similar fashion, due to being doomed in similar environments.

But many peculiar things stand out about Murmuring John's account that the official history likes to ignore. The ship that found him, the Yume, stated they had been in the atmosphere of the moons around Leiptr for two days when John's signal suddenly came through. The ship's captain went on record stating: "Either his suit just miraculously turned on right next to us, or he appeared out of nowhere." The captain is right to be confused. Even if John's suit just happened to fire back on, the Yume's scanners were working fine; they were tracking all objects, alive and dead, in a six hundred kilometre radius. It would have seen an atmospheric anomaly not consistent with the rocks and dust common to Leiptr's moons long before the signal popped on-screen.

The Yume went into immediate high alert, believing the signal to be one of their own untethered. After a quick roll call, done three times over, confusion set in. Imagine how much more so when they expected to find a live person, as opposed to what they did?

Of course, the photos themselves are on public record, just like John's story. Many believe that the tatters and tears in his suit are from colliding with debris during his journey, thus ending his life by opening him to the vacuum. Some experts, however, have written whole dissertations on the findings of John, on how the suit's ruptures aren't consistent with any known effects of atmospheric debris damage. Exposure to the vacuum was still the cause of death, no doubt.

Most of these experts, all with reputations to uphold, will reluctantly agree that his suit appears to be slashed in a way that's more consistent with something…claw-like. Most backtrack, of course. All their responses can be paraphrased into: "There's a lot we don't know about the universe and how it affects the human species in different cosmic situations."

To add to the oddity of his situation, John's decomposition—or lack thereof—was inconsistent with where he was found compared to where his crew determined he became untethered. Where he was first lost, out in the depths between systems, he should've frozen over after exposure. Where he was found, mummification should've taken hold with how close in proximity he was to the star, Pan. In fact, his body had hardly begun to freeze, much less dehydrate, with no other decomposition present.

The first responders on the Yume even tried to resuscitate the corpse, right there in decompression, before realizing whom it was they found. Had they known straight away, no vita-stims would have been administered, no CPR bots would have been issued for chest compressions, since at that point, all of Earth and its colonies knew John's ship reported him missing over five Earth-years prior to the

Yume finding him. Five years, four months, and fifteen days to be exact.

His suit is kept locked away and has been thoroughly examined a thousand times over. The voice recordings are public, so who knows how many people have listened to them throughout our expansion. But the one thing many skim over are the findings he claims were picked up by the scanners within his suit. John's descriptions of the anomalies he observed were difficult to discern. Between the archaic, broken language he spouted, to his reminiscing about cooking meals for his own family again, he did give some details.

Amorphous, blob-like entities took shape as glowing, yellow lights on his scanners. He stated that nothing physical was present with him, or at least that he could see through his visor. The lights slowly came together and spread as far wide as the scanner's periphery and crept up across his screen. He spoke of other figures with a more solid shape darting around the wall of light. He described the scanner picking up their movements as "strobes, flashing here and there, but with devilish purpose behind the front line."

Nothing was ever officially documented from those same scanners to even come close to his testimony. There isn't five years' worth of data on them to study. His suit stopped functioning months in, not years. But even in the months it was active, it received next to nothing. The path he is theorized to have followed didn't come close enough to the nearest planets to pick up on moons, planetary debris, or meteors. There was nothing out there. He was the only spec for millions of kilometres. Therefore, many believe his brain was just giving him a final show—one so convincing it would eventually lead him to saying: "I am among them."

This is where most truly sympathize for a man gone mad, as the majority of humanity thinks we may never come across any complex life. How long have we spent, reaching further and further, and have yet to find anything? Especially in the middle of space. In the middle of virtually nowhere. John knew this. So did I. Or, so, I thought I did. I admit, it's difficult not to give in to the facts of history out here, but I still believe it's simply too vast to house a lone intelligent species. We may never find any, but that doesn't mean they don't exist. How arrogant to think so?

Then on the recording, John screamed.

I've never heard any living thing, on Earth or in the stars, that compares. His wailings were a final call refuting the infinite. As hard as his diaphragm could push, and as long as the air in his lungs allowed him, John cried out. I've listened, more than once, to the full three hours and forty minutes of screaming, until I heard the cracking and tearing of his vocal cords. I listened as he attempted to continue to scream for two more hours, when nothing but a hoarse scratch against his throat forced itself out. I listened to it all, every moment, because his scanners *did* pick up something.

There is no evidence proving space amoebas, or tele-porting lieutenants among other-worldly ranks. But, for a mere .0054 seconds, just as he claimed he was with them, just before his yelling began, records indicate that every single pixel of his visor's scanner lit up. One final flash for the man adrift.

I stopped eating a day after my panic attacks. A calm blanket of acceptance laid on me. My mind, drained. My body, useless. I let a slideshow of my loved ones play on repeat for nearly a week until darkness took me. What better way to fade into nothingness than on pleasant memories?

Yet here I am awake, pulled back into consciousness not but two hours ago. What woke me was not an insatiable need for sustenance, or a nightmare of what the afterlife may be, but something else; the one thing above all I was horrified of the most. I did my best to ignore my fear while I floated, tucking it away like a child pretends the darkness underneath their bed no longer scares them, convincing themselves there is no monster. But to my utmost, unnerving alarm, my scanners blinked a soft, yellow light.

A dot appeared on my visor, representing something in the far, far distance. It jolted me back into survival mode. I checked my systems. They were all green. They hadn't faltered a bit while I was teased with my ending. How long had I been out? I checked my time adrift, and I distinctly felt my hair stand erect over my entire body.

Fifty-four days.

A ship going maintenance speed travels at around sixty-thousand kilometres per hour. I can't be travelling much slower in this frictionless hell. That's twelve hundred and ninety-six hours. Or roughly, seventy-seven million, seven hundred and sixty thousand kilometres.

How could this be? Surely my systems were malfunctioning, but no. The new solar suits rarely fail, especially with myself so close to Eras. It took me more moments than I'm proud to admit to regain my composure. Especially since the dot on my visor, as I came ever closer, began to expand into a faint line. Constantly flashing, always reminding me that as every second ticked, I came closer. As the line spread far past my peripheral vision, it opened in other directions to make a wall. A gate to greet me. To engulf me.

It was then I heard them, but to hear them doesn't exactly do the experience justice. The only way to describe the phenomenon is to take a phrase from John's encounter I have fixated on my entire life and reiterate: "I can *feel* them."

Their voices—if you can even call them that—started swishing between my own inner voice about an hour ago, and continue as I speak now. I am finding it compelling, but in the way cheese is on a mousetrap. It is taking everything within me, every ounce of my resolve, not to repeat it. The old, lost language could not be fathomed by John, and I am also failing. It's as if I am learning histories upon histories in mere moments, and to do so, it is tearing apart the very fabric of everything I know.

In my final moments, I mean to send a message to my family. Brellah, my beautiful star, how I wish I could have given you the comfort you gave me. I say the stars were my serenity, true, but they are but a small fraction of what you are to me. Even in these final moments, I am using the memories of you to maintain the man you always knew I could be. To my daughters, Ayleah and Thea, I never knew love, true unconditional love, until you were born. I am sorry I won't be there for your achievements, your successes, but, more importantly, I am sorry to miss the lows, the heartbreaks, the failures. You two are already so strong together and must remain so. I have no doubt there are no limits for my two little moons. To the three of you, every moment spent out here I have had you with me. I will keep you until the end, and you have made me the proudest man in the cosmos.

* * *

If I am found, I ask you to return my body to the GEA, as they have been good to me and my loved ones. I beg those at the GEA to please, under no circumstances, allow my family to hear anything past the previous message to them. Use my recordings, my corpse for research. Please. But they need no part of what's to come. I want them to remember me for the man I tried so damn hard to be, because I have now come to my journey's end. They are everywhere. I am among them.

And now, I'm afraid, I am going to scream.

CONTENT WARNINGS

Profanity
Pregnancy
Violence
Death
Loss of a child